DRIPPING CHOCOLATE

KEITH THOMAS WALKER

KEITHWALKERBOOKS, INC

KEITHWALKERBOOKS

Publishing Company
KeithWalkerBooks, Inc.
P.O. Box 690
Allen, TX 75013

For information write
KeithWalkerBooks, Inc.
P.O. Box 690
Allen, TX 75013

ISBN-13 DIGIT: 978-0-9850500-1-6
ISBN-10 DIGIT: 0985050012
Manufactured in the United States of America

Second Edition

Visit us at www.keiththomaswalker.com

CONTENTS

DRIPPING CHOCOLATE

MORE BOOKS BY KEITH THOMAS WALKER

Blurred Lines: The Monster
Blurred Lines: Cop Killer
Blurred Lines: Copycat Killer
Blurred Lines: Mister Me Too

Asha and Boom Part 1
Asha and Boom Part 2
Asha and Boom Part 3

Backslide
Backslide 2

The Realest Ever
The Realest Christmas Ever

Prom Night at Finley High
Fast Girls at Finley High
Bullies at Finley High

Jackson Memorial
Jackson Memorial 2

Brick House
Brick House 2
Brick House 3

Threesome
Threesome 2

Take One of Mine
Take one of Mine Part 2

Fixin' Tyrone
How to Kill Your Husband
A Good Dude

DRIPPING CHOCOLATE

Riding the Corporate Ladder
The Finley Sisters' Oath of Romance
Blow by Blow
Jewell and the Dapper Dan
Harlot
Plan C (And More KWB Shorts)
Dripping Chocolate
Sleeping With the Strangler
Life After
Blood for Isaiah
One on One
Election Day
Evan's Heart
Poor Righteous Poet
Might be Bi Part One
Harder
Primal Part One
Hotline Fling

Visit www.keiththomaswalker.com for information about
these and upcoming titles from KeithWalkerBooks

**PROLOGUE
INSECURITIES**

CHAPTER
1

"SO, UM, WHAT color panties you got on?"

Nicole smacked her lips. "Boy, stop."

"For real," Byron said, his voice deep and wannabe-sexy. "You don't wanna tell me?"

Nicole actually didn't want to say because it wasn't a good time of the month for her, and her undergarments weren't sexy at all. Plus she was at work. Supposedly her outgoing, personal calls weren't monitored, but it was no secret that all of her business calls were. What was to stop her manager from listening in on any call she pleased?

"You know I can't talk like that at work," Nicole said. She leaned back in her swivel chair, her eyes flicking from her computer screen to the compact in her left hand. Her phone was secured to her head with a stylish headset. She applied a coat of lipstick with her right hand and then used the same hand to type a quick email to one of her co-workers. Nicole was often praised for her multitasking.

"You not working late?" Byron asked.

"Nope," she said. Nicole checked the time in the bottom right corner of her computer screen. It was a quarter 'til four. In fifteen minutes she'd lead a mass exodus to the time clock, and she wouldn't return to this brightly lit office for *two whole days*. She sighed, her heartbeats already quickening. Weekends-off had to be the sweetest perk a company could offer its minions.

"Can I come by?" Byron asked. "I wanna see you."

Nicole smiled. She brought her mirror closer to her face and rubbed her lips together, spreading her lipstick evenly. "Okay," she said. "What you got in mind?"

"Nothing," Byron said. "What you making for dinner?"

Nicole frowned at that. She checked her whole visage one more time before she closed her compact and dropped it into her purse. Maybe she wasn't the prettiest girl in the whole, wide world, but Nicole was no ugly duckling either. Her face was thin, her eyes large and her lips were full. Her nose was a little European, but it matched the angles of her face perfectly.

Carla Nicole Cook had smooth skin that was dark like an Almond Joy. Her real hair wasn't very long, but her hairdresser was a magician, and it was hard to tell where the extensions started in her ponytail.

Nicole was always a thin girl, but she had some nice curves nowadays. Her hips started to spread after high school, and her breasts swelled and maintained their B-cup status when she had the twins two years ago. Nicole's best feature had always been her perfectly onion-shaped ass. Men were often taken aback to see such a beautiful backside on a skinny girl like her.

Maybe she wasn't *all that*, but Nicole thought she deserved more than another Friday night at home on the couch.

"I don't feel like cooking," she prompted.

"What, you want me to bring y'all a box of chicken?" Byron guessed.

Nicole shook her head. "No. I don't want that either."

"So, um, you want me to get some burgers?"

In addition to her terrible-two year old twins (a boy and a girl), Nicole was the single mother of a nine year old named Shawn. It was nice of Byron to offer to feed her family, but she could do that just fine by herself.

"Have you heard of any good movies lately," she hinted.

"I can't afford to take everybody to the movies," Byron said right away.

Nicole rolled her eyes. Why did he have to be so stupid? It was getting to the point where she couldn't ask Byron for anything without him thinking he had to provide for her whole brood. She started to tell him, *I didn't ask you to do nothing for my kids, did I?* But she bit her tongue and said, "I can get a babysitter. I was talking about just me and you."

"I just, I don't really feel like going out tonight," Byron replied. "Can't we rent a movie or something? I'll bring a bottle of wine, for when the kids go to bed. You can light some of them candles, if you want..." She could hear him grinning over the phone.

Her period aside, Nicole was not impressed with Byron's half-assed attempt at romance. What was wrong with a nice restaurant or a twilit promenade downtown? Nicole had a few dresses in her closet that she hadn't worn in over six months because Byron never took her anywhere. And it wasn't like–

"Aww hell." Nicole's eyes grew large as she fished her daily planner from her purse. "I can't see you tonight," she told Byron. "I'm supposed to help my friend move."

There was a slight pause as Byron's brain (laced with insecurities) processed her statement and determined it was not true. "You what?"

After eight months together, Nicole understood the flawed workings of her boyfriend's mind. "Don't start."

"You ain't finna help nobody move," Byron stated.

"Yes I am," Nicole said. "My friend Angie's moving to a new house, and I told her I'd help her today."

Byron knew Angie was a real person, but he also knew that women generally included real persons, places and things in their lies. "Don't nobody move on Friday night," he deduced.

"You don't know what people be doing," Nicole said

"Alright, I'll take you to the movies," Byron offered.

"I told you I got something to do tonight."

"Who you going out with?" Byron demanded.

Nicole's eyes narrowed, and her body temperature began to rise. She and Byron had enough problems in their relationship already. His jealously might be the tremor that made the whole deck of cards come tumbling down.

"I gotta go," she told him, checking the clock again. "I'll call you later."

"You ain't gotta go."

"I'm at work," Nicole said with unveiled annoyance. "I got stuff to do."

"Just tell me why you lying," Byron pleaded. "You know you ain't gotta help nobody move."

"You don't know what I got to do!"

"Don't be talking to me like that," Byron warned.

Or what? Nicole wondered. She worked for APEX Teleservices, which was a large company that took incoming customer service calls for a variety of businesses, including UPS and Sony. She didn't have a direct number to her phone, and Byron would have to go through the main operator and a couple of supervisors if he tried to reach her through APEX's main number. By then Nicole was sure to be gone for the day.

"I'm hanging up," she said calmly. "I'll talk to you later."

"Don't hang up this phone," Byron growled.

Nicole weighed her options and said, "Bye."

"You bet not–" Byron's voice was interrupted by a dial tone.

"*Dumb ass,*" Nicole mumbled, referring to herself just as much as her crazed boyfriend.

One of her coworkers peeked around her cubicle wall with a concerned look on her face.

"What happened?" Stella asked.

Nicole chuckled, knowing her friend had been listening to the whole conversation.

Stella made up ¼ of a group of women at APEX who were so close they were affectionately known as "the rat pack." Well, mostly *affectionately*. Nicole met Stella, Twyla and Blanca during a training course on her first day at the job. The girls became fast friends, helping each other learn the ropes – mostly with jokes and trashy gossip that ensured the repetitive nature of their work never got too stale.

When Nicole first heard that some people in the building were calling them *the rat pack*, she took it as a badge of honor, thinking she was a member of a respected clique, like the group that once included Frank Sinatra and Sammy Davis Jr. When Nicole later learned that the term originated as an insult (a homely bitch named Lisa Nevels was secretly calling them *hoodrats*), she brushed the hate off her shoulders and kept doing her thing. God made haters just like He made rats and roaches. They were all ugly nuisances, but pretty much harmless.

"Was that Byron?" Stella asked. She was well aware of the problems in Nicole's current relationship.

"Yeah," Nicole said, rubbing away a tense spot between her eyebrows. She removed her headset and tossed it casually on her desk. She hadn't done any real work in the past ten minutes, and she didn't plan on doing any in the next five.

"Why you still with him?" Stella wondered. She removed her headset and placed it on her desk as well. Stella was an attractive woman with short, auburn tinted hair that was styled in a bob. Stella was a foot taller than Nicole, and she was ten years older. Despite being married to the same man for fifteen years, Stella considered herself an expert on relationships. Sometimes Nicole wondered if she'd been out of the game for too long.

"You don't have to break up with somebody every time they get jealous," Nicole said.

"Yes you do."

That voice came from Nicole's right. She looked that way and saw Twyla peeking around her other cubicle wall. This was another member of the rat pack who had no qualms about eavesdropping on Nicole's personal calls. Twyla was closer to Nicole's age, and they usually saw eye-to-eye on more issues. Plus

Twyla was a single mom herself, except she only had one child to Nicole's three.

"Don't you have a call?" Nicole asked her friend.

"Yeah, I got them on hold," Twyla said, expressing no shame for her slacking.

Nicole shook her head. "Are you sure they're on hold? You remember last time that lady listened to you bitching for almost five minutes…"

"Yeah they on hold," Twyla said with a frown. "Don't you think I know how to work a phone?" But she pulled her mouthpiece down and checked anyway. "Hello…" Twyla's eyes suddenly grew large, and her jaw dropped. "Ooh, I am so sorry, Ma'am! Hold on just one second, I'm looking that up *right now*…" She kicked her feet, and her chair disappeared around the corner again. After a moment, Nicole heard fast typing on Twyla's computer.

"Oh my God," Nicole said with a hand over her mouth. She tried but couldn't stifle her laughter.

"She gon' get fired," Stella predicted.

"No she's not," Nicole said.

"If it wasn't for Blanca, she would," Stella said, and Nicole knew she was right about that.

Blanca Puente was the fourth member of their clique. Unlike her cohorts, Blanca used *hard work and integrity* to elevate herself to a supervisor position at APEX. Blanca was the only reason Nicole, Stella and Twyla still sat next to each other after three long years of their shenanigans.

"But your boyfriend, that nigga do need to get fired," Stella said, back on the subject at hand.

"He not that bad," Nicole assured. "He gets a little jealous, but he loves me."

"That's not love," Stella said, shaking her head. She wore glasses with bold, black rims. Her outfits were always prim and proper, like a teacher, or a pastor's wife. "If he don't trust you, that's not love, baby. That's *obsession*."

"Everybody got their ways," Nicole said, trying to placate her. "Like you believe your husband every time he says he's going somewhere."

"Of course I do," Stella said.

"Well, what about before you got married," Nicole said. "He never got jealous, of any of your old boyfriends?"

"Old boyfriends is one thing," Stella said, her lecture mode in full swing. "You told him you were going to help your homegirl move. He don't got no reason not to believe you – unless you been lying to him about other stuff."

Stella raised an eyebrow, and Nicole shook her head.

"I don't got no reason to lie to Byron."

"Then you need to wise up," Stella advised. "What do you think is gonna come out of this, huh? What do you honestly believe is going to happen? He gonna wake up one day and not be crazy no more?"

"He's not *crazy*," Nicole said, even though she gave Byron a similar label a few minutes ago.

"Don't be no fool," Stella cautioned. "You got three little kids at home. If he don't trust you, he gon' start trying to control you. And if you let him get away with *that*, the next thing is for him to start hitting you. That's the way it goes."

At thirty-eight, Stella wasn't an *older woman*, but she was Nicole's elder, and Nicole knew when to pipe down and heed wise counsel. Byron never hit her, but he was already showing signs of his controlling nature.

Don't hang up this phone.

That was both an order and a threat. At some point Byron would have to show her he meant business, wouldn't he?

"Don't be no fool," Stella said again, noticing she was getting through to her dear friend. "I know you got three kids, but you don't have to settle on no man, Nicole, pretty as you are. You need to nip this in the bud *right now*, while you still got control of the situation."

Nicole nodded, giving her friend's words the consideration they deserved. She and Byron had been together for almost a year. They had their share of good times, but lately the bad outweighed the good. It was sheer folly to think things would go back to the way they were.

And Stella was right about something else: Nicole was good-looking and by no means desperate. It was nice to find a man who accepted her *and* her crumb-snatchers, but she had a lot to offer the relationship, too. Byron was lucky to have a good woman like her. If he didn't know that by now, maybe he didn't deserve Nicole.

With her dilemma almost solved, Nicole checked the clock again and saw that it was 4:01 pm.

"Aww hell," she told Stella. "It's time to go!"

Both women logged off of their computers and rushed to straighten up their work stations before they left. Nicole had to pick up her oldest child at 4:30, but his school was only fifteen minutes away. She wasn't pressed for time, but you'd never know it by the way she hurried to get out of the building.

"Y'all not gon' wait for me?" Twyla called as she watched her best buds speed-walking to the time clock.

Nicole and Stella looked back at her, and then they looked at each other and laughed. They didn't slow down one bit.

"Trifling heifers," Twyla murmured with a big scowl on her face. "Oh no, not you Ma'am," she told her caller and then returned her attention her computer screen. "Can't you talk faster?" she urged her. "I'm supposed to be gone already..."

CHAPTER
2

NICOLE WAS STILL feeling good about her weekend off when she rolled to a stop in front of Piedmont Elementary. But the look on her son's face as he marched to her Civic melted the smile right off her face. Nicole was singing along with Jazmine Sullivan, but she turned the radio off and girded herself for more bad news when the nine year old boy opened the door and climbed into the passenger seat.

Shawn was tall for his age, with rich, dark skin like his mother. Nicole kept his hair shaved low, and she always made sure his wardrobe was stylish – even if it meant she had to put off a trip to the hair salon or a new pair of jeans for herself.

Shawn was handsome and healthy and smarter than most of the other kids in his grade level. But he rarely received kudos from his teachers because Shawn also had "emotional" and "behavioral" issues. Nicole had been aware of these issues as early as pre-k, but they weren't a big problem. Like most mothers, she hoped her son would level out as he aged. Instead, Shawn grew progressively worse. He had two fights last year, and his first two months of third grade were off to a shaky start.

Nicole put her Civic in DRIVE, headed for the twins' daycare center in the Stop Six neighborhood. She remained quiet for nearly half a mile, and Shawn did the same.

"Did something happen today?" she finally asked.

Shawn shrugged and looked out of the passenger window. His expression was deadpan, but his large eyes were fearful and contemplative.

"Did your teacher give you a bad mark?" Nicole asked.

The boy bent to dig through his backpack, and Nicole's heart sighed. Shawn handed her his new progress report. Nicole looked it over briefly as she drove. A quick scan of his number grades provided good news; mostly B's with a couple of A's sprinkled in. The citizenship category wasn't any different from last time, but it broke Nicole's heart all over again.

She took a moment to consider her approach as she handed the paper back to him. Sometimes she got frustrated when she encountered a dilemma she couldn't figure out. Frustration never worked with Shawn, though. And if Nicole pushed too hard, she knew he'd shut down completely.

"I guess we're still not ready to start your allowance," she said.

Shawn didn't say anything. As a last resort, Nicole offered him cold, hard cash if he could bring home a progress report or report card with no N's or U's on it. At the time, Shawn seemed excited about the prospect. But he had yet to collect one dime of his "be good money."

"I know it's not your teachers," Nicole said, "'Cause you got two new ones..."

Shawn didn't have a comment for that.

"You been getting into it with them same boys from last year?" Nicole asked.

Shawn shook his head. He still hadn't made eye contact.

"You're gonna have to say *something*," Nicole demanded. "You can't keep bringing home progress reports like this. You know they're thinking about putting you in a special class..."

Shawn's throat caught, and he looked his mother in the eyes. He knew he was smarter than most of his peers, and he didn't like the idea of being ostracized because of his behavior.

"I didn't, I didn't do nothing," he said.

Nicole watched his eyes, and she knew that, in Shawn's mind at least, he was telling the truth. Her son's behavior problems weren't necessarily disruptive, and Shawn knew better than to talk back to his elders. According to his teachers, Shawn's problems ranged from lack of cooperation to an all around *funk* that made them wonder if Shawn might be depressed.

Nicole invested a good amount of time in in-school and after school counseling. But time after time the counselors came up short. One thought Shawn might be jealous of his new brother and sister, born two years ago. Another thought it might be the lack of a father figure in his life that made the boy so moody. A third counselor suggested prescription drugs that would make Shawn "happy." Nicole would only try that as a last resort.

"I know you didn't do nothing," she told him. "That's the problem, Shawn. The teachers want you to talk more in class, but you won't. How come?"

The boy shrugged, his head lowered, chest sunken.

"The special classes might not be a bad thing," Nicole said. "If you don't like to talk, they can–"

"I'll talk," Shawn promised.

"I don't want to *make* you talk," Nicole said. "I wanna find out why you so closed up. School's not supposed to be fun all the time, but it's okay to laugh every now and then. You have a beautiful smile. Don't you want the girls to see it?"

He shook his head.

"What about me?" Nicole asked. "Can I see it?

He looked up at her with a slight smirk.

Nicole smiled. "I know you can do better than that."

She reached and rubbed the top of his head, and Shawn's smile brightened. It was a beautiful smile. So tragically beautiful.

"If you could take that smile to school with you tomorrow," Nicole said, "we wouldn't have no more problems. But since you can't, it looks like we have to figure something else out..."

Shawn's smile quickly vanished. "I have to go to some more counselors?"

"I don't know yet," Nicole said. "We'll see."

She was wondering if maybe she could find a mentoring program for her baby. It was slightly painful, to consider that a perfect stranger might have the solution to a problem she'd been trying to solve for years. But Nicole was past the point of thinking *mother knows best*. If a mentor couldn't help Shawn, Nicole would even call her doctor to get more info about those happy pills she rejected last year.

She reached to squeeze her son's hand, and he squeezed back, and that strengthened her resolve.

CHAPTER 3

NICOLE'S NEXT STOP was at Mama Rose's Day Care where her two year old twins Keisha and Kevin were running their caregivers ragged. Nicole was aware of the phrase "terrible twos," but she always thought it had more to do with parenting than anything else. Shawn, for example, didn't exhibit any unsavory antics at the two year mark. And Nicole had a few girlfriends who had wonderful two-year-olds.

But Keisha and Kevin were something else. Totally unaffected by sugar, rest or even spankings, these twins were as rowdy as they come. They assaulted Nicole with hugs when she entered the daycare, and then they bolted from the building when Nicole turned to say hi to one of the other parents. Nicole rushed outside with her heart high in her chest, hoping neither of her babies was crazy enough to run into the street, but there was no need. Shawn was already out of the car when she got there. He held his sister by her wrist and his brother by the forearm.

"Quit playing around, before you get hurt!" he told them.

"I gotta pee," Keisha replied.

"I wanna sit front!" Kevin shouted and pulled in that direction.

"You sitting in the *back*," Shawn said sternly. He looked up and grinned when he saw his mother approaching. "She say she gotta pee."

Shawn let go of Keisha, and she sprinted to Nicole with her strange, little-people run that made onlookers smile.

"Why didn't you use the bathroom before you left?" Nicole scolded as she scooped her up.

"I didn't have to," Keisha said.

"I'll be right back," Nicole called, but Shawn didn't answer. He was busy strapping Kevin into his car seat, like a good big brother should. Despite his progress report, Nicole was constantly appreciative and proud of him.

WITH THE WHOLE family in the car, Nicole felt like her life was calm and complete – and that was strange, considering the racket the twins kept up in the back seat. Even with their limited vocabulary, Nicole's babies could talk your ear off. And when they talked to each other, they were like two old biddies at a bingo game. Most of what they said was gibberish, but Nicole loved to hear it just the same. She once recorded them embroiled in a heated argument that they settled peacefully all by themselves, with nary a word of real English spoken.

While the twins told her about their exciting time at the daycare center, Nicole kept stealing glances at her son as she drove. She was looking for him to roll his eyes or sigh or show some sign of irritation with his siblings. But Shawn didn't look upset at all. He wasn't totally *in love* with the twins' banter like Nicole was, but it didn't get on his nerves, either.

Shawn didn't even get upset when they rounded the corner onto their block and saw Byron's black and gray Buick parked in front of their humble abode. Rather, it was Nicole who exhibited apprehension over the unexpected guest. She told Byron she couldn't see him tonight, yet there he was. And instead of the joy a girl might feel at the sight of her beau, Nicole felt a deep sense of foreboding that made her eyes narrow and a cluster of goose bumps sprout on her forearms.

She turned and watched Byron's face as she drove slowly past him. Byron locked eyes with her as well. Nicole's stare was cold and clearly frustrated with the way things turned out between them.

Byron's stare was exactly the same.

PART ONE
OBSESSION

CHAPTER
4

AFTER SEEING THE look in Byron's eyes, Nicole pulled casually into her driveway and killed the ignition. She looked over at Shawn who didn't expect anything out of the ordinary. Shawn knew Byron well, and Nicole believed he liked – or at least tolerated Mama's boyfriend for her sake. The twins were also unfazed by Byron's appearance, and Nicole wanted to keep it that way. She offered Shawn a weak smile as she unfastened her seatbelt.

"Hey, can you take them inside for me?"

Shawn frowned. He knew as well as Nicole that getting the twins inside and quieted down was a job for two people, or at least one angry adult.

"Are you leaving?" he asked.

"No. I need to have a private talk with Byron."

That was red flag #2, but Nicole didn't stick around for more questions. She exited the Civic and went around to pull Keisha from her car seat. She hoped Byron would remain in his Buick, but when she looked up, Nicole saw that he was out of his car as well.

He took a few steps in their direction, and Nicole shot him a look that said *You stay right there!* Byron read it perfectly. He stopped in his tracks and stuffed his hands in his pockets.

Nicole looked back to her son, hoping he didn't catch the exchange. But Shawn was as quick as a whip. He looked from his mom to Byron's sour disposition and asked, "What's wrong?"

"Nothing, baby. Just help me get these two in the house."

Nicole tried to lead Keisha by the hand, but the toddler was much too slow. Nicole picked her up and fumbled with her keychain as she hopped onto the porch. Shawn was right behind her, but Byron had his full attention now. The boy ran into the first step and stubbed his toe because his eyes were glued on Mommy's friend – who might not be a friend anymore.

"Come on, boy. Watch where you going," Nicole chided.

She pulled Shawn's hand who in turn pulled Kevin's hand, and after a few seconds Nicole had all three of her children safely inside. The twins took off as soon as their feet hit solid ground, but Shawn lingered in the doorway.

"Can you help them get their shoes off," Nicole asked him.

"Okay," Shawn said, but he didn't move.

"You, um…" Nicole sighed. She sensed that any attempt to get him away from the door would only make him more suspicious. "Alright. I'll be right back."

Nicole stepped outside and pulled the door closed. Shawn grudgingly moved out of the way at the last moment. When she turned and faced her boyfriend, Nicole knew their relationship had already been damaged irreparably. She didn't like the way she had to herd her children inside, like Byron was a big bad wolf – no longer hiding in sheep's clothing.

She stepped towards his Buick, and he met her in the middle of the front yard.

Byron was a tall man with caramel brown skin and soft eyes that rarely reflected the look of scorn he now wore. Byron kept his hair short, styled in a fade, and he was always a nice dresser. Today he wore black jeans with a white collar shirt and dark-colored Polo boots. Byron was clean-shaven. His lips were full. His nose was a little pudgy, but overall he was handsome. He was a thin man with large hands and feet. His voice wasn't very deep, but it was stern and assertive.

"What the hell you trying to pull?"

Nicole was more than a foot shorter, but she didn't cower at all. In fact, she bucked-up to him as much as possible.

"Man, what the hell are *you* trying to pull? I told you I had something to do today. Why you come over here?"

"You not finna play me like that," Byron stated.

"Who the hell is trying to play you?" Nicole wanted to know. "Why you always thinking somebody's lying to you? You get on my nerves with that shit!"

"What?"

"You know you heard me!"

"You trying to front me out?"

Nicole looked around, her eyes large and exasperated. "What are you talking about, Byron? Ain't nobody out here! How I'm trying to front you?"

"Let's go in the house," he said and tried to head that way.

Nicole cut him off. She folded her arms under her breasts. "You not going in my house, Byron. I done told you, I got something to do tonight."

"Who in there?" Byron asked, looking over her shoulder.

Nicole's eyes and mouth grew big at the same time. "What the hell are you talking about? Are you, are you serious?"

"Why I can't go in if ain't nobody in there?"

Nicole stared deeply into his eyes, hoping this was a joke, but knowing it wasn't. And at that second she experienced a moment of clarity. She never experienced one before – never heard of them outside of a book she read once – but she knew what was going on right away. It was as if her peripheral vision had been foggy for a long time, but with a snap of her fingers, everything was suddenly crystal clear.

Nicole saw the beauty in Byron. She saw his compassion, the way he cared for her children and the way he sometimes pushed his own needs aside when he made love to her. But Nicole also saw how the jealousy twisted up his brain and made his heart spew sick venom. She saw the conniving in his eyes and the slight twitch in the corner of his mouth. She saw the darkness in his soul, and it made her fearful of him, for the first time ever.

In that second, Nicole knew, without a doubt, that her man was *not right* in the head. And if she didn't put an end to this right now, someone would get hurt before it was all said and done.

"I can't be with you no more."

Byron didn't seem 100% shocked by this. "So. You still ain't finna disrespect me."

"I'm not disrespecting you, Byron."

"Then how come we can't go inside and talk?"

"'Cause I don't want you in my house."

"I been in there before," Byron said, looking over her shoulder again. "Why I can't go in there now?"

"'Cause we not together no more." Nicole spoke calmly.

"You, you gon' break up with me, just like that?" Byron's expression didn't change, but the twitch in the corner of his mouth grew stronger. And a fat tear leaked from his left eye. It rolled slowly down his cheek, but he didn't reach to wipe it away.

"I'm sorry," Nicole said. "I think you're a good dude. I care for you."

"No you don't."

"I do, Byron. Why you think I stayed with you this long? It's, but your jealousy…"

"I love you." His face and his voice cracked simultaneously, and Nicole's heart melted like a candle.

"I'm sorry," she said.

"I love you so much." Both of Byron's eyes were leaking now.

He stepped to her, and Nicole let her guard down. She allowed him to put his strong arms around her. With their chests pressed together, she felt him shudder. She felt his heart stutter. Byron lowered his head and nuzzled her neck, breathing hard.

"You not gon' leave me."

Nicole felt so bad about the breakup, she almost didn't hear what he said. By the time his statement registered, it was too late. She pushed away from him, but Byron locked his hands behind her back. His grip was not immediately vice-like, but the more Nicole struggled against him, the stronger he became.

"Let me go."

She wiggled and then fought violently. But Byron was a grown man. And even though he was sniveling like a little bitch right now, his muscle mass was perfect for his height and weight. Nicole's arms were pinned down to her sides, and she was too small to escape his anaconda grip.

"Man, let me go!"

Her heart knocking, Nicole began to kick as well as scream. A hard foot to the shin made Byron take a step back. Nicole used her forward momentum to send him falling to the ground. But not only did Byron maintain his bear hug, but he managed to shift his weight during their decent, and Nicole found herself on the bottom of the twisted pile of arms and legs. She met the earth with a thud that made all of the air exit her lungs with a surprised *OOF!*

Before she could take another breath, Byron came down hard on top of her and pressed her flat on the recently mowed lawn – which wasn't nearly as soft as Nicole thought it was. The pain was immediate and horrifying, and if she could've, she would've screamed again. But she still couldn't breathe. Her eyes were wide and bulging. She saw gray and black dots circling before her pupils.

Possibly sensing he'd gone too far, Byron began to scramble to his feet, and Nicole sucked in the greatest breath of air *ever*. She exhaled quickly and sucked in another mouthful of life-saving oxygen. And then she went on the offensive. With a guttural growl that didn't sound human at all, she wiggled one arm free and socked Byron as hard as she could, right on the temple.

She didn't get much leverage behind the punch, and he looked down at her with more anger than pain. Before he could react, Nicole brought her knee up and caught him squarely on the testicles. This time Byron cried out in pain. His eyes widened and nearly crossed. His grip on her loosened completely, and Nicole was shocked to see a dark blur, roughly the size of her nine year old son, rush in from the left.

"Leave my Mama alone!"

Shawn jumped on Byron's back and began to pound away with little fists that were as hard as rocks.

"OW!"

Byron reached for the boy as he made it to his feet and staggered aimlessly around the yard. Nicole stared in shock for a moment, thinking this scene was too bizarre to be really happening. Byron lurched to and fro like a zombie, while Shawn clung to his back like a monkey, somehow managing to hold on with his legs while he peppered the tall man with blow after blow.

"SHAWN!"

Nicole shook the last of the cobwebs from her head and shot to her feet just as her boyfriend decided he'd had enough. Byron reached back with one hand and grabbed Shawn by the back of the neck. With a burst of strength that could only be the product of an adrenaline rush, he flung the child across the yard as effortlessly as he would toss his hat on the sofa.

"SHAWN!!"

Nicole's heart split in four pieces as she watched her son tumble through the air. She reached for him and ran, but she was no wide receiver, and the boy was no football. Shawn collided with the earth at an awkward angle, his head and forearm taking the brunt of the impact, and Nicole let out a wail that was nothing like anything anyone within earshot had ever heard. She fell to her knees when she reached her son, and she cradled him to her chest, even though Shawn had already shaken off the fall and he tried to go after the bad man again.

Byron watched them with a special blend of remorse and fear. His chest rose and fell erratically. Blood glistened on his face from a busted nose and a few deep scratches – all inflicted by

Nicole's little boy. The pain in his groin was still very powerful, but nothing hurt as much as Byron's heart at that moment. He didn't have a specific plan when he came to Nicole's house this evening, but this... This was definitely not how he thought things would go. He opened his mouth to tell her he was sorry, but he never got the words out. Out of nowhere he was blindsided once again. This time his attacker meant business.

"Nigga, you wanna hit a little kid?"

WHAP!

Byron's head was rocked by a mean right cross to the jaw. He spun around, expecting Tyson or Holyfield, and he was shocked to see a woman standing there, her fists raised in a perfect boxing stance.

"Come on, punk!"

BAP! BAP!

She caught him with two lightening quick jabs. The first busted his bottom lip. The second snapped his neck back like whiplash.

"Come on! Let's fight!"

POP! POP!

She followed the jabs with a left cross and an uncanny uppercut that sent Byron reeling. His head swam and the earth swam too, and Byron barely had time to register that he was being beaten up by a girl before he hit the ground and rolled slowly onto his back.

He looked up weakly. Angie stood over him with her fists still balled. Byron wiped the tears from his eyes, and he realized he knew this woman. This was Nicole's best friend. Apparently Nicole wasn't lying about helping her move today.

Seeing who knocked him down, Byron didn't feel too embarrassed about getting whooped by a girl. Angie was as tall as him and about forty pounds heavier. She was fair-skinned and more handsome than pretty, about two hundred and thirty pounds of big-mama fun.

She kicked Byron hard in the leg and dared him to get up.

Byron laid his head back on the grass, indicating he wanted no parts. Besides Angie's threatening pose, there were now a few neighbors in Nicole's yard, drawn by her blood-curdling scream a few moments ago. One of the neighbors said she called the police already. Another said he'd make sure Nicole's attacker didn't get away before the authorities arrived.

Damn, Byron said to himself. He closed his eyes so he wouldn't have to see any of the people who were literally and figuratively looking down on him.

CHAPTER 5

TWO HOURS LATER Nicole and Angie sat in Nicole's living room, shoulder to shoulder on her black, leather sofa. The twins were in one of the back rooms. They were as rowdy as ever, but Nicole didn't have the energy to go yell at them. Shawn sat between his mother's legs. He leaned back with his eyes closed and enjoyed the affection as she tenderly rubbed his head with her soft hands.

Shawn didn't have any physical bruises, but Nicole was sure there were emotional scars that wouldn't manifest until later, maybe even years from now. Shawn already had enough emotional problems. Nicole hated Byron for pulling such an ugly stunt. If she ever went out with another man who was even *slightly* unbalanced, she vowed to drop his dusty ass long before she invited him to her home, let alone allowed him to meet her kids.

"I'm sorry you didn't get to move today," Nicole told her friend when the 6:30 news went to a commercial.

"Don't worry about it," Angie said right away. She wore denim Capris with white sneakers and a tank top. Her skin was fair like a glazed donut. Her long hair was braided to her scalp in neat cornrows. She never wore makeup.

Nicole and Angie had known each other for five years, from back when they were next door neighbors at the Falcon Crest Apartments in Woodhaven. Nicole was the first to move into a house, two years ago. Today was supposed to be Angie's first day in her new home.

"I'll help you tomorrow," Nicole promised. "Sunday too."

"I know you will," Angie said with a chuckle.

Nicole smiled too.

"If I wasn't so mad at the time, I think I woulda laughed my butt off, when I saw you fighting Byron like that," Nicole said, careful to keep her language PG for Shawn's sake.

"I thought he was gonna throw at least *one* punch," Angie said with a grin. "That skinny punk just dropped and folded up like a chair."

Nicole laughed. She was still a little tense from the wild episode, but she was safe now, and it was okay to smile again. It might even be therapeutic.

"How about you?" Angie asked Shawn. She nudged the boy with her foot. "I see you got in a few good licks too."

Shawn nodded. "Don't nobody mess with my mama," he said, and Nicole's heart swelled.

"You alright though?" Angie asked him. "I know you not hurt, but you not scared either, are you?"

Shawn shook his head. "I'm not scared."

"That's good," Angie said. "Do you feel like going to get me some Kool-Aid? My mouth's as dry as a desert."

Shawn got up obediently and disappeared down the hallway. Angie took that moment to ask her friend, "So, what the police say? Same old, same old?"

Nicole nodded. "Domestic abuse. Bail won't be that high. I can go downtown tomorrow or Monday to get a restraining order."

"You better do it."

"I am," Nicole said.

"What you gon' do if he come back?" Angie wondered.

"Wally's bringing me a gun tomorrow."

Wallace was Nicole's big brother and only sibling. Most gangsters would probably think he was a *square*, but Nicole preferred to call him *smart*. Just because Wally didn't go around starting trouble didn't mean he wouldn't handle his business if trouble came to him.

"You'd shoot that punk?" Angie asked doubtfully.

"I'll shoot anybody who put his hands on me or my kids," Nicole said confidently.

Angie nodded and then smiled. "You might not have to shoot nobody if Shawn runs into him first. Did you see the way he was boxing that nigga's ears?"

"Yeah, but I was scared to death," Nicole said. "I didn't know you saw that."

"I had just pulled up," Angie said. She shook her head, giggling. "You know, I don't think Byron will ever come back here. Between me and Shawn, that nigga got to' up from the flo' up!"

Nicole laughed nervously, hoping that was the case.

"You lucky to have that boy," Angie said as Shawn returned with her Kool-Aid.

Nicole looked her son in the eyes and smiled. "I know that. I been knowing that."

CHAPTER 6

THREE WEEKS LATER, Charles Dwayne Hester, sometimes know as Chuck or Chuck D, lounged in his west side apartment with an old friend named Michael Cooper. Mike was sometimes known as MikeyMike, but he was trying to get away from the childish moniker. So Charles only called him that when he was trying to get under Mike's skin.

Charles' apartment had two bedrooms, but it was just him living there most of the time. Charles allowed Mike to sell drugs, mainly crack cocaine, from his apartment, but he always put Mike out if he caught his friend dozing on the couch or trying to creep into the spare bedroom with a blanket in hand.

"Yo, you need to move around," Charles would tell him.

"Aww, come on, Chuck. It's just now getting busy out there. The fiends is coming," Mike would say.

"Then you need to get out there and find them," Charles would respond. "I done told you: I don't want nobody in here while I'm sleep."

"This some bullshit," Mike would say, but he would leave. He didn't have a choice in the matter.

Not only was the apartment in Charles' name exclusively, but Charles had a good fifty pounds on Mike. And a recent stint in prison left Charles cut up like Jai White. Mike was an okay fighter in his own right, but Charles just got out of the pen. The fights Mike was involved in while Charles was locked up were nothing compared to the punishment Charles inflicted in the last four years.

Charles left the living room couch and went to look out of the only window in the room. It was nearing four o'clock on a warm Friday afternoon. Soon the hard-working men and women in his apartment complex would come home with their pay for the week.

Back when he was in the crack game, Charles would have a field day on Friday nights. The fiends would come so fast, he couldn't cut up the dope fast enough. Charles would take their hard-earned money. He would take their clothes and electronics and rent their cars when the money ran out. Charles would even take crackhead women to the back room sometimes, if they weren't *too* cracked out. Charles thought most of the female crackheads were utterly disgusting nowadays, but back before he got locked up, you could still find a few dime pieces who had just started using.

Outside of his living room window was the usual scene: Charles' apartment was on the second floor overlooking the pool, but it was already closed for the winter. Even if the pool was open, no one would get in it because the water was mostly green.

To the right of the pool, Charles saw Rufus, their 45 year old maintenance man. He was sweating profusely, working on one of the neighbor's AC units. Rufus was a good handyman, but he was also a crack smoker. All of the dealers in the complex had the best appliances and AC units because Rufus gave extra attention to anyone who donated to his habit. On the other side of the pool, Charles saw Mama Mary, another middle-aged crackhead, walking her skinny Rottweiler.

Charles frowned. Come to think of it, nearly every tenant in his apartment complex was either selling or smoking crack. He only charged Mike $50 a day to work his dope out of the apartment. He didn't know how much Mike was making, but it must've been a lot because he paid the $350 every week – never once complaining about Charles' overhead.

"Yo, nigga," Mike called. "I know you ain't on no gay shit, but this shit looks gay as *fuck*." He laughed.

Charles turned with a slight sneer on his face. "Then put it down, nigga. Ain't nobody told you to mess with it. You keep touching it, maybe you the one on some gay shit."

"Hell naw," Mike said and tossed the G-string on the coffee table. "I'm just saying, I can't see no straight nigga wearing this shit."

Charles' jaw clenched for a moment, but his friend didn't notice. Mike was only twenty-five years old. He got locked up few times here and there for various crimes over the years, but Mike never did any *real* prison time – not four years flat like Charles just did. Mike had been throwing around his gay insults for the past thirty minutes – not knowing that Charles would've broken his neck if Mike said something like that in prison.

The G-string in question was a male stripper thong. It had a six-inch furry tube attached to the front, presumably for the man to insert his penis when he put it on. The thong was still in its original packaging, but Charles already knew he'd need a couple more inches on the furry sock if he became fully erect while wearing it. But then again, an erection didn't seem likely at all. Who could get hard while prancing around half-naked in public? Charles had plenty of reservations already, and Mike wasn't helping at all.

"You just don't wanna see a nigga come up," Charles guessed. He went to the kitchen and took a soda from the fridge.

"Give me one," Mike called when he heard Charles pop the top on his.

Charles grabbed another pop and tossed it to the living room couch. Mike caught it, and he was smart enough to know there'd be a big mess if the opened it right away.

"Yo, why you throw it?" he whined. "Shit gon' spray everywhere." He held the can away from his body as if it might burst open on its own.

At five-eleven, Mike was shorter than Charles by three inches. His skin was dark like Charles' but it wasn't as smooth. He certainly wasn't as muscular. Mike had long hair that was styled in skinny dreadlocks. He wore a black tee shirt with blue Dickey pants. His arms were covered with tattoos, most of them indicating he was a member of the "Hoova Land Crip" gang.

Interestingly, before Charles got locked up, he was a member of the Davis Street Crip gang, and they were at war with Hoova Land. But the beef started over something trivial, most likely a woman, and both the Davis Street and Hoova Land leaders got locked up at the same time. The remaining gang members squashed the beef, and for the last three years there had been an easy truce.

None of that really mattered to Charles, because he didn't consider himself a gang member anymore. To him, Mike was just an old friend from the neighborhood. He was one of the first people Charles hooked up with when he was released four months ago, and Mike had been riding his coattails ever since.

"I ain't got no problem with a nigga trying to make it," Mike said, now tapping the lid of his soda. "I just can't see one of my homeboys being no stripper."

"You ain't got to see it," Charles told him. He downed his Coke is seven big gulps and tossed the can into the wastebasket.

Charles went back to the living room and took a seat on his recliner. At six-two, two hundred and thirty pounds, he was an imposing figure. His black tee shirt was an extra large, but his traps were still bulging through the fabric. His skin tone was dark. He had to keep a fresh crew cut while he was in prison, and he maintained the habit once he was released.

Charles had small eyes with bushy eyebrows that were perfect for the hard looks of disdain he often directed at the dopefiends in his neighborhood. When he was younger, Charles didn't like his LeBron James-snout, but he learned to appreciate it as he grew older and learned more about his culture. Charles had full lips that were a little pinkish. Inmates were required to keep a clean-shave in the joint, and Charles preferred to remain that way when he got out.

"Why you get so sensitive about your little g-string?" Mike asked. He finally felt comfortable enough to crack his soda open and take a sip.

"I see you ain't gon' let it go," Charles said. "You trying to get me hot?"

"Naw," Mike said right away. "I'm just wondering why you get so mad about it. You the one chose to do it. If you don't like it, you ain't got to be no stripper."

"I ain't say I don't like it," Charles replied. "Today my first day. How I know if I like it or not?"

"That's why–"

"But you ain't said nothing constructive since I told you about it," Charles said, cutting his friend off. "Sitting in my house cracking jokes... Don't you know you can get violated over that?"

Charles was 31 years old. His voice was deep and virile. A *violation* could mean anything from an ass-whooping to a cold-blooded murder. Mike didn't think Charles would really harm him, but Charles might kick him out of the dope house if he was mad enough. Mike could sell his rocks on the streets, if worst came to worst, but he wasn't really built for that. He didn't have the heart. On the streets, you have to watch yourself from every angle; 360 degrees. In a dope house on the second floor, all you had to watch was the front door.

"Alright, man. I ain't gon' clown you no more," Mike promised. "But can you tell me what possessed you to go buy some drawers like that? I been knowing you since the fifth grade. You ain't never said nothing about wanting to be a stripper."

"I didn't buy that thang," Charles said, still a little irritated. "The man at the club gave it to me. And you know I don't wanna be no goddamned stripper. I'm just trying to make some paper, as much as I can with as little risks as possible."

"But who turned you on to stripping?" Mike wondered.

"This girl I met at the store," Charles said honestly. "She saw how a nigga got all swolled up in the pen, and she asked if I had a job. I said, 'Nope,' and she handed me a card for the strip club. She said her brother was the manager, and he was looking for some niggas that was cut up, like me."

Mike didn't say anything because it was embarrassing to talk about Charles' physique. Mike hadn't done a push up since his high school P.E. teacher made it a requirement. Charles did no less than 250 push-ups a day when he was locked up, and he kept up the regimen since his release.

"I swung by there," Charles continued, "and the dude was liking me right away. He said the girls always like new faces, and they was gonna go crazy when they saw me. He made me take my shirt off and was looking at me real hard, like I was a slave on the auction block. This nigga was grinning so much, I thought I was gon' have to whoop him, but then he said I was hired – just like that. He said I could make about $200 on the weekdays and probably more than $500 on Friday and Saturday. All I got to do is wear that damned sock on my dick and rub up on some old ladies. That's easy money."

Mike fought really hard to stop from laughing. "You ain't just got to rub up on 'em," he said. "You got to dance for 'em, Chuck, just like the girl strippers do."

"Nigga, how you know?"

"I saw it on this video once."

"Man, what the hell you doing watching some stripper video with *dudes*?"

"Hey, chill with all that gay shit," Mike said. "It was on HBO. They was talking about female strippers, but then they showed a couple of man strippers. It was just for a second, and it wasn't like I was jacking off to that shit or nothing. Just 'cause we talking about some gay shit, don't mean either one of us is gay, my nigga. You need to get off that."

"Alright," Charles said, realizing he did have a few homophobic tendencies.

"Anyway," Mike said, "I know for a fact you gotta dance for them ho's. You got to wave yo shit all in they face, and you got to get on the stage and do some of them grinding dances them bitches like."

Charles tried to minimize his actual stripper duties, but he knew Mike was right. Before Charles left his interview at *Peeping Jane's*, the manager took him to the main floor to let him get a peek at some of the strippers currently working at the club. Charles almost threw up at the sight of a light-skinned dude humping the stage like there was an invisible female lying under him.

But twelve hundred dollars a week is a lot of money, especially if you're fresh out of prison with a couple of felonies on your record. Charles had been looking for a regular job ever since he got out. Stripping was a last resort, and the fact that he was currently in possession of a thong with a furry sock attached to it was testament to just how desperate he was to go legit.

"I used to could dance a little when I was in middle school," Charles said. "Ain't nothing changed. It's all about humping. I can hump the floor, or I can hump a chair, or I can hump directly on a bitch. It all add up to the same thing; money in my pocket."

"Yeah, but you got to be damned near *nekkid!*" Mike said with a grin. "Ass out!"

Charles felt his anger starting to rise again. "Say, my nig, don't you think I'm embarrassed enough about this shit already? If you ain't gon' give me twelve hundred dollars a week, then you ain't got shit to say about how I get it. I done told you: I don't wanna be no stripper. This is just some shit I got to do. If you wanna keep cracking jokes, then you can crack your skinny ass out in that heat and sell your shit on the corner, like a real goon."

It was mid December, but still nearly eighty degrees in central Texas. Mike knew Charles wasn't kidding about putting him out, so he piped down.

"Alright, my nig. Chill. It ain't that serious, yo."

There was a knock at the door.

Mike started to get up, but Charles motioned for him to remain seated.

"Why you think it's for you?" Charles asked as he pushed off of his recliner.

"It's about that time," Mike said, rubbing his hands together. He removed a fold top baggie from his pocket. It was almost half-full with ten dollar pieces of crack.

Charles went to the door and checked the peep hole. "I told you it wasn't for you." He opened the door to reveal a short man with brown skin and a full beard.

The visitor wore baggy jeans with new Jordan sneakers. His long-sleeved Polo was without a wrinkle. His fitted cap was clean and crisp.

"Yo, what it do?" Charles asked him, offering a brief handshake.

"What's up, Chuck D?" the visitor asked, smiling brightly. He walked inside and looked around the ugly apartment. "You got it ready?"

"Naw, not yet. You can come in here."

Charles led the man to the kitchen where he had a scale waiting on an otherwise bare counter. Charles reached to one of the higher cabinets and removed a large freezer bag that was filled with greenery. It was so potent, you could smell the marijuana before he opened it.

The customer's eyes lit up. "Can I see it?"

Charles popped the bag open and removed a bud that was lime green with strands of red throughout. To the average observer, the weed appeared to be covered with a thin coat of mold. But to those in the know, this was the finest grade of bubba Kush marijuana.

The visitor took the bud and examined it and then took a hearty sniff while Charles weighed out his purchase on the digital scale.

"Ooh wee! This shit smells *nice!*"

Charles bagged one ounce of weed and handed it to him. "Don't get no better."

"What about this?" the man asked, still holding the sample bud.

"You can throw it in there," Charles said.

The customer was happy to hear that. He reached into his pocket. Charles quickly ran through his options, should he try to pull out a gun, but the baller produced a wad of one hundred dollar bills; squeezed together with a rubber band. He counted out four notes and handed them to Charles.

"'Preciate it, Chuck. You my man!"

"For sure," Charles said and led him out of the apartment. The whole transaction took less than sixty seconds.

"What you on now?" Mike asked when the customer was gone.

"Kush," Charles said. He counted his money again and folded it with the considerable stack he already had in his front pocket. He returned to his seat in the living room and kicked his legs up on the coffee table.

"What you charge him for a zone?" Mike asked.

"Four hundred."

Mike grinned and shook his head.

"What?" Charles asked him.

"Why don't you just get down with the crack game?" Mike asked, waving his baggie.

Charles shook his head. "You know I don't fuck with 'caine no more."

"I don't see why not," Mike said. "You taking the same risks."

"How you figure?"

Mike sat up with his elbows on his knees. "You started off selling *regular* weed," he explained. "Then you moved up to popcorn, then 'dro and now Kush. Don't you know you get just as much time selling Kush as you do for selling crack?"

Charles hated his friend's knowledge sometimes. When he first got out, Charles was determined to not sell drugs at all. Prison was the worst thing he ever experienced. Charles would do damned near anything to avoid going back – not because he was a punk, but because a man can't accomplish anything in life if he's locked up. He can't see his kids, his family. He can't make any money. He can't go to the park or even sit on his porch and watch the cars go by.

But after two months with no luck finding work, Charles decided it wouldn't be too bad if he started selling a little marijuana here and there. He bought a pound of weed for $400 and made $1,200 without even breaking it down into dimes. He later learned he could make twice as much (with half as many customers) by selling "popcorn" weed. He then graduated to selling hydro and eventually "Kush," that had supposedly come all the way from Afghanistan.

Charles only needed to make four to five Kush sell each week, which hopefully kept him under the radar. The only drawback was the "High-Potency Marijuana Sentencing Enhancement Act of 2009." That law made it possible to get from five to 25 years in prison for selling certain types of high quality weed. So in essence, Mike was right about Charles taking the same risks as a crack dealer.

"Naw," Charles shook his head. "The difference is my customers ain't all ugly and cracked-out like yours. Niggas who buy my shit are G's; with nice clothes and rides. Them crackheads you mess with will tell your enemies *and* the police all about you for ten or twenty dollars. Plus I got *waaay* less traffic."

"But you selling drugs," Mike insisted. "Me and you is exactly the same."

Charles continued to shake his head. "I told you I'm going legit, Mike. I'ma stop selling everything if this stripping thing pans out, till I can get a real job. I'ma move outta here, and ain't gon' be nobody knocking on my door but my family." Charles eyed his apartment with contempt.

Mike frowned, not liking his goals at all. The dope game was always going to be the best game. Charles was stupid to think an ex con could get a break – in the middle of a recession, no less. "You just made four hundred dollars in thirty seconds," he said. "Stripping ain't never gon' be that good."

"I'm just stacking my paper right now," Charles explained. "When I get a regular job, I'm good. Fuck them get-rich-quick schemes, homey. Everybody wanna get out of prison and go *right* back. I don't know what for."

"I feel you." Mike said. "So, what they say your stripper name was gon' be?" he asked, still hoping he could change his friend's mind with good-old fashioned peer pressure.

"Dripping Chocolate," Charles said with a sigh.

Mike didn't stop laughing for thirty seconds.

CHAPTER
7

AROUND THE SAME time Charles was looking out of his apartment window, passing judgment on the dopefiends below, Nicole and her friends at APEX were counting down the minutes on another hellacious Friday afternoon. Nicole was the center of attention, mainly because she sat between her buds Stella and Twyla, but also because yesterday was Nicole's 29th birthday. After two days of haggling, her friends finally talked her into letting them take her out for a little partying.

Nicole was never one to frequent the many night clubs in Overbrook Meadows, and she went out even less after the twins were born. Plus Christmas was just a few days away. All of Nicole's extra money was spent already; wrapped nice and neat in different size boxes under her Christmas tree at home. But her girlfriends promised she wouldn't have to open her wallet at all tonight, so Nicole reluctantly agreed to let them spoil her.

"Did you pick out your outfit yet?" Stella asked her. It was a quarter till four, but she had her headset looped casually around her neck, a clear indication that she was done taking calls for the day.

"I did," Nicole said with a smile. "It's a black and red skirt with a slit up the side. I haven't worn it in a while."

For her party tonight, Nicole's hair was down, in loose curls. Her lipstick was fiery red. She was thin and beautiful. Nicole's swivel chair was turned completely away from her computer, a clear sign she was done working for the day as well.

"I hope it's *tight*," Twyla said. "We don't want none of that conservative mess tonight."

Twyla was probably the prettiest member of their clique. She had golden brown skin like a dinner roll. Her breasts were 32 C's, but even they couldn't draw attention away from her big, brown eyes and moist, pink lips. Twyla had been dating her current boyfriend for four months, but he was just a semi-wealthy drug dealer. Everyone knew Twyla wouldn't settle down until she found a serious baller, preferably a Maverick or a Dallas Cowboy.

"It's alright," Nicole said about her dress.

"You should wear something *real tight*," Twyla advised. "You got ass for days. Don't be scared to put it all out there."

Stella laughed.

Nicole did too. "You tripping."

"No I ain't," Twyla said. "You haven't gone out in, like, six months. Been broke up with that buster for three weeks. It's time to get your sexy back."

Nicole's smile faded a little at the thought of Byron. He was another reason her friends were so insistent she go out with them tonight. After the eight months of stress she endured with her crazy ex, they wanted her to let her hair down, to feel wild and oh so *free*.

"Is he still calling?" Stella asked, unaware that Nicole wanted to forget about Byron completely.

"Forget that punk," Twyla said. "We don't need to talk about him no more."

"I'm just asking," Stella said. She was only ten years older than the rest of the crew, but she had motherly vibes that could not be denied. Nicole was often thankful for her comforting touch.

"It's cool," Nicole said. "I think he called last night, but he didn't say nothing. The caller ID said it was a private call. I don't know... I didn't use to get prank phone calls before we broke up."

"You know it was him," Stella said. She pushed her glasses higher up her nose and pursed her lips. "What the police say? How many times do he have to call before you can get him arrested again?"

"I think once is enough," Nicole said. "But he didn't say nothing last night, so I don't think that counts."

"You shoulda called the police when he showed up at your door last week," Stella said. "I told you: You can't let him slide with that, Nicole. Not even *one* time."

Nicole's face grew warm. She sighed in anticipation of the hell Stella just unleashed.

"He came by your house?!" Twyla was just as loud as she wanted to be. Some of their coworkers looked in their direction, but they looked away with a roll of their eyes when they saw who it was. It was no secret the rat pack accumulated a good deal of animosity over the years. Few people bothered to complain to Blanca, the floor's supervisor, because she was a card-carrying member of the rowdy crew.

"It's alright," Nicole said. "Didn't nothing happen."

"But why you let him come over your house?" Twyla demanded. Her big, brown eyes were bigger than usual.

"He was in jail for two weeks," Nicole explained. "When he got out, he came to talk to me, to see if I was still mad and if I didn't want to see him no more."

"You told him that when you called the law on his punk ass," Twyla said with a sneer.

"That don't mean nothing," Nicole said. "The police said half the girls that get beat up let their man come home when he gets out of jail."

"That's why you shoulda called them when that mark showed up at your house," Twyla said, "to show them you ain't stupid."

"Didn't nothing bad happen," Nicole said. "I told Byron I had a restraining order, and he could get arrested right now for coming to my house. I told him we wasn't never getting back together, and he better leave."

"And he left?" Twyla was skeptical.

Nicole nodded. "Yeah. He left."

"Good."

Nicole agreed that it was, and she wished things had really gone that smoothly. In truth, the sight of Byron on her doorstep scared the bejesus out of her. So much so, Nicole ran to her bedroom and retrieved her brother's pistol before she even considered asking Byron what he wanted.

With gun in hand, Nicole had to make one of the hardest decisions of her life: Should she yell at Byron through the door while her son watched, or should she step outside where she was 100% more vulnerable?

But she wasn't vulnerable, was she? She had a firearm, and she knew how to use it. The gun gave her strength, and she stepped out of her den to meet the threat head on, like mama bears have been doing for centuries.

Once outside, Byron's eyes quickly locked on the weapon. He looked more offended than frightened.

"Why you, why you got that? I'm not, you think I'm gon' hurt you, Nicole?"

She held the gun at her side. She felt bold, but her heart was hammering. Her voice rattled when she spoke. "You hurt me before."

"That was an accident," he said, almost pleaded. Byron wore dark jeans with a dingy tee shirt. The whites of his eyes had a red and yellowish tint. He was a mere shell of the man Nicole knew before. She knew she could never love or trust him again.

"It wasn't no accident," she said.

"I didn't hit you," Byron told her. "Why you tell them people I hit you?" His voice cracked, and his eyes quickly filled with tears.

"I didn't tell them that."

"I didn't hit Shawn either," Byron whined. "I love Shawn. I would never hurt him."

"It don't matter 'cause you not even supposed to be here." Nicole's features were hard and cold. "I got a restraining order, Byron. You can go to jail right now."

"I know," he said. "They gave me them papers. I just wanted to see if you and Shawn was okay. I didn't know who was on my back, Nicole. I swear to God. I wouldn't never do nothing to hurt Shawn – you either." He stared deeply into her eyes. His tears flowed freely.

Nicole saw that his fingers were trembling. His chest rose and fell heavily. She felt bad for him, but the last time she let her guard down, she ended up in a terrifying bear hug. No way would she let him get that close again.

"Just leave," she said. "I don't wanna call the police on you, Byron. But I will..."

He shuddered. He nodded and wiped his nose with the back of his hand. "I didn't mean to hurt you," he insisted. "I just wanted to hold you. I don't know why you started kicking."

"You need to leave."

"I didn't know it was Shawn on my back," he said. He looked down at his shoes and sniffled. "I just pushed him off. It was a reaction." He met her eyes. "I didn't hit nobody that day, Nicole. I didn't deserve to go to jail for that. They saying I beat up on women and kids, and it ain't true. You know it ain't true. You need to tell them. You need to tell them you drop the charges."

With that, the slight sense of remorse she was developing was gone in a flash. Nicole tightened her grip on her brother's pistol. "Get out my yard, Byron. We ain't got nothing else to say to each other."

He gasped. He sensed he'd made a mistake, but he wasn't sure how. "You don't have to drop the charges, Nicole. I just, I want us to try to work it out. I wanna see Shawn. I wanna tell him I'm sorry."

Nicole removed her cellphone from her pocket. "You think this a joke?"

"Alright, alright." He put his hands up. "I'm gone, Nicole. Dang. I'll leave."

She stood on the porch and watched until he got in his car and made good on his promise. When she went back inside, Shawn was waiting for her.

"What he want?"

"Nothing," Nicole said. "He wanted to say he was sorry. He didn't mean to hurt nobody."

"Y'all still together?"

"No," she said. "And if you ever see him again, you need to tell me right away. He don't got no business coming over here no more."

Shawn waited a second and then said "You gon' miss him?"

Nicole hesitated, surprised by the maturity of his question.

"No," she said. "Not at all."

"You don't need no boyfriend," Shawn told her, and Nicole smiled at that. It wasn't entirely true, but she understood her son's knee-jerk response: Boyfriend hurt Mama, so boyfriend = bad news. He was too young to see it any other way.

That visit from Byron was over a week ago, and he didn't make the mistake of coming by Nicole's house again – not that she knew of, at least. He did call once to ask if she was doubly sure they couldn't work it out. Nicole told him she was going to show the police her caller ID if he kept it up. She got a call last night from an unknown individual who didn't speak at all. He just listened and breathed. Nicole called the phone company and requested they block all private callers from contacting her. She doubted if that would solve her problem, but it couldn't hurt.

"What the hell?" A familiar voice snapped Nicole out of her daydreaming.

She looked up and saw the fourth member of their clique rounding the corner. Blanca Puente was short and round, as cute as a cherub. Nicole had the most fun with Blanca back when all four of them used to sit next to each other because Blanca had an awesome sense of humor. She would crack up at the lamest jokes, and if she saw something that was *really* funny, Blanca would get red in the face and nearly choke on her chuckles.

Blanca was 27, married with four kids. Her youngest child was already out of diapers by the time she talked her baby-daddy into jumping the broom – but she wasn't resentful at all. *Better late than never*, she said. Nicole reserved a little resentment for any man who would knock a girl up *four times* and still be reluctant to get married. She never met Blanca's husband, but Nicole suspected he was a lowlife.

"What's up?" Twyla asked when their supervisor got closer.

"Why y'all making so much noise?" Blanca wanted to know. "I can hear you all the way across the room."

If it was anyone else, the ladies would've felt guilty and rushed to take another call. But Blanca's friendly smile let them know there was nothing to fear.

"I'm sorry," Nicole said. "You know that was Twyla. That girl don't have an inside voice."

"Who complained?" Twyla asked, ready to cut her eyes at a snitch.

"Nobody," Blanca said with a giggle. "I heard you myself."

"We'll be quiet," Stella said, but Blanca waved her off.

"It's okay." She checked her watch. "It's almost time to go. You ready for tonight?" she asked Nicole.

"Yeah. I wish y'all would tell me where we going..."

Blanca giggled, her cheeks growing crimson. "I'm not saying *nothing*," she assured, but everyone knew she was the weakest link.

"Tell me," Nicole urged, "so I'll know what to wear."

"It, you could wear anything," Blanca said. She had long, beautiful hair with tighter curls than Nicole. Her eyelashes were naturally long. She wore the perfect amount of shadow.

"Is it a dancing club, or a mingling club?" Nicole asked. "'Cause I don't wanna wear high heels if–"

"Stop," Twyla said. "You ain't slick. You know she gon' mess around and tell you."

"I think I have a right to know where I'm going," Nicole said. Her smile was delightful. In truth, she enjoyed the mystery very much. She couldn't remember the last time she was so excited about her birthday party.

"I'll just say there's a lot of men there," Blanca said.

"Shut-*up!*" Twyla told her. "Dang! You can't keep your mouth shut for nothing!"

"What?" Blanca asked. "I didn't tell her where we're going."

"You're about to," Twyla said. "You don't need to give her a bunch of hints."

"Alright, I'll stop asking," Nicole said, playing mediator as she often did. Although the four women were all friends, it was no secret some got along better than others. Twyla was somewhat of a bully, and Blanca didn't stand up for herself as much as she should.

Nicole checked the clock. "It's time to get out of here anyway," she said as she rolled back to her computer. "As long as we not going to a strip club or nothing, I'm cool."

No one responded to that. Nicole frowned. She looked back and saw that her friends had disappeared behind their cubicle walls. Only Blanca remained in view.

"I said, '*As long as we not going to a strip club...*'" Nicole repeated.

Blanca turned abruptly and headed the other way. "Alright, I'll see y'all later."

Nicole's jaw dropped. She rolled quickly and peered around Stella's cubicle wall. "Girl, where we going tonight?"

"I don't know," Stella said with a blank expression. "Ask Twyla."

Nicole headed that way, but Twyla's voice cut her off. "It's a surprise, Nicole. *Dang!*"

"Alright, whatever," Nicole said. She grabbed her purse and stood and straightened her skirt. "But I ain't going to no strip club, so I hope that ain't the big surprise..."

Once again no one responded, which of course spoke volumes.

CHAPTER 8

NICOLE WAS STILL in a good mood an hour later when she dropped her kids off at her brother's house. Wally had to be the best uncle around. And he was one of few people who could get the twins in line with just his words. Nicole had no idea how he accomplished this feat, and she didn't ask too many questions. Kevin and Keisha were always happy and healthy when she picked them up from Uncle Wally's, and that was good enough for her.

Wally had dark, brown skin and a thick goatee. He wore old school, horn-rimmed glasses like Malcolm X. Wally lived alone in a nice house on the southwest side of the city. He worked with computers, but his title changed so often, Nicole couldn't say exactly what he did for a living. She knew he created software for a number of large companies, and he liked to work alone, preferably from home.

Wally wore sweat pants with a dazzling white tee shirt when he answered the door. He took the diaper bag from Nicole and told the twins, "You bet not!" when they took off in the direction of his office. Kevin and Keisha looked back at him, looked at each other, and then they took off again, headed for the game room instead. Shawn was right behind them. Wally had a full size pool table and nearly every gaming system every invented in there.

"Do you be whooping them?" Nicole asked, always surprised by the twins' obedience to her big brother.

"It's something in their genes," Wally said. "They're hot-wired to submit to the alpha male."

Wally was skinny and somewhat dorky, so Nicole guessed it was his deep, manly voice they responded to.

"That nut been back to your house?" Wally asked.

Nicole shook her head. "Nope."

"He still calling?"

"Uh uhn." Nicole shook her head. She almost told him about the unknown caller last night, but there was no sense in getting him upset about something she couldn't prove.

"You sign up for them classes yet?" Wally asked.

"I'm going to," Nicole said. Her brother had no problem with giving her a pistol, but Wally was straight and narrow all the way. He wanted Nicole to take classes, so she'd be aware of the laws regarding when she could and couldn't use deadly force. He thought it would be pretty silly if Nicole went to jail for a pistol charge when the only thing she wanted was to protect her family.

"Why you gotta procrastinate?" Wally wondered, but that was something he'd been asking her for years. Wally always thought NOW was the best time to do everything. Nicole always believed LATER was much better.

"I'ma take care of it," she promised and stepped closer to give him a hug. "Thanks for watching them for me."

The siblings had always been close, mainly due to their parents' divorce when Nicole was nine years old. Surprisingly, it was their mother's infidelities that led to the split. She had an affair with a co-worker and a neighbor while Nicole's father was far away, combing Afghani caves in search of Osama bin Laden.

When he got discharged from the Army, Nicole's father was a heavy drinker. The divorce turned him into a raging alcoholic, and Wally and Nicole had to stay with their mother (whom they fully blamed and somewhat despised during their teenage years).

As a result of these parenting issues, Wally and Nicole learned to depend only on each other, and they continued to do so today.

"You want me to keep them all night, right?" Wally asked when Nicole released him and backed out of his doorway.

"I can pick them up," she said. "My friends are going to try to get me drunk, but I don't have to–"

"Naw, it's cool," Wally said. "You never go out. Have fun. I'll see you tomorrow."

"Okay," Nicole said, happy for the night of freedom.

"Where y'all going?" Wally asked.

"I think they're gonna try to take me to a strip club," Nicole said. "But I'm not going. They gotta come up with something better than that."

Wally shook his head, chuckling. "You might as well go."

"That's just *nasty*," Nicole said with a frown.

"Get off your high horse," Wally told her. "Strippers need love too."

CHAPTER 9

NICOLE DIDN'T THINK she was on a high horse (whatever that meant), and her opinion of strippers hadn't changed four hours later when she, Blanca, Stella and Twyla all piled in Angie's SUV. The atmosphere was immediately crunk. Angie was somewhat of a Tomboy, and she invested a lot of time and money in her truck's sound system. She had two twelve-inch speakers in the back, pushed by a 1200 watt amp. Beyonce's new song belted from the speakers with enough bass to rattle the bones of all five ladies.

Nicole didn't see her coworkers outside of the office very often. Whenever they did hook up, they were as wild as they wanted to be. Everyone wore skirts with heels. Their legs were long and creamy. Their push-up bras created a cornucopia of cleavage. Their lips gleamed with gloss and lipstick. Their perfumes mingled with their sex pheromones, creating a new scent that would draw men from miles and miles if someone figured out a way to patent and bottle it.

Angie's music wasn't *too* loud, but the girls had to raise their voices when they spoke. No one drank anything yet, but they were all animated; laughing and sometimes yelling at each other as Angie piloted her SUV to a still undisclosed location.

Nicole sat in the back seat between Stella and Twyla. Blanca was riding shotgun, but she turned in her seat so she wouldn't miss out on any of the juicy girl talk behind her.

"I swear it was as big as a cucumber," Twyla was saying. "And it wasn't even hard!"

"Bullshit!" Nicole told her.

"I swear!" Twyla said, her grin big and toothy.

"I don't get it," Stella said, shaking her head. "How he go from knocking on your door one minute to showing you his thing the next?" Stella was the only one who wore a loose-fitting skirt, but she still looked really nice. Nicole predicted her husband would jump her bones as soon as she made it home that evening. Well, that was *if* she made it home.

Nicole's girlfriends all met at her house at nine-thirty. They left their cars there and jumped in Angie's ride. Since Nicole had the house to herself, she told them they could spend the night when they got back if they were too tipsy to drive home. Angie didn't mind being the designated driver because her tolerance was so high, she could still have a couple of drinks without getting drunk.

The current topic of discussion was Twyla's indecent episode with one of her boyfriend's best friends. Supposedly J Mart came to her house last night looking for his main man Tron. When Twyla told him Tron wasn't there, J Mart professed his love for her. More accurately, he expressed his desire to "beat it out the frame."

"Big dick niggas like him, they don't care," Twyla told Stella. "I told him, 'If you serious, let me see it,' and he whipped it out, just like that!"

"Why you tell him that?" Nicole wondered. She loved dick just as much as the next girl, but she didn't think she ever told a man to *whip it out*.

"He was rubbing on hisself while he was talking," Twyla recounted. "I wanted to see what he was working with."

"Wait," Stella said, shaking her head.

"Yeah, wait one doggone minute!" Nicole said. She thought she heard the worst of it, but this story kept getting better. "What do you mean he was rubbing hisself? Who does that?"

"A pervert," Blanca said.

"He ain't no pervert," Twyla said. "J Mart looks good. He fine as hell, *and* he got paper."

"So, how did this play out?" Nicole wondered. "You opened your door, and he's standing there with his dick in his hand?"

Blanca laughed.

"Naw," Twyla said. She laughed too. "I opened the door, and he was like, 'Yo, Tron over here?' And I was like, 'Naw, he ain't here.' And he was looking me up and down, 'cause I had just got out the shower, and I didn't have nothing on but a long tee shirt. His eyes got real low, and he said I had some sexy legs. I told him, 'Yeah, I know,' and the next thing I know he was rubbing on hisself. He said, 'When you gon' let a nigga hit that?' I told him he was tripping, and he said, 'I'm serious. I'll beat it out the frame.' I checked him out a little and said, 'What about Tron,' and he said, 'That nigga ain't gotta be all in our business.'"

"Jesus," Stella said.

Nicole was thinking the same thing, but she was too enthralled to speak.

"So then I said, 'If you serious, let me see it,'" Twyla went on. "And he just pulled it out."

"Just like that?" Nicole asked.

"Just like that," Twyla confirmed. "And he was still standing outside too. I reached out and grabbed it a little, and I was looking him in the eyes the whole time. He got hard in, like, two seconds. I was getting wet too, but I didn't know what kind of game he was on, so I told him, 'Maybe later,' and closed the door."

Nicole shook her head, no longer surprised by any of this. "Okay, I'm..." She sighed. "Yeah. So anyway, when are y'all gonna tell me where we're going?" Looking out of the window, Nicole saw that they left Overbrook Meadows five minutes ago and were now in the fair city of Arlington.

Angie took the next exit at Division and said, "We almost there. You can wait."

"Yeah, I can wait," Nicole said, feeling antsy. "But if we're going to a strip club, you can turn around right now. It's plenty of regular clubs in Overbrook Meadows. We can go to one of those."

"What's wrong with a strip club?" Twyla asked.

"Are we going to a strip club?" Nicole countered.

"If we is, what's wrong with it?" Twyla said, and Nicole knew for sure.

"Man, what's wrong with y'all?" she asked, no longer smiling. "What made y'all think I wanted to do something like that?"

"I keep asking you what's wrong with a strip club," Twyla said. "You still ain't said nothing."

"I don't want some half-naked man rubbing all on me," Nicole said with a sneer.

"If you didn't want that, you wouldn't have no kids," Twyla said.

Blanca laughed.

"Ain't that the truth," Stella said.

"I'm serious," Nicole said. "I don't wanna go to no strip club."

"*Why*?" Twyla nearly shouted.

"Because the men in strip clubs are *freaks*," Nicole said. "They nasty. They grind on women all night with their thongs, and they let people touch them. They're like *prostitutes*."

"How are they like prostitutes if they don't have sex?" Blanca wondered.

"Oh, don't think they don't have sex with some of those girls who go in there," Nicole said. "If they'll shake their ass for five dollars, what you think they'll do if you offer them a hundred to meet you at a motel?"

"Well, don't offer them a hundred dollars and you won't have nothing to worry about," Stella advised.

"I still don't wanna go," Nicole said, but Angie was already slowing down, about to make a right into a crowded parking lot down the street. The building was unremarkable, but a huge marquee attracted hundreds of women to this location each week, like moths drawn to a bright flame. The marquee read "PEEPING JANES."

"You can keep right on going," Nicole pouted. "This supposed to be *my* party. How come I don't have a say in where we go?"

"If you really don't like it, we'll leave," Twyla said. "But we done drove all the way over here. We might as well get some drinks before we go. Is that okay?"

Nicole shrugged. It was clear she didn't really have a choice in the matter. "Whatever."

CHAPTER
10

OH MY GOD.

Peeping Jane's lobby was no bigger than a walk-in closet. A handsome brother wearing a white collar shirt directed Nicole's crew to push through a set of dark curtains that led to the main floor. Nicole had a lot of expectations, most of them bad, and she wasn't too surprised when she followed Angie inside. But still.

Oh my...

Nicole knew she was still in Arlington, Texas, but she felt like the curtain was actually a portal, delivering them to a parallel universe where the laws of physics, gravity and decency were thrown to the wayside. The huge room was dimly lit. The strobe lights disoriented you further. But at the same time, Nicole could see it all. And it was a lot. The shock made her heart flutter and her eyes dilate.

Peeing Jane's was a dark business with dark walls, dark carpeting and dark, illicit desires at every table. In the center of the room was the main stage, which was currently occupied by a high yellow fellow with curly hair and a pencil thin moustache. The dancer didn't have a stripper pole to swing on, but he didn't need one.

Nicole watched as he crawled across the stage (on all fours) towards a woman at the other end. She had a ten dollar bill in her hand, and the dancer clearly wanted it. When he reached her, he dipped his head low and then pushed up on his sinewy arms, revealing a chest and torso with more cuts than a Jack-o-Lantern.

The dancer then began to hump with a passion. He kept his eyes glued on his sponsor for the moment as his pelvis pounded the stage to the beat of *Ride my Pony*. Nicole was still walking, but she was transfixed on the scene. From the side, it looked like his spine was as limber as a snake's. Every muscle on his back glistened with a thin coat of stripper oil. The man was completely nude except for a thong that disappeared fully down the crack of his ass – and what a nice ass it was.

As he humped the stage, Nicole could imagine two creamy thighs spread beneath him. She could've imagined more, but the dancer stood on his knees suddenly, exposing his genitals – which were thankfully sheathed by a furry tube attached to his thong. He appeared to be fully, or at least three-quarters erect, and the woman tripping him was tickled pink to have his manhood close to her face.

She reached for it. The dancer let her get a nice squeeze before he gently pushed her hand away and shook his head slightly. He didn't look angry. In fact, he looked like he would love for her to fondle him – and then some – if not for Peeping Jane's pesky rule. Nicole didn't see the rules posted anywhere, but she knew that patrons could touch any part of the dancer they wanted – *except* his penis.

The tipper knew this too, and she was completely satisfied with her one sneaky feel. She stuffed her ten dollar bill into the front of the dancer's thong (making sure to brush her hand along his shaft one more time for good measure) and then she placed both hands on his chest and felt her way down to his thong again before he backed away. The woman was forty-five years old and slightly overweight. She had two friends with her who were around the same age.

Nicole didn't realize she was staring so hard until she ran into Angie who had stopped at a table she thought they could all sit at.

"I thought you didn't like strip clubs," Stella told her.

"I don't," Nicole said.

"Your mouth says no," Stella noticed. "But your eyes, they're saying something totally different."

CHAPTER
11

THE GIRLS STARTED their evening with a round of hurricanes for everyone. Nicole never had one before, and she was startled by the alcohol content. Her eyes widened at the first sip. She stirred the drink with her straw and sipped from the top of the glass, but it was still very strong.

"Damn, this is what we're starting with?" she asked their designated driver as Angie took two hefty gulps of the same concoction.

"Might as well," Angie said when she put her glass down. "I figure the more you drink, the sooner you'll stop tripping."

Blanca laughed at that. Stella did too.

The five friends sat around a circular table built for four. There was a new dancer named Explicit on the main stage. This was another fair-skinned brother, but he wasn't as fine as his predecessor. His muscles weren't as defined, but Explicit had a huge barrel chest. His hair was long, braided to his skull in cornrows.

There were too smaller stages in the room, and they were both occupied by brown-skinned men in varying stages of undress. Nicole could already tell the most popular dance was the *dick slang* – if you could even call that a dance. She was pretty sure that if she had a penis, she could make it flop around with minimal effort.

The strip club was nearly full with over fifty happy and tipsy women. The dancers who weren't on stage mingled with the crowd, hoping someone would call them to their table or ask to go the "Champagne Room" for a lap dance. Rumor had it the men would unsheathe their swords in the Champagne Room and let you touch it and possibly take their manhood into your mouth back there. Nicole doubted if that was true, but either way, she knew she would never find out.

"You ain't got to get her drunk," Twyla said to Angie. "Nicole know she like it here. I don't know why she fronting."

"I'm not fronting," Nicole said. "If I liked it, I would tell you."

"We seen the way you was looking at ol' boy when we first came in," Twyla reminded.

"He's fine," Nicole admitted. "But I just can't get into this..." She looked around uneasily. "This whole vibe." She shook her head. "It's not for me."

"Me neither," Stella said. "I haven't been to a place like this since before I got married. But I can still have fun here if I want to."

"What don't you like about it?" Blanca asked Nicole. "I know you don't care about how those dancers live their lives. They're getting paid, and they're having fun."

"I *don't* like the way they're living their lives," Nicole said. "But it's not just them, it's *us*. It's every woman here. What do we expect to come from this?"

"Nothing," Twyla said. "It's pure entertainment, like the movies."

"More like a porno," Nicole said.

"And people buy those, too," Twyla replied. "Even in the recession, porn stars get *paid*."

"I guess it's 'cause I don't got no man at home," Nicole said. "I bet a lot of these women don't. They get all hot and heated, and go home to what?"

"They vibrator," Angie said with a snicker.

Nicole took a big sip of her drink, totally unwilling to discuss her masturbation habits.

"Maybe you can meet somebody here you can go home with," Blanca said.

Nicole coughed and had to swallow hard to avoid choking. "*What*?!"

"They mens," Twyla said. "They fucking somebody when they leave here. Why can't it be you – or me, or anybody else that want them?"

"That's disgusting," Nicole said. She couldn't believe her friend would suggest such a thing.

"Why it's disgusting?" Twyla asked.

"Because they're *freaks*," Nicole said.

As if to illustrate her point, the dancer on the stage closest to them made eye contact with Nicole and licked his lips. He flicked his tongue at her as he rolled his glistening abs in a *Come get me* gesture. Nicole rolled her eyes at him and looked away. The dancer frowned, and he rolled his eyes too. He muttered something that looked like, "Bitch, what you come here for?" But it was impossible to hear him over the music.

"They probably know how to fuck *real* good," Twyla said. She eyed the dancer Nicole just rejected, and he seemed equally attracted to her.

"That's the game they play," Nicole said. "They make you think you got a chance, and they'll let you get closer and closer. After four lap dances, you might have them buck naked, talking about how bad they want you. But when your money's gone, they're gone too."

"That's why you have to play them just like they playing you," Angie said. "Let me show you how to do this thing..."

She found nine singles in her purse and then called the closest dancer to their table. He was tall and brown-skinned with a lot of tattoos scrawled across his chest and arm muscles. Nicole thought he was attractive until he opened his mouth to speak and she saw that he was missing one of his canines.

"What's up, ladies."

All five women at the table devoured him with their eyes at the same time. They looked from his face to his chest to his stomach (which was nice and flat) and down to the mysterious package behind his thong attachment.

"Damn, you got it going on!" Angie said. "Lemme see that ass!"

The stripper turned obediently revealing a perfect bubble butt.

"*Jesus!*" Angie said, shaking her head. She reached and squeezed one butt cheek while she tucked one dollar into the waistband of his thong.

"Ooh, and it's soft too!" Angie told her friends. "Feel it, y'all!"

Stella and Nicole declined, but Twyla and Blanca reached to squeeze the Charmin.

"Ooh, it is soft," Blanca said as she sat back down. She looked so happy, Nicole almost gave it a try.

"Turn around," Angie instructed.

The stripper turned to face them, and Angie slipped another dollar in his waist band.

"Show us some moves," Angie ordered.

The stripper began to dance for them – nothing big, but it was quite a show for just the five of them.

"I like him," Angie said to her friends. "What's your name?" she asked the stripper.

"Diablo," he said with a grin.

"Is this all you in here?" Angie asked as she went in for the kill. She groped his manhood fully and removed her hand before he had to do so himself. "That's all him," Angie told her friends with a laugh. "Diablo got it going on!"

Diablo's smile brightened and he waited for his next instruction, but that was it. He'd been had.

"I'ma find you later," Angie told him and then turned her back on him completely. "I might get one of them lap dances, too."

Diablo stood there looking foolish for a moment before he said, "Alright, I'll hook up with you later," and walked away.

The girls burst into laughter when he was gone.

"So who's running what?" Angie asked as she returned her seven singles to her purse. "I gave that nigga two dollars for a dance, a feel on his booty *and* I grabbed his dick! Yeah, they will try to play you if you let them, but you can play them just as good. The only reason he did that is because he thought he was gon' get the rest of the money in my hand. But I don't have to give that nigga shit!"

The girls laughed again, and they agreed Angie just scored a huge victory for womankind in general. With the game plan set, the ladies set forth to get as much as possible for as little as possible for the rest of the evening.

Men were used to being the predators when it came to sex, but on that night, at Nicole's table at least, the women refused to play the victim. Dancer after dancer was drawn to their table, lured by fistfuls of dollars the girls were clutching. And one by one the men left dejected, lucky to get a fraction of the exposed bankroll.

Even when word got out that table six was filled with cheapskates, the men kept coming because they had no choice. Two dollars was better than no dollar, and surely one of the girls would slip up as the night wore on and their alcohol intake increased.

The dancers vowed to send at least one of them to the ATM before it was all said and done.

CHAPTER
12

CHARLES' FIRST NIGHT at Peeping Jane's started out much worse than Nicole's. He arrived early, thinking there was some last minute training he needed, but there was nothing. The club manager asked if he had his thong, Charles reluctantly told him he did, and that was it. The boss man said, "Alright, well, you're ready to go. The house is packed tonight, so you should make a killing. Do you want to start off on the main stage, or you wanna take a look around first?"

Charles was hesitant to jump right into it.

"I wanna look around."

"Alright," his boss said, his smile big and greasy. "Go change, and I'll get Johnny to show you the ropes. You can work the crowd for a little while, and then we'll get you on one of the side stages. We prolly won't put you on the main stage until after midnight. That cool?"

Charles shrugged. His employer was a fat man with curly hair that was as dry as a haystack. Charles didn't think he'd ever get used to the way the man looked him up and down, like Charles was his dinner or something. "Yeah, that's cool," he said.

"Cool," the manager said. He stood and slapped Charles on the shoulder. "You the man. You gon' kill 'em tonight. You'll see! You 'bout to get paid, my brother!"

Charles nodded. "I hope so, man. I can't be doing this for no chump change."

"Don't even worry about that," the manager said. "You the man, Charles. You 'bout to set this place on fire. Hey, Johnny!" he yelled into the hallway. "Johnny in there?"

They waited a moment, and a large shadow rounded the corner, followed by a black man who was nearly as big. Johnny was topless, but he had on a pair of basketball shorts. He was fair-skinned with a huge chest that was almost as big as Charles'. A tattoo on his right pectoral read *Explicit*.

"What up?" Johnny said. He looked Charles over with little interest. His eyes were low and bloodshot. He sniffled and wiped his nose with the back of his hand.

"I want you to show the new guy around," the boss said. "This his first night. He never danced before."

Johnny eyed Charles again and said, "Alright." He turned and headed back in the direction he'd come.

Charles already regretted his choice of professions, but after a moment he followed his new coworker.

Johnny led Charles to a locker room that was more like a trauma unit because Charles got burned twice in the first five seconds. He took a seat on an empty bench, his face set in a deep sneer that made his peers avoid conversation.

When he was in prison, the convicts took their sexuality very seriously. They wouldn't prance around showing their ass unless they wanted someone to put something in it. The inmates would say they got "burned" if they accidently glimpsed another man's genitals. It was common to hear things like, "Damn, cuz! You burnt me! Next time tell me when you changing clothes over there," when the prisoners were locked down for the night.

The locker room at Peeping Jane's was one of the worst things Charles ever experienced. Everywhere he looked was BURN! BURN! BURN! Brothers were walking around in their thongs. Some were changing and not even attempting to turn away from the crowd. Charles finally snapped when a pretty-boy walked by and his bare bum came within three feet of Charles' face. He rose to his feet and shoved the man hard in the chest, sending him flying into a row of lockers.

"Get yo ass out my face, punk!"

The man he pushed registered shock and then anger. He regained his balance and met Charles head on. "Better keep yo hands off me, boy!"

The stripper looked like he could handle his business, but Charles knew he was a pussy. A real man would've thrown a punch instead of making idol threats.

"Say, cut that shit out!" The man called Explicit was between them in a heartbeat. He grabbed the aggressor by the shoulders, and Charles allowed him to push him back a couple of feet. "What's your problem?" Explicit asked him.

"This nigga got his ass all in my face!" Charles spat. "All y'all acting like you gay or something."

Charles looked meaner than a junkyard dog, but to his surprise the man he pushed chuckled.

"You just got out the joint, huh?"

Confusion replaced Charles' anger. "Yeah, why?"

"Every nigga who get out the pen be acting like that," the man said. "Ain't nobody in here gay, my nig. You ain't gotta prove your manhood all the time."

"I ain't trying to prove nothing," Charles said. "But I don't like seeing all this ass everywhere I look. Y'all ain't trying to turn away or nothing!"

A small crowd had formed. Most of the faces were grinning, shaking their heads.

"I'm Otis," the man Charles shoved said. "I been working here three years. When I first started, I was just like you. I was ready to fight somebody if they didn't wrap a towel around they waist when they was back here. But after awhile, you get used to this shit. You ain't in prison no more, homey. Look at it like it's a football locker room. I ain't trying to show you my shit, and I know you ain't trying to look at my shit, so we go on about our business."

Charles found it hard to gain knowledge from someone who was wearing a thong, but he knew Otis was telling him right.

"Alright, my bad," Charles said. "But until I'm used to it, can y'all please try to keep your ass out my face? I'm still getting adjusted to life in the free world. Shit, I haven't even bought an iron yet. I still press my clothes under my mattress."

The men standing around him laughed, and Charles felt good about the situation ending without any more violence. It was hard, but he really did want to change. He could do it too. He just had to take it one day at a time.

CHAPTER 13

BY THE TIME Charles felt comfortable enough to take his turn on the main stage, a full hour had passed, and he felt like he knew more about the stripping business than he ever wanted to. The sad thing was Charles was trying to get away from trouble, but nearly every aspect of the strip club was illegal.

The dancers were all hustlers and addicts. They sold cocaine, heroin, weed and ecstasy to each other as well as to some of the female customers. Explicit, the man who showed Charles around the place, snorted one pill of heroin every couple of hours. There was another guy who had a full injection kit in his locker. And of course there was also some prostitution.

And Peeping Jane's customers were supposed to be the driving force behind the business. But rather than see them as valuable commodities, most of the guys looked upon them with disdain. They thought the women were ugly or fat or desperate, yet they had no problem sucking them dry, preying on them until their purses were completely barren. Everything the strippers did was a scam to get more money from the "dumb broads" who dared to come to the club on Friday night.

Charles was determined to not develop any of those holier-than-thou attitudes, so he kept an open mind when the DJ introduced him to the crowd:

"Alright, ladies, we got a special treat for you right now. Coming to the main stage is a face I know you ain't never seen nowhere before because he ain't been nowhere before! Get your tips ready and show him some love y'all! It's *Dripping Chocolate!*"

The DJ put a record on, and Charles sauntered to the stage as sexy as possible when the first notes of *Feeling on Your Booty* began to play.

The club owner told Charles to bring his own personality to the performance, so he wore jeans and a wife-beater rather than one of the cowboy outfits or break-away tuxedos they had in the back. None of the women in the club rushed the stage right away, but that was okay. Charles met most of his comrades by then, and he felt he was the pick of the litter. No one was as handsome as him. Charles was the only one who wasn't drunk or high, and he also had the best physique.

He began his show with a gentle rocking of his hips that gradually included his shoulders and head. He didn't really know what to do with his arms, so he flexed his muscles a little and heard a few oohs from the crowd. He wanted to smile, but he kept his face stern because that's what all of his coworkers did. He lifted his wife-beater to show off his six-pack, and three women stood and floated quickly to his stage.

Encouraged, Charles pulled his shirt off completely, and the ladies started to cheer. At that moment Charles realized he didn't have any more dance moves, so he dropped to his hands and knees and worked his hips like he was making slow love. That brought even more screams and a few more women to the stage.

Oh, they like that, Charles thought, and he couldn't help a smile from brightening his face then.

"Ooh, he so pretty!" one of the girls standing before him said. She clapped and stared into his eyes, but Charles became nervous and he looked away.

He dropped down lower and spun to the side and began to pump the stage in earnest. The chatter in the audience grew louder, but Charles was too embarrassed to look at them. He had forgotten how Explicit told him to remove his pants. *Fuck it*, he thought and rose to his feet again. He popped the button on his jeans and rolled his stomach as he lowered the zipper. He turned his back on the crowd before he let the pants fall past his butt. The explosion behind him was enormous.

Charles couldn't make out everything that was said, but the consensus was clear: His ass was a thing of beauty. He faced the crowd again, and there was a second eruption when they saw how well he filled out his thong attachment. Charles summoned the courage to look the women in their eyes, and what he saw made his chest swell two times its normal size. The women were way past enamored. Some stared at him in awe. They screamed like he was a rock star. And they weren't all ugly and fat either. Some of them looked good, damn good, and something happened that was so shocking Charles had to look down at himself before he fully believed it.

As unlikely as it was, he grew a mighty erection. The rest of the dancers were so used to the game, they never got hard enough for their dick to stand at even half-attention. But Charles' penis stuck straight out, and it wasn't done yet. It began to point skywards as it became engorged with blood, and nearly a hundred eyeballs were glued to it. Money began to rain on him before Charles got his jeans fully off.

By the end of his song, Charles was still rock hard and he had nearly sixty dollars strewn about his feet. His heart and brain were racing, but he forced himself to scoop it up casually, like it was no big deal.

CHAPTER 14

AFTER HIS TIME on the main stage, Charles had to dance on the second stage and then the third one before he could mingle with the crowd and hopefully be asked for a lap dance in the Champagne Room. Most of the other dancers made this transition with no trouble at all, but Charles had a virtual mob of women to contend with.

"Dripping Chocolate!"

"Dripping Chocolate, come over here!"

He placated them as best he could: "I'll be back. I'll come holler at you in a minute." But there was one group of women who would not be denied. A large girl with beautiful cornrows grabbed Charles by the wrist and yanked him to her table. Charles saw that she was sitting with some of the most beautiful women in the club, and he has eager to see what they wanted.

"Hey, it's my girl's birthday," Angie told him. "Can you give her a quick dance?"

"I, uh, I'm supposed to be on the other stage," Charles told her. He was wearing nothing but his thong, and his erection was still very powerful.

"Come on," the other girls at the table urged. "It won't take that long."

"Alright, who's birthday is it?" Charles asked. He checked the women out one at a time, hoping it was the slim chick. For as long as he could remember, Charles had a thing for short, skinny women. Both of his baby-mamas fit that description to a T.

"It's hers," Twyla said, pointing at Nicole.

Charles looked the birthday girl in the eyes and his smile was genuine. She was very pretty. And even though she was sitting down, Charles saw that her hips were spread just right. He knew she had a nice ass, and he was eager to get his hands on it.

"Happy Birthday," Charles said as he grooved his way to her chair.

Nicole grinned and then laughed with both hands hiding her smile. She was clearly intoxicated, but that wasn't a turn off. Charles worked his body like a snake and eased closer and closer until his penis brushed her knees. She looked down at it and laughed again. Charles grinned as he put his large hands on her thighs and pulled her legs apart. Her eyes widened and she threw her hands down to hide her panties – but Charles was already moving closer and her fingers brushed his throbbing manhood.

Nicole's jaw dropped and she looked into his eyes again. Charles nodded slightly, still smiling, still dancing, and Nicole felt her hands open on their own accord. They closed with a slight grip on his penis, and her mouth went completely dry. She wasn't sure how they got to this point, but she squeezed harder and stroked slightly, amazed by how much of him she could feel through the thong attachment.

But then reality struck, and she quickly withdrew her hands. Her eyes were wide, mouth open. Charles chuckled at her unease and continued to work himself closer. When his penis encountered her panties, he thought he might shoot his load in front of everybody, but the birthday girl was a prude. She pushed his chest back and forced her legs closed at the same time.

Charles laughed at her again, and she looked around wildly before meeting his eyes and giggling herself.

"I can't believe I just did that."

"I can't believe you stopped me," Charles said as he backed away from the table. "I'ma get at you later," he told her, and then he turned and made his way to his designated post.

Five minutes passed before Charles realized the birthday girl got a free feel and didn't give him on dime. When he was finally free to mingle with the crowd, Charles went looking for the thin beauty at table six. He was disappointed to find that her whole crew was already gone.

81

PART TWO
SECOND IMPRESSIONS

CHAPTER 15

A WEEK LATER, Christmas had come and gone, and Nicole was in the recuperating phase. The holidays had never been that special when she was growing up, mostly due to her parents' divorce, but Nicole went out of her way to give her children a different experience. Shawn got the new Nintendo DS he'd been hinting about, and the twins got a bundle of flashy toys they would no doubt break or lose interest in by Valentine's Day.

December 29th was a sunny Saturday, but the northern winds were starting to bring chills that would graduate to a full blown freeze in the next couple of weeks. The twins needed new winter coats, and Nicole was disgusted to find only seven dollars and eighty-three cents in her checking account. She needed the twins' father to provide for his seeds, so she gritted her teeth and loaded the family into her Civic for a trip to the north side of town.

Clifford Washington was a 34 year old no-goodnick with bow legs, five baby-mamas and a silver tongue that would've done the snake oil salesman of yore proud. Nicole had half a dozen meaningful relationships in her lifetime, and Clifford was the only boyfriend she considered a MISTAKE.

When she met him, Cliff told her he was a delivery truck driver for FedEx. He had FedEx shirts and stocking caps lying around his living room, and he had his own car and apartment, so

Nicole had no reason to believe otherwise. She was charmed by his wit and the sense of security he offered her, and she soon found herself seriously smitten. Cliff doted on Shawn like he was his own child, and when he made love to Nicole, he explored every inch of her body with such passion she still got tremors whenever she thought about it.

Sure there were warning signs, but Nicole wanted to see the best in Cliff. She wanted to believe in him. She began to envision their future together. She wasn't even upset when she learned she was pregnant with twins.

But like all fairytales, Clifford was too good to be true. Nicole discovered he was cheating on her. And if that had been it, she might still have a little respect for him today. But Cliff's magic show went *way* past his one infidelity. Nicole later learned that Cliff didn't really work for FedEx. He didn't have a job at all – other than his 9-5 shift at a crack house on Baltimore Avenue. In that neighborhood, no one knew Cliff by his real name. Everyone called him Skimo.

And if *that* wasn't enough, Nicole learned that her accidental pregnancy was not so accidental at all. Cliff liked to *feel* 100 percent of his sexual experiences, so he started slicing his own condoms a few years before he met Nicole. Using a razor blade, he'd cut through the condom wrapper (and condom), leaving a small slit none of his sexual partners noticed. Cliff's condoms would indubitably "break" during intercourse, and he'd throw his hands up in a *Who me?* gesture if his partner complained.

"It ain't my fault my dick big."

Nicole kicked Cliff to the curb when all of his darkness came to light, but the damage was already done. Keisha and Kevin were born six months later. At that point Nicole had three children and no father in the home, but at least all of her STD tests came back negative.

A few months ago she heard Cliff contracted herpes from one of his many skeezers. Nicole didn't have one ounce of sympathy.

"I'm surprised you don't got AIDS," she told him during a heated argument. "You sick dick bastard!"

NICOLE KNOCKED ON Cliff's door at 2:32 pm. He answered with a groggy expression that spoke volumes about his lifestyle. He was topless, but thankfully he threw on a pair of basketball shorts when he staggered out of bed.

"What's up?"

"Daddy!"

The twins rushed from Nicole's side and grabbed on to their father's legs. Kevin and Keisha were both fair-skinned, like their sorry-ass dad. Kim didn't understand why they loved him so much, but she never interfered with their affection. When they got older, they would realize what a loser Cliff was. Until then, they could believe in him if they wanted, the same way they believed in other fictitious beings, like Santa the Easter Bunny.

"Why you ain't answer your phone?" Nicole asked. "You just got up?"

Cliff frowned and looked over his shoulder at his cable box. He looked down at his children and a smile brightened his face. "Yo, what up, son?" he said to Kevin. "How you doing, pretty lady?" he asked Keisha.

Cliff was a slim man with a plethora of tattoos marring most of the skin between his neck and waistline. The tats should've been Nicole's first big clue that Cliff might not be all he said he was. But her nose was so wide open back then, she believed him when Cliff said he used to be a bad person, but he turned over a new leaf.

He looked up at Nicole with a grin. "What's going on? Where y'all finna go?"

Cliff had a slight moustache and goatee, but he was usually clean shaven. His hair was long, not styled at all at that moment. But as rough as he looked, he was still handsome. Cliff had the cutest lips and the most beautiful eyes Nicole had ever seen on a man.

"I'm going to Walmart," she said. "I need some money to get them some coats. And you didn't get them nothing for Christmas. You can give me some money for that too, if you want."

At the mention of Christmas, Kevin asked his father, "Where my present?"

"Where my present, too?" Keisha piped in.

"Who said I didn't get them nothing?" Cliff asked. "I got you something right here." He backed away, and the twins reluctantly loosened their grip on his legs. They followed him to the kitchen where he had a few bills lying on the counter. He plucked two twenties and handed one to each of his children.

"Ooh!" Kevin said as he stared at the dead president's picture.

"How much this?" Keisha asked.

"That's *twenty dollars*," Cliff told her. "You can buy whatever you want with that."

Nicole took a few steps into his apartment and shook her head in disappointment. She folded her arms over her stomach and had a nice frown waiting when Cliff turned back to her.

"What?" he said.

"That's straight-up *sorry*," she told him. "What they supposed to do with that?"

"Take 'em to Family Dollar," Cliff suggested. "They can get a lot of stuff with that."

"Why don't *you* take them," Nicole countered. "I'm sure they would rather go with you."

"I wanna go with Daddy!" Keisha said, and she grabbed hold of his leg again. Clifford bent and picked her up.

"You wanna go with Daddy?" he asked her with a crocodile smile pasted on his face.

"Me too!" Kevin said. Upset that he didn't get picked up, Kevin pulled on Cliff's shorts until they came sliding down his thin frame. Cliff looked into Nicole's eyes and took his time pulling them back up.

"Hold on, boy," he told Kevin. "You pulling my clothes off, man!"

Keisha laughed at that. Kevin did too.

Nicole couldn't help but smile a little herself. Daddy may be a screw up, but it was clear the twins loved and missed him dearly. "Gimme the money for their coats," she told him.

Cliff rolled his eyes and turned back to the pile of money on his counter. He found two more twenties and offered them to Nicole. She took them and held her hand out again.

"This ain't enough."

"How come it ain't?" Cliff asked. "That's eighty dollars."

"No, that's *forty* dollars," Nicole said. "You can't count their Christmas money – or their *guilt* money, whatever you wanna call it."

"Watch your mouth," Cliff told her. He turned again and came back with two tens. "There. Now that's sixty dollars. I know you can find some coats for thirty dollars apiece."

Nicole was sure she could too, so she turned without another word and headed out of the apartment.

"Wait!" Cliff said. "Where you going? What you doing?"

"I'm told you I'm going to Walmart," Nicole said. "I'll be right back."

"Why you ain't taking them?" Cliff asked, looking down at his son.

"You can keep them for awhile. I'll only be gone an hour, two at the most."

"*Two hours*?!" Cliff said it like a judge was sentencing him to twenty years.

"You haven't seen them in a month!" Nicole reminded him. "I know you ain't tripping about two hours."

"You didn't even ask if I had something to do," Cliff said. "Hold on a minute."

"Boy, I don't have time to play with you," Nicole said. "Shawn waiting on me in the car."

"That's why you needed that other twenty," Cliff wondered, "so you can get something for him too?"

Rather than respond, Nicole's nostrils flared and her eyes became hard and cold. Cliff quickly realized he had gone too far.

"Alright. Alright, chill," he said. "You say you gon' be back in two hours, right?"

"Yeah," Nicole said and then she turned and left the apartment. The only reason she brought the twins over there was because she was positive Cliff never sold drugs from his home.

He was smart enough to value his safety. He was also smart enough to keep all of his women ignorant of each other. But when it came to practical things, like being responsible for the children he brought into the world, Cliff had to be the dumbest man ever. Nicole wondered if she was equally dumb for letting an asshole like him knock her up.

CHAPTER 16

AT 2:36 P.M. on the same Saturday afternoon, Charles "Dripping Chocolate" Hester fought valiantly to free himself from the clutches of his baby-mama Stacy Cook. Stacy heard that Charles had been stripping. She didn't understand how Charles could show his bare ass to a room full of strangers, but he wouldn't even take his shirt off for the mother of his child.

She cornered him in the bedroom and tugged at his zipper while peppering his neck and face with warm, breathy kisses that used to get him as hard as a rock. Now Charles was acting so tight with the dick, he refused to let her give him a blow job – and he knew Stacy had mad skills in the blow job department.

"C'mon, Chuck. Why you acting like that? Mama need you, baby. You got me so wet. Feel it."

She took his hand and tried to pull it between her legs, but she was a petite woman, and Charles was a hulk of a man. Stacy couldn't do anything with his body unless he allowed it to happen.

"Watch out, girl," he told her.

He pushed her arms away, but they kept appearing in a different spot. He never knew Stacy was part octopus. He wanted to grab her by the shoulders and shake the hell out of her, but that could be considered domestic violence. If she called the police and showed them fresh bruises on her arms, they wouldn't listen to

Charles' excuse about how she was the one trying to rape him. They would look at how much bigger he was and formulate their own conclusions. Once they ran his license and saw what a bad apple he was, Charles would go to jail for sure.

And besides that, Charles' five year old son Charles Jr. was in the room with them. Big Charles couldn't believe Stacy was trying to jump his bones while Little Charles was standing right there. Big Charles wondered if Stacy behaved this way on a regular basis, when her real boyfriends stopped by for some late night action. Actually Charles didn't have to wonder at all. He was certain Stacy was always this freaky.

When he first met her, Charles thought he hit the jackpot. Stacy was a hood chick with a smart mouth and plenty of sass. She was high-maintenance, but that was okay because Charles liked how she took care of herself. Stacy always had to have her hair and nails done. She was brown-skinned and pretty, but most importantly she was short and slender with a perfect ass that looked good in everything she put on.

When they made love, Charles could lift her into the air with no problem at all, so standing up became their favorite position. If Stacy had a skirt on, they could make love in a restaurant bathroom or on the side of MikeyMike's grandmother's house. Stacy's freakiness was her best attribute back in the day, and the fact that she was barren was even better. Charles didn't go raw-dog very often, but when he and Stacy became a serious couple, he never wore a condom with her.

And he loved it – up until the day she told him she was pregnant.

Charles was nearly belligerent when she delivered the frightening news. He demanded to know how, after nearly six months with no rubber, she wound up pregnant all of a sudden. What happened to the female surgery she had when she was younger that supposedly messed up her uterus? What happened to, *I don't even make no eggs*?

Stacy further angered Charles with her nonchalance about the matter.

"Boy, I don't know what happened. I ain't never been pregnant in my life. And you see how long it took for you to get me pregnant. I don't know why it happened, but it happened. Now deal with it."

Charles had no choice but to do just that, but before he could deal with it, he had to do some real soul searching to determine what his child's life would be like with Stacy as a mother. Sadly, Charles decided things wouldn't be good at all.

It was one thing to have a freaky girl he could lay pipe to after a hard day of hustling. But when Charles took a step back and evaluated Stacy's parenting skills, he knew that he had made a grave mistake indeed. Stacy wasn't just a hood chick, she was a hood*rat*. Stacy liked to raise her voice to the point of screaming during an argument, especially if she was in a public place. She would kick off her shoes and fight at the drop of a hat, and she was always interested in a welfare or a hot check scam.

Charles decided that it was okay to have fun with Stacy when it was just the two of them, but under no circumstance could their relationship continue on its current route with a baby in the picture. Charles tried to change Stacy, but she resisted with a passion. After awhile, Charles became frustrated. Every time he saw his woman cursing at someone while tilting back a 40 ounce of Old English, Charles imagined his son or daughter sitting on her lap while she got drunk. It nearly drove him crazy.

He ended the relationship when Stacy was four months pregnant. Four and a half months later she got the last laugh. Stacy delivered a healthy baby boy at Jackson Memorial, and from that day on she and Charles were shackled together for life.

That was five years ago. Charles might not be fighting her off today if he didn't get lonely in prison and start writing love letters to his baby-mama. Stacy jumped on the opportunity to get him back, and she gave him the best sex of his life the day he got out of prison. But after a few weeks Charles remembered why he broke up with her in the first place. Three months ago he ended the relationship a second time, but Stacy had yet to accept it.

"I waited for you all this time while you was locked up," she told him.

"You didn't wait for me," Charles had said. "MikeyMike told me you been fucking with a lot of niggas."

"Whatever," Stacy had said. "We still together. We got this baby. And you ain't leaving me."

Charles wondered how she planned on keeping him against his will, and he found out fairly quickly. Every time he went to visit his son, Stacy would do everything she could to get in his pants. She was certain that if Charles took a dip in her forbidden waters *one more time*, she could whip it on him so good he'd forget all about how crazy she was.

Charles didn't think he'd mind so much if his son wasn't standing there watching each time Stacy pulled her nympho routine.

TODAY SHE WORE a short white tee shirt with a pair of g-string panties. That was all. Charles still found Stacy attractive, and he knew he exacerbated the situation sometimes by staring at her juicy ass when she flaunted it around her apartment while she got Charles Jr. ready for his visits with his dad.

"Come on, baby. Don't be like that." She reached between his legs and grabbed his manhood, which, despite his frustration, was starting to respond to Stacy's rough advances.

"You getting hard," she noticed. Stacy bit his bottom lip and raised one leg on his thigh.

Charles fought an urge to grab her leg and lower her onto the bed. He knew she was soaking wet, and his dick knew it too. Stacy was a lunatic, but she could fuck like nobody's business. Her head game was better than any girl Charles had ever known.

But it could never be just sex with Stacy. She wanted a full-time commitment. Charles knew he could never go that route again, so he pushed her away and then grabbed her arms to restrain her.

"Stop, girl! The baby standing right here!"

The baby was tall and intelligent and nowhere near a *baby* anymore, but Charles was finding it hard to accept how quickly Charles Jr. grew up while he was in prison. When he got locked up, his son was in diapers. Now the boy could talk, run, dress himself and use the television remote.

Stacy didn't look down at her son. She stared into Charles' angry eyes, and *finally* accepted that she failed yet again. Like many hoodrats, she didn't take failure well. She sneered and then snapped at Charles, like he was the one pressuring her.

"Get yo hands off me, nigga!"

She pushed away and stormed out of the room. Charles was glad their fight was over, but he wished it didn't end like this every time. He looked down at his son and the boy looked up at him with the same sullen expression he always wore when they were around his mom.

Charles Jr. had large eyes and a large head. He was surprisingly smart, given the lack of intellectual development at his home. Charles knew his son obtained most of his knowledge from Sesame Street, because Stacy hadn't read a book in years.

"I'm, sorry about that," Charles told his son.

"It's alright," Charles Jr. said.

They left the bedroom together and found Stacy in the living room, digging through her purse for a Newport.

"Alright, I'ma take him to get something to eat," Charles told her. "I'll be back in a couple of hours."

"Fuck you," Stacy snapped.

"Don't be talking like that in front of my son," Charles said.

Stacy turned and looked him in the eyes. "Fuck you, Charles. You ain't gon' do shit about it."

A brief rage made Charles' muscles twitch, but he didn't wrap his hands around Stacy's throat like she wanted him to. He never hit a woman, but he was known to shake the hell out of one.

He hadn't done that since he got out of prison, and he wasn't going to backslide now, definitely not for an instigating witch like Stacy.

"You want me to go back to the pen," he said.

"Might as well. You ain't doing nothing for me since you got out," Stacy said. "You ain't doing nothing for your son either."

This time Charles had to take a deep breath to avoid putting his hands on her. Stacy knew he was trying his best to be a good father. She had a bad habit of using Charles Jr. to hurt him.

"Alright, whatever," he said and headed for the door. "I'll bring him back in a couple of hours."

"Why don't you keep him?" Stacy spat. "When was the last time he spent the night with you? Don't you think I want some time to myself? Maybe I wanna go out."

Stacy was attacking him on two fronts now. She wanted to make Charles feel inadequate as a father. She also wanted him to know that she was going to have sex with *somebody* today. Charles could solve both of these problems by spending the night with her.

But he was too smart to fall for these tricks. He said, "Alright. I'll keep him tonight," and Stacy nearly flipped. She threw her lighter at him as Charles exited the apartment.

"Fuck you, nigga! Get yo ass on then! Don't nobody need you!"

Charles paused at the porch and looked down at his son again. He wanted to tell the boy to wait there while he went back inside and manhandled Stacy for disrespecting him like that. He wanted to teach her a lesson so badly his fingers trembled.

But Charles Jr. took his dad's hand and led him down the stairs. "It's alright," he said, and Charles felt like a fool for letting Stacy get to him again. If his five year old son could live with that wretched woman every day, then Charles could certainly tolerate her for ten to fifteen minutes a week.

In fact, if Charles could get his life on track, he was sure he could get a judge to grant him full custody of his son so Charles Jr. wouldn't be subjected to that madness. Charles was an ex crack dealer, an ex gangbanger and an ex con, but he was still a better parent than Stacy.

"I guess we gotta go to Walmart," he told his son when they got down to the parking lot. "Get you something to wear this weekend."

Charles Jr. smiled for the first time that day. He had smooth, dark skin, like his father.

"Will you buy me a big wheel?"

Charles grinned. He made over four hundred dollars last night at Peeping Jane's, so money was no problem. "Yeah, man. Whatever you want."

They piled into his '88 Bonneville and left the parking lot with the system turned down low, so they could have some man talk. Stacy called Charles' cellphone before they made it to the freeway.

"You didn't get no clothes for Lil' Charles," she said, trying to play nice. "I'm packing his bag for him."

Charles used to wonder how she could go from full-blown rabid dog one minute to being soft and sweet the next. Now he no longer cared. MikeyMike often told him, "That bitch crazy." No further explanation was needed.

"I don't need his bag," Charles said. "I'm taking him to Walmart to buy some clothes for today and tomorrow."

"Oh," Stacy said. When she wasn't fiending for sex or cursing you out, she sounded like a regular person. "Don't you got to work tonight?"

"I'll call in," Charles said.

"Didn't you just start working there?" Stacy said. "They'll let you miss a day already?"

"Ain't like I work for the bank," Charles replied. "It's a club. Anything goes in that place."

"Oh," Stacy said. "I'm sorry I yelled at you. You is a good father. I just be getting mad 'cause we ain't together no more. You can come get his clothes. I'll be good, baby. I promise."

Charles rolled his eyes and told her, "Naw, I'm alright. We already done made plans."

"But–"

"Let me get off this phone so I can drive," he said. "I'll holler at you tomorrow."

"Okay," Stacy said. "I love–"

Charles hung up before she could finish the sentence.

CHAPTER
17

NICOLE FOUND MATCHING jackets for the twins for thirty dollars each, but they were on sale for $19.99. So technically Cliff was right about her not needing the extra twenty bucks, but he was a fool for sure if he thought Nicole was going to return his change.

In addition to not seeing his kids very often, Cliff was not keeping up with his child support payments. Nicole took him to court last year, but there's not much the system can do if the deadbeat dad doesn't have a legal source of income. Nicole warned Cliff that he would get arrested once his arrears reached a certain dollar amount. But he didn't care about that either.

"How I'm gon' get a job if I'm in jail?" he asked her once.

"You're not in jail now, and you're not looking for a job," Nicole replied.

"I don't need no job," Cliff had told her. "I got paper. I give you money all the time. I gave you a hundred dollars last month."

"But you didn't give me *nothing* the month before that!" Nicole snapped. "And you supposed to be paying *four hundred dollars* a month for two kids."

"Well, I can't pay you shit if I'm in jail."

"It ain't even about you paying at that point," she told him. "It's about you sitting up in there, washing your drawers in the sink, thinking about what you did."

"I ain't scared of no jail," Cliff said defiantly.

And that was that. He continued to neglect his financial obligations, and Nicole waited for his inevitable incarceration. She wished it didn't have to come to that, but she agreed with the child support laws. Plus she thought Cliff should go to jail just for slicing his own condoms so he could trick women into letting him hit it raw.

Sick dick bastard.

NICOLE DIDN'T PLAN on buying Shawn any clothes with the money left over from the twins' coats, but she did stop at the McDonalds inside Walmart so they could dine on Cliff's dime. After they ate, Nicole had to buy her son a few pairs of school pants so he could make it through the second semester. She'd have to use a $40 gift card Blanca gave her for Christmas, but that was nothing new. Nicole rarely had a desire that was more pressing than her children's needs.

When Shawn was mostly done with his burger, Nicole broached a sensitive topic that she knew he'd been thinking about.

"New Year's is coming…"

Shawn's whole demeanor changed. He looked down at his tray and stopped chewing the food in his mouth.

"Did y'all do something at school?" Nicole asked, "for the first?"

Shawn nodded vacantly.

"You wanna tell me about it?" Nicole said.

He shrugged and shook his head.

Nicole got up and moved to his side of the bench. "I talked to your teacher," she said. "He said you didn't want to do your New Year's project."

Shawn wouldn't look at her. Nicole allowed him to flake on his New Year's school work last year, but she warned him that it was never going away. New Year's Day was a major holiday, and his teachers would always make a big deal out of it.

"You were supposed to draw a poster," Nicole went on. "You could've drawn anything you wanted; Baby New Year or a calendar, or some fireworks…"

Shawn's eyes glossed over at the word *fireworks*. Nicole felt bad for him, but she didn't think she was wrong for bringing it up. Shawn was only nine years old – way too young to develop a complex over such an innocent word.

"Grandma said I can see my dad in the fireworks," Shawn said.

Nicole sighed and put her arm around him. She knew her mother told him that. It didn't seem like a big deal at the time, but Shawn was young and emotional. His curious mind warped the comment and turned it into something negative.

Nicole was a senior in high school when she became pregnant with Shawn. His father was her high school sweetheart, a handsome and funny kid named Elliott White. The pregnancy was an accident, and it was laced with immaturity: Nicole and Elliott had been sexually active for months, and Elliott asked if he could try the withdrawal method versus a condom on Valentines' Day.

It seemed like a romantic thing to do, but Elliott was drowning in pleasure when the crucial moment to pull-out drew near. Nicole knew he was cumming inside her, and she wrapped her legs around him and urged him to go deeper.

Shawn was born in November, and he lost his father before he learned how to walk. Elliott was stone-sober when he left a New Year's Eve party in the wee hours of the morning, but the 40 year old man who hit him was as drunk as a skunk. Elliott's injuries were so severe, he had to have a closed casket funeral. Nicole sat on the first church pew wearing all black. Shawn sat on her lap and grinned at the mourners as they stopped to give their condolences.

When Shawn was five, he began to desire greater details about his father's death. Nicole told him about the drunk driver and the holiday, but the questions kept coming, especially around New Year's.

On New Year's Eve, when Shawn was six, Nicole's mother took them downtown to see the fireworks display at the ballpark. Shawn's eyes dazzled as he watched the bright explosions high in the sky, and his grandmother told him, "You know your daddy's up there, don't you?"

Confused, Shawn looked away from the fireworks and listened closely to her explanation.

"Elliott died on New Year's Day," his grandmother said. "So every year, on January 1st, you can see his spirit in the sky. You can see him in the fireworks, you just have to find the right one..."

Nicole didn't think there was any harm done at the time, but she did notice that Shawn didn't smile anymore for the rest of the night. Each time there was an explosion overhead, he craned his neck and stared intently into the purple sky, trying to find his deceased father.

Over the next couple of years, his enjoyment of the holiday took a severe decline. Simply mentioning *New Year's Day* or *fireworks* was enough to put him in a funk. Nicole used to feel the same way, but she eventually learned to move on with her life. Shawn needed to do the same.

She pushed the McDonald's tray away from him and plucked a few napkins from the dispenser. She offered them to Shawn, and he took one and blew his nose.

"You know," Nicole said, "I can't say for sure if your father is in those fireworks on New Year's. I know your grandmother told you that, but no one really knows what happens when people die. That's something you can never be sure about while you're alive."

Shawn looked into her eyes, to see if she was being honest or trying to placate him. "You don't think my dad's in the fireworks?"

"I don't know what to believe," Nicole said honestly. "I know he's in heaven, and I know he looks down on us sometimes. But I don't know if he comes back to earth on New Year's. Why would he want to do that? He definitely don't want you to be sad when you see fireworks."

Shawn watched her a while longer. "I think I saw him once, in the fireworks."

Nicole thought hard before she responded to that. She didn't believe in ghosts, but she didn't want to influence Shawn's thoughts on the matter.

"Did it make you happy," she asked, "to see your dad in the fireworks?"

Shawn shrugged.

"I think whatever you decide to believe in should be something that makes you happy," Nicole suggested. "If your daddy is in the fireworks, then that's a good thing. He's making everything bright and pretty for you, because he wants to see you smile. He doesn't want you to get sad every time you think about him or New Year's. He loves you. He never wants to see you cry."

Shawn nodded. He seemed comforted by her words, but New Year's Eve was a couple of days away. Nicole didn't plan to stay home that night because depression had to be addressed, not avoided. She didn't need a psychologist to tell her that.

CHAPTER 18

CHARLES ENTERED THE Walmart on the McDonald's side. Nicole and Shawn were looking for new school pants by then. Charles asked his son if he wanted to stop and get a burger. Little Charles was too excited about the shopping trip to care about his stomach.

"I'm not hungry."

"When'd you eat?" Charles asked him.

"This morning."

"That was a long time ago. What about lunch?"

"I'm not hungry," Charles Jr. said again. He grabbed Big Charles' hand and tugged him in the direction of the toys. "Come on!"

Charles chuckled and sped up a little. "Hold on, man. We gon' get there."

When they got to the toy aisles, Charles tried to pry a little information from his son as they searched for the baddest big wheel.

"So, what's been going on at the house lately? You doing alright?"

Little Charles continued down the bike aisle, looking right and left. "Yeah."

"You been eating good?"

"Mmm hmm. What about this one?"

"That looks good, but don't you think you ready for a real bike?" Charles asked.

"I can't ride a bike."

"You almost six," Charles said. "You can get one with training wheels. It won't be that hard."

"I'll fall off," his son predicted.

"That's cool. I'll get you one of them helmets. You can't learn how to ride a bike without falling off a bunch of times."

"You'll teach me how to ride it?" Little Charles asked.

Big Charles felt his blood grow warm with pride. He missed so much of his son's youth. He'd be honored to take part in something so memorable. "Yeah, man. I'll teach you how to ride it. Shit, I might get me a bike too, so we can ride together."

"You said shit," his son noticed.

"My bad," Charles said. He turned and looked at some of the adult ten-speeds. "Do your mom be cursing a lot?"

Little Charles sensed a trap. "She told me not to tell you what she be doing."

Charles frowned at his son. "When she tell you that?"

"She always tell me that," Little Charles said, now looking for a small bike with training wheels. "What about this one?"

"That's a *tricycle*," Charles said. "You don't wanna ride that. So, why yo mama tell you that? Do she be doing something bad?"

His son looked him in the eyes, deciding how he should respond. Charles didn't know why his son was so smart. Sometimes he wasn't sure if it was a blessing or a curse. With Charles Jr., you couldn't pull any of the tricks most stupid kids fall for.

"She gon' ask me what I told you," he said.

"I don't wanna hear nothing about her boyfriends," Charles said. "I just wanna know if she be drinking and smoking over there. Do she be feeding you right and treating you good?"

The boy shrugged and looked away, and Charles knew to drop it.

"Well, the reason I'm asking is 'cause I been thinking about getting a better place, so you can stay with me more."

His son lit up. "For real?" He stared into his father's eyes, and he was so hopeful, it broke Charles' heart.

"Yeah, man. I wouldn't say it if it wasn't true. You wanna stay with me more?"

"Yeah!"

Charles Jr. nodded vigorously, and Charles again wondered if there was something bad going on at home. But he didn't push it.

"Alright, man. I'm saving up some money now. Then I gotta move into another apartment..."

Charles trailed off because his son looked like a deflating balloon.

"I'm serious," Charles said. "I'ma take care of my business. It won't take that long."

"Okay," Charles Jr. said, but it was clear this kid had his dreams dashed many times in the past. If the phrase *I'll believe it when I see it* was in his vocabulary, he would've told his dad just that.

"I'm serious. I'ma take care of business," Charles said again, but he was mostly trying to convince himself at that point.

HE FOUND A bike for himself and a smaller bicycle for his son. He decided to pick them up on their way out rather than lug the huge boxes around while they continued shopping. He formulated a list of essentials Charles Jr. would need for the next two days and grabbed the first unattended buggy he found. There was a pair of pantyhose and a dress already in the cart. Charles tossed these items on the first display he came to.

"You stole that lady's buggy!" his son informed with a snicker.

"You snooze you lose," Charles told him and continued on his merry way.

He enjoyed spending time with his son, and when they located the boy's clothing, he found that there was something else he liked about shopping at Walmart.

The women.

They were all around him, as far as the eyes could see. Charles saw big women, little women, tall women and short women. They were young, old, Mexican, white and mostly black.

He wasn't looking for a girlfriend or even a sex partner, but he had no problem approaching a dime piece if someone special caught his eye. As he pushed his basket deeper into the maze of clothing, Charles scanned the area and then did a double-take when he saw the exact woman he was looking for – but not really looking for.

He stopped and stared because she had her back to him and the view was absolutely lovely. She stood no more than five-feet-two, with smooth skin that was dark and lovely. She had a thin waist and thin arms, but her backside was quite the opposite. Charles didn't know why he had such an attraction to plump booties, but his buggy was moving in her direction within three seconds of spotting it.

He hadn't seen her face or her breasts yet, but those things weren't as important as the onion she had on display. As he got closer, Charles picked up on smaller details like the fact that she had on Capri pants, her tee shirt was pink and her canvas shoes were not new. Charles saw that her hair was pulled back into a ponytail, and her hoop earrings had fake diamonds.

None of that stopped or even slowed him, but when a small boy approached the woman with a pair of pants in hand, Charles came to an abrupt halt.

Damn. She got a kid. Charles had to reconsider because the crumb-snatcher changed everything. And it was rare for a black woman to have just one child. Charles had to assume she had one or possibly two more little ones.

The sight of a child didn't necessarily deter him, but it did change Charles' whole game plan. He hadn't yet decided what he wanted from this woman (a one night stand vs. something more), but the introduction of a kid meant a one night stand was not an option. Only a scumbag would treat someone's mother like that. Charles was a lot of bad things, but he wasn't that.

He started to push his buggy again, knowing he had only a few moments to make a decision about this woman. Her body was banging. She wasn't thick enough to star in a music video, but she was just right for him. If her face and her conversation were equally pleasing, he wouldn't mind her kid(s) at all. Hell, he had two snot dragons himself.

"Excuse me..."

She turned and all sorts of shit hit the fan. But it was internal. Shawn didn't notice the tornado spinning through his mother's head, and Charles Jr. didn't realize his father was stunned silent.

Recognition was immediate, and it was scary. And then it was funny. Nicole chuckled and then put a hand over her mouth and laughed. Charles' heart hammered. He didn't know what to say, so he played dumb.

"Do, don't I know you from somewhere?"

The woman was beautiful, there was no doubt about that. And apparently she had a great sense of humor. These were both pluses, but Charles was pretty sure this wouldn't go well. What do you say to a woman who has already seen you in a thong *and* touched your penis? Two seconds ago Charles was as cock strong as ever. Now his underarms broke out in a sweat like a pubescent boy.

"I don't think I know you," Nicole said, and that was perfect. She was lying, and Charles knew she was lying, but he liked how she was protective of the children.

"Oh, my bad," he said. He looked away and started to walk away as well, but when he looked back at Nicole, her big brown eyes were captivating. So what if she saw him naked before? He was still a man with wants and needs. And so what if she was a customer at a strip club? That didn't mean she was a weirdo. *Look at her; she's just a regular person shopping at Walmart with her son.*

Charles only came across a couple of women in his time who had the perfect size, looks and personality that he desired, and he fathered a child with both of them. If he walked away from this one, he knew he'd curse himself later when he stopped feeling like a scary sixth-grader.

"Do you mind if I ask your name?" he said.

Nicole's heart thudded as well. She couldn't believe he didn't walk away when they recognized each other. Was he seriously hitting on her? Charles was a fine man (*yes, Lawd!*), but she already saw him *naked*, for Christ's sake. He pushed his *thing* between her legs. Nicole was drunk that night, but she remembered touching and squeezing it before she pushed him away. You can't go out with someone *after* touching their dick, can you?

If it wasn't for Charles Jr., she would've told him to get lost. Nicole had a strong opinion about strippers, but the fact that this one brought his son to Walmart with him meant something. He wasn't a sex-craved drug addict, totally void of responsibilities. Or maybe he was, but today at least he cared enough about his son to want to spend time with him. That already put Dripping Chocolate leagues above other deadbeats she knew, like Clifford.

"I'm Nicole," she said. "Is this your son?" She looked down at the boy, and he eyed her curiously.

"Yeah, this is Charles Jr.," Charles said. "He's five. Is that your boy?"

"Yes," Nicole said.

"I'm almost six," Charles Jr. said.

Shawn kept quiet.

"I, uh... I'ma let you get back to your shopping," Charles said. "But I wanted to stop and say hi. You looked like somebody I know, but I can see you ain't her."

Nicole nodded. "Okay."

He turned and his conscious kicked him in the ass. *What the hell's wrong with you?* He turned back to her and smiled nervously. "You, uh... You think I could have your number? Maybe we can go out sometimes..."

He felt like an idiot. This wasn't him at all. Charles, aka Dripping Chocolate, was as smooth as a cup of warm cocoa. He was a ladies' man. They came to him. They piled up at his stage every weekend. He didn't like how Nicole stole all of his confidence, but thankfully she gave it back just as easily.

"Okay."

Charles dug his cellular from his pocket and she took it from him. Their sons waited impatiently while Nicole dialed her own number, let it ring once, and then hung up. She gave the phone back to Charles, and only then did she take a moment to admire his physical beauty. She loved his thick eyebrows and his smooth, brown skin. Dripping Chocolate was definitely the right name for him. She thought about his thong attachment between her legs and giggled again.

Charles didn't know why she was laughing so much, but he figured it had something to do with their first encounter.

"Cool," he said. "I'll give you a holler."

"Alright," Nicole said, still snickering.

Charles hoped she'd walk away first, so he could get another look at her ass, but he had to remind himself that she was more than just a big butt and a smile.

She got a kid, homey.

Yes she does. And to a real man, that meant something.

"Come on, boy," Charles told his son. "Let's get you taken care of, or we'll be in here all day."

CHAPTER 19

CHARLES EXITED WALMART thirty minutes later with his basket full of way more clothes and toiletries than his son needed for just two days. And he still had to pull around to the main entrance before he left to load up his new bicycles. They weren't assembled at all. Charles didn't have any tools, but he was sure he could get his apartment's handyman to put the bikes together for five dollars apiece. It was surprising how people devalued their services when they got hooked on crack or heroin.

Charles took his son to Wendy's on the way home, but they had to cut the meal short. MikeyMike called his cellphone with disturbing news.

"Yo, what up?"

"We got hit up, my nigga."

Charles looked over at his son who was sipping a Frosty without a care in the world.

"What you mean?"

"Somebody jacked us," Mike elaborated. "We got robbed, cuz."

"When?"

"Just now. I went to this little freak's house for a minute. When I got back, the door was kicked in."

Charles was a lot less surprised than he should've been. He knew he lived in a bad neighborhood. The majority of his neighbors were drug addicts, and most of them knew Charles and Mike sold weed and crack out of the apartment. It was a bold move to rob two dealers, but crackheads were like brain dead zombies. Consequences don't mean anything if you're fiending badly enough.

"What they get?" Charles asked.

"They got your living room TV," Mike reported. "They got your shit out the cabinet too. I think that's it. You really didn't have nothing in here. I think they grabbed some CD's off the coffee table. I had my shit on me, so they didn't get nothing from me."

Damn. Charles gritted his teeth. His TV was an older model, and the CD's were probably bootleg. The weed though, that was nearly a pound of some of the best Kush in the city. Charles paid $3,500 for it, but the retail value was $6,400. He'd have to do a lot of stripping to make up for that money. Plus he'd been splurging on his son all day. The bikes alone cost him $340.

He considered going to work tonight, but another glance at Charles Jr. made him scratch the idea. He promised the boy he'd keep him until Monday. And the idea of taking him back to crazy ass Stacy wasn't appealing at all.

"I'm on my way," he told Mike.

"I'ma find out who did this shit," Mike promised. "We gon' get them niggas, for sure."

WHEN HE GOT home, Charles saw a couple of police cars in the parking lot. They filled him with a sense of dread even though he didn't have any warrants and his car was clean. He regretted having a small child with him. Charles Jr. put up with enough drama with his mama. Charles didn't want to be another source of strife, but tonight it couldn't be avoided. His only saving grace was he planned to move away from there soon. Hopefully

Little Charles was too young to remember stuff like this when he got older.

When they got up to his apartment, the police were headed out. They didn't say anything to Charles, and he didn't volunteer any information, either. What was he going to tell them? *They stole my weed!* Yeah, right.

There was a crowd of onlookers watching Rufus, the apartment's maintenance man, repair the damage to Charles' door. Rufus was on his knees, working diligently. He looked up with sweat running down his face and offered a weak smile.

"I'm sorry about this, man. These folks around here don't got no sense. They don't care about nothing. But I'ma take care of you. I'll have you hooked up in ten minutes. I'ma put an extra plate down the side of this doorframe so they can't get in here so easy next time. I don't do that for everybody, but I'ma do it for you."

Charles knew what he was getting at. Rufus was like the valet who stood there clearing his throat after he returned your vehicle. Charles reached into his pocket and pulled out a ten spot.

"'Preciate it, man."

Rufus snatched the money as quickly as a bullfrog snagging a dragonfly.

"Thanks, Mr. Charles. I sho' thank you."

"I got some more work for you later on," Charles told him. "I got a couple of bikes need putting together."

"I got you!" Rufus said. He was dark-skinned with a salt and pepper shag. "I'll get on it as soon as I finish this door."

"Alright," Charles said. He and his son stepped by the cracked-out craftsman on their way inside the apartment.

Charles expected the worst, but things didn't look bad at all. There was wood and splinters on the living room floor, and all of the cushions on the couch were pulled up, but nothing else was damaged. Charles checked his bedrooms and found the same pattern: Some of the dresser drawers were dumped, the mattress on his bed was not aligned properly, but nothing was broken.

"You got robbed?" Charles Jr. asked as he surveyed the scene.

"Yeah, but it ain't nothing," Charles told him. "They didn't take nothing. We'll be alright."

"The man that stay next to us got robbed," Charles Jr. recalled. "Mama say they going to hell, whoever rob people."

Charles nodded, glad to hear Stacy was passing along some core values.

"Yo, Chuck! You in here?"

Charles looked into the hallway and saw Mike entering the living room.

"Yeah, I'm back here."

"I had to bounce when them laws got here," Mike said. "Oh, shit. I see you got your son with you. What's up, Lil Chuck?"

Charles Jr. said, "Hi."

"Yo, I already found out who got yo shit!" Mike said. He was loud and animated, gesturing wildly with his long arms. "It's that crackhead ass nigga Shawty! That nigga on some *other* shit. They say this bitch named Janie got him for two hundred dollars, and Shawty went crazy! He beat up a couple mo' crackheads, trying to rob them. When he didn't get nothing, that nigga decided to run up in *yo* shit! He done flipped-out, cuz, but I know where he at. We can go get that bitch ass nigga right now, cuz. Hem his ass up!"

Charles frowned and stepped towards his friend. "Say, chill with all that noise, man."

"What you talking about?"

"Nigga you see I got my son with me," Charles said, still walking. He led Mike back to the living room where Rufus was working hard. Rufus didn't look at them, but Charles knew he was paying close attention to everything.

"Come over here, nigga," Charles said, heading out of his apartment. "Wait right there," he called to Charles Jr. who had poked his head out of the hallway.

"What's up?" Mike asked. He followed Charles down the hall, to the stairs that led to the lower units.

Charles finally stopped and faced him. "Yo, you need to chill with all that noise, man. You see I got my son with me. And you talking all that shit in front of Rufus. You know that nigga smoke crack with everybody around here. You think he ain't gon' give Shawty a heads up?"

"How he gon' tell?" Mike wondered. "He in there fixing your door. I know where Shawty is right now. We can go get him *now*!"

"Nigga, I keep telling you I got my son with me. I ain't finna do no shit like that."

"Why not, cuz? That little nigga can wait in there. We'll only be gone a minute. We need to hurry up and get yo shit back before he sell it."

Charles shook his head. "Dog, what I look like leaving that boy here while I'm gone doing some shit like that?"

"Why not, cuz?"

"Anything could happen," Charles said. "I already got another crackhead fixing my door–"

"Rufus can watch him."

Charles frowned. "What? Nigga I'll leave him by hisself before I leave him with Rufus' ho-ass." Charles was talking loud enough for Rufus to hear them, but he didn't care. Even Rufus would have to admit that he was irresponsible.

"Tell Rufus to leave 'til we get back," Mike suggested.

"What if something go down with Shawty," Charles asked him. "What if I get jammed or shot?"

Mike stared at Charles like he had no idea who he was. Going to jail or getting shot was all part of the game. Charles sounded like a dentist saying, *I hope no one gets a cavity today*.

"Nigga, what you mean?"

"I'm watching my son tonight," Charles growled. "I ain't saying it no more."

"What about your weed?" Mike asked.

"You can go get it if you want to. Otherwise, I'll see that nigga Shawty when I see him."

"It'll be gone by then," Mike assured him.

"Fuck it," Charles said. "Charge it to the game."

"You getting soft, my dude," Mike said and turned to go down the stairs.

Charles grabbed his shoulder and spun him back around roughly. "What, nigga?"

"Nothing," Mike said. He shrugged Charles' hand off.

"How I'm getting soft?" Charles demanded.

"Man, since you got out, you been different," Mike whined. "You don't wanna get down with the dope game – and that's cool. I ain't got no problem with that. But you started stripping and shit. And now you don't wanna bust this nigga's head for running up in your place." Mike shook his head. "I'm just saying, man. You changed."

Charles nodded as he listened. He understood what Mike was saying, and his old friend was right. Charles made a point to change when he got out, and he was trying to stick to it. He didn't want to be a part of the high recidivism rates for black convicts. He made a vow to be a better father to his two children.

The problem wasn't that Charles had changed, it was that MikeyMike hadn't changed at all. Mike would probably leave a one-year-old alone so he could go *handle his business*. Mike could care less about what happened to Charles Jr. while they were gone. If they got arrested or killed, surely someone would find the boy sooner or later.

Charles knew he couldn't explain himself to someone like Mike, so he didn't bother.

"Whatever, cuz," he said and turned back to his apartment. "And don't come back over here tonight," Charles added. "Ain't shit going down while my son here."

Mike was distressed to hear this, but he didn't show it. He skipped down the stairs two at a time, trying to think of an alternate location to sell his dope tonight.

When Charles got back to his apartment, his son was waiting in the hallway just as he told him to. Rufus was done with the door. He was picking up the scraps of wood from Charles' floor.

"I'll get it," Charles told him. He stood with his hand on the door until Rufus backed out of the apartment.

"Okay, Chuck. I got your door fixed. You still want me to fix them bikes?"

"Yeah," Charles said. "They in my car. Go wait down there, and I'll meet you in a minute."

"Okay. I'll, I'll meet you down there." Rufus nodded quickly like an old slave and then hurried down the hallway.

Charles Jr. walked cautiously into the living room. "Your friend gone?"

"Yeah," Charles said. "I told you it was just gon' be me and you tonight. Ain't nothing to do over here, but I got cable, and I got another old TV in the closet back there. Or we can go get a new DVD player and watch some movies."

"I thought you was leaving me," Little Charles said.

His innocence gave Big Charles a lump in his throat. "Naw, man. I left you for four years already. I just got back. I ain't going nowhere."

CHAPTER
20

LATER THAT EVENING, Nicole was at home and as restless as ever. She didn't know what was going on with her two-year-olds, but they were taking their terrible antics to a new height. If she didn't know any better, Nicole would swear Cliff gave them nothing but cotton candy during their visit. But that was more than four hours ago. They would be coming down by now if it was a mere sugar high.

Nicole was trying to get Keisha out of the tub and ready for bed, but Kevin was running around the house like a trapped animal. Nicole screamed at the top of her lungs when she heard her younger son slam into something hard and then start crying.

"SHAWN!"

Nicole's oldest child peered into the bathroom a few moments later. He had his new Nintendo DS in hand.

"Huh?"

"Don't '*Huh*,' me, boy! You better say, '*Yes, ma'am.*'"

"Yes, ma'am."

"What the hell is going on in there?" Nicole asked him. "What's wrong with Kevin?"

"He ran into the refrigerator," Shawn explained nonchalantly.

How the hell does one run into the refrigerator? Nicole wondered. It wasn't like she just bought the appliance. It had been there since they moved in. "Is he hurt?" she asked Shawn.

He shook his head. "I don't think so."

"Well you better go check!" Nicole snapped. "You see I'm busy with her. Why you not watching your brother? I'ma take that damned game back to the store if you don't wanna do nothing else around here!"

Shawn eyes grew wide as he backed out of the restroom.

"And what's that noise?" Nicole asked him.

"That's your cellphone."

"And you just sitting there listening to it ring? Bring it in here!"

"Okay." Shawn turned off his game and rushed to do what his mother asked him to. He returned a few moments later with Kevin on his hip and Nicole's phone in his hand. Kevin wasn't crying anymore, and he didn't have any visible bruises. Nicole still gave Shawn a look of disapproval as she took her phone.

"Hello?"

"Hey."

Nicole couldn't believe her ears. She checked the phone's display and shook her head in amazement. "Do you wanna go to jail?"

"No," Byron said. "Please, Nicole. Please, can't you hear me out?"

"What the hell do you want, Byron?! You not supposed to be calling me. I ain't got nothing to say to you!"

"I'm sorry," he pleaded. "I don't want to harass you. I love you, Nicole. I need you. I can't live without you. I want you back."

"I'm not coming back to you, man. What you think, I'm stupid?"

"No, I didn't say that. I know you not stupid."

"Then stop calling here! You think I won't get you locked up?"

"*Please, Nicole.*" He was moaning and crying. Nicole guessed he was slouching on the couch with his face in his hand. She had a *little* sympathy, but at that moment she was too frustrated to care about a grown man's hurt feelings.

"You shouldn't have did what you did, if you love me so much."

"I do love you! I can't, I'ma die without you, Nicole. I'ma kill myself."

Nicole didn't like to hear things like that, but it was definitely better for him to harm himself than anyone in her household. Besides, it wasn't like he was really going to do it. This was no doubt another ploy to make her take him back.

"Do what you gotta do," she said.

Byron was stunned. "You want me to kill myself?"

"I didn't tell you to do that!" Nicole said. "You said you were going to do it."

"But you don't care?"

"Byron, I got my own life and my kids to look after right now. I don't got time for this. I told you don't call me no more. If you decide to do something stupid, that's on you. You ain't finna make me feel guilty, and I ain't changing my mind. Stop calling me!"

She disconnected and took a stunned Keisha to the bedroom to finish drying her off and get her PJ's on. When her cellphone rang again, Nicole stomped back to the bathroom with fire in her eyes. She snatched her phone off the floor mat with every intention of calling the police this time.

"*Didn't I tell you to stop calling me?!*"

"Damn," Charles said. "That's one hell of a way to answer the phone. I ain't never called you before."

"Who is this?" Nicole asked.

"This is Charles. I met you at Walmart today..."

"Oh..." Embarrassment cooled her body like a cold shower. "I'm sorry. I thought you was somebody else."

"What, you got a stalker or something?" Charles asked.

"No," she said. "Just this boy I broke up with a *long* time ago."

"What, he–"

"Can I call you back?" she said. "I'm kinda busy right now."

"That's cool," Charles said. "I'll be up for a while."

SHE DIDN'T CALL Charles back until 11:00 pm. She checked her clock just as he answered the phone.

"Hello."

"Hi, Charles?"

"Yeah, this me."

"This is Nicole. I'm sorry for calling back so late. I didn't know what time it was. Do you got to go to work?"

"What you mean?" he asked. He sat on his loveseat watching an animated movie he ordered on cable. Little Charles was lying on the sofa, already starting to doze off.

"I thought you worked nights," Nicole said.

"Oh, so you did recognize me?" he said. A slick smile parted his lips.

"You recognized me too," Nicole said. "I saw it in your eyes." She was in her bedroom stretched out across the mattress. The twins were still awake, but they were in their beds at least. Shawn was in his own room, stuck on his Nintendo.

"How come you played like you didn't know me?" he asked.

"Prolly the same reason you did," Nicole replied.

"I was kinda embarrassed," he admitted, "with my boy standing right there. He don't know where I work at."

"Me too," Nicole said. She thought about their encounter and said, "You looked like you didn't remember me until you got close. You really thought I was somebody else?"

"Naw," he said. "I didn't know who you was at all, not 'til you turned around."

"So what made you approach me, if you didn't see my face?"

He thought about her delectable ass and grinned. "I don't know. I thought you had a nice figure."

Nicole's chest grew warm. Skinny Minnie's like her were losing popularity these days. But there were still some men who preferred them over thick chicks.

"I went looking for you," he went on, "at the club last Friday..."

Nicole was still too self-conscious to talk about her visit to Peeping Jane's. "Why you not going to work tonight?" she asked as a distraction.

"I got my son," Charles said. "He spending the night."

"You're not married?" That should've been a common sense question, but Nicole wouldn't put anything past the brothers she met these days.

"Naw, I wasn't married to either of my baby-mamas."

"How many kids do you have?"

"Two. What about you?"

"Three. Shawn's my oldest – that's the one I was at Walmart with. I got two-year-old twins too..." Normally Nicole would've felt anxious when she dropped this bombshell on a new suitor, but she honestly didn't care what Charles thought about her children. It wasn't like there could ever been anything between them.

"I got a daughter. She's my oldest," he said. "She's eight. Did you–"

"You been to prison?" Nicole asked.

"Damn, shorty," Charles said with a chuckle.

"I'm sorry. You don't have to answer."

"I'ma answer," Charles said. "But you making me feel like I'm on a job interview."

She waited.

"Yeah, I been to the joint," he said. "I did four years. Just got out about five months ago."

Another strike. Nicole rolled her eyes and then checked the clock again. There was absolutely no way this was going anywhere. She wondered what she should say to get off the phone with him.

"Did you hear what I said?" he asked.

"About what?"

"I told you I went looking for you at the club last Friday, after you left."

"For what? To get your tip?"

He chuckled. She was feisty. He liked that in a woman. "Naw. I went looking for you because I liked you. I thought you was cute."

"A bunch of women at the club were cute," Nicole recalled. "Why you come looking for me? I'm sure you could've had your pick out of any of them."

"Maybe," he admitted, "but you the one I wanted."

"I don't see what for."

"Damn." He frowned. "Why you so hostile? If you didn't wanna holler at me, why you give me your number? Why you even call me back tonight?"

"I don't know," she said honestly. "I guess a part of me did want to talk to you – even though I knew better."

"What you mean by that?"

"You prolly just wanna get some," she said frankly. "And I ain't down with that."

"Who said that's what I wanted."

"Anything past that ain't gon' work either," Nicole said.

"You thinking too much," Charles told her. "You don't know what could work."

"I'm single with three kids," Nicole informed. "I gotta think like this. I gotta protect myself, and my family. I don't got no time to play around with no man."

"You tripping 'cause I'm a stripper, ain't you?" he guessed.

An ex-con, a stripper, two baby-mamas... Nicole had plenty of reasons to trip.

"What if I said I don't wanna holler at you 'cause you got three kids?" Charles asked.

"It happens all the time," Nicole said. "They may not come right out and say it, but I know what it is. It ain't nothing new."

"But it's wrong though," he said. "You know it's wrong. You know how it makes you feel, but you gon' sit there and do the same thing to me."

Nicole sighed as she thought about what he said.

"When I saw you at Walmart," Charles said, "I felt like Prince Charming. When you left the club last Friday, I wanted to find you. All I had was a glass slipper. Then I found you, and the slipper fits, but you got an attitude. That's cool. I'll let you go, shorty. I ain't gon' sweat you."

Nicole almost said *Bye*, but she was hesitant. His Prince Charming analogy made her feel really special. And it said a lot about his level of intelligence, too. Common sense told her he was feeding her lines, but her romantic side couldn't have been more intrigued.

"Wait."

Charles waited.

"I'm sorry," Nicole said. "I was wrong. I shouldn't talk to you like that."

"Damn skippy," Charles said.

Nicole giggled. "The nice thing would've been for you to say, *I forgive you*."

"But I don't know if I forgive you," he said. "You hurt my feelings, girl. I think you should make it up to me."

The smile slipped off Nicole's face. She shook her head.

"...by going out with me," he said. "Yeah, I bet you thought I was gonna say something else."

"You still prolly thinking like that," Nicole said with a chuckle.

"Tell you what," Charles said, "why don't you stop trying to figure me out until you know for yourself, and I'll do the same thing for you? I'm not none of them dudes you been with."

"Okay," Nicole said. *Why not?*

"Alright, I'll give you a call sometime next week," he said. "Get you some sleep, shorty. You got a busy day tomorrow."

"What am I doing tomorrow?"

"Hell, I don't know," he said. "But you got three kids. I figure everyday's prolly a busy day for you."

Nicole laughed. How right he was. "Bye, Charles."

"Bye, Cinderella," Charles said and disconnected.

PART 3
THE OLD AND THE NEW

CHAPTER
21

ON SUNDAY, CHARLES began his bike-riding lessons with his son, as promised. There weren't any good sidewalks in his neighborhood, and his apartment's parking lot was full of crackheads and dope boys, so Big Charles loaded the bikes up and took Little Charles to a huge park on the east side of town. They went to the movies afterwards, and Charles made dinner that night himself. It was nothing special; spaghetti with garlic bread, but Charles felt good as he prepared the meal. It was the first time he slaved over a stove for his boy. Later, Little Charles asked if he could please stay *one more day*, and Big Charles couldn't deny him.

Monday was New Year's Eve. The last four times Charles celebrated this holiday, he was with a bunch of stinky inmates in the Texas Department of Corrections. This year Charles celebrated with his family. He took Charles Jr. to a small town called Joshua, where he was born and raised and the fireworks laws were a lot less strict. Charles bought a bag full of Black Cats and bottle rockets from a roadside vendor and lit them up that night with his son and a crowd of seldom-seen cousins.

Charles Jr. had never met most of his relatives on Charles' side of the family, and he had a lot of fun with those "country folk." Charles' mother died from heart disease while he was in prison, but his grandmother still made the best buttermilk pies in the state. Little Charles ate 'til he couldn't fit anymore in, and he slept like a baby during the ride back to Overbrook Meadows later that night.

On Tuesday Charles Jr. wanted to stay *just one more day, please*, but Big Charles didn't want his son to get too comfortable in his drug-infested environment.

"Wait 'til I get my new place," he told him. "Then you can stay for a whole week – or a month if you want."

"I like it here," Charles Jr. said, with total disregard for the neighborhood's degradation.

"I know you do," Charles said. "But I don't. It's not safe over here. People get hurt all the time. I don't want you around this place too much. But don't worry. I'm moving out pretty soon. I'm gonna have a better life, me and you."

Little Charles nodded, but he was upset about leaving. Big Charles felt bad about taking him home, but the truth of the matter was his son was blocking his money in a few directions. MikeyMike hadn't been selling dope from the apartment all weekend, which was cutting into the rent Charles charged his old friend. Plus Charles hadn't bought or sold any weed since his son got there. And he hadn't worked at the strip club either.

He spent nearly five hundred dollars since he picked up his son on Saturday, and not a dime of it had come back. He tried not to see Charles Jr. as a hindrance, but when you look at it on paper, having kids can be a financial burden.

WHEN THEY GOT to Stacy's apartment, Charles wasn't surprised to find her car missing from the parking spot. She hadn't answered the phone all day. Charles ran up and knocked on her door anyway, but there was no answer.

"Where you think she at?" he asked his son when he got back to his car.

"Prolly at Grandma's," Charles Jr. said. Big Charles gritted his teeth as he headed that way.

Stacy's mother was strung out on heroin the last time Charles saw her. She was too old to be selling her body on the streets, but she was doing that too. Charles didn't see Stacy's car when he got to her mother's house, but he got out and knocked, just to be sure. A creepy zombie with short, graying hair and sunken fish eyes answered. Charles couldn't stop the revulsion from showing on his face.

"Uh, Stacy over here?"

"Naw," her mom said. Her voice was hoarse and mannish. Behind her Charles could see that she still had a hoarding problem. "I ain't seen her since last week."

"Alright," Charles said and tried to hurry off.

"You Charles, ain't you," the half-dead woman said.

"Yeah," Charles said, but he kept his feet moving.

"I heard you was out," Stacy's mom said. "Why you ain't come see me?"

Charles turned back to her reluctantly. "I'm sorry, Ms. Cook. I meant to stop by."

"Lemme hold ten dollars." The older woman coughed roughly and spat a loogie on her porch.

"I ain't got it," Charles said reflexively.

"Nigga, you got ten dollars," Stacy's mom countered. "I be watching your son all the goddamned time. You can give me ten fucking dollars!"

Charles' stomach twisted again. Why the hell would Stacy bring his boy to this woman's house? But just as quickly, Charles blamed himself. He wasn't there to raise his son, so he wasn't in a position to complain about anything Stacy did.

But still.

He reached into his pocket *again* and parted ways with another twenty dollar bill. He approached Stacy's mom and stretched his arm out as far as possible so they wouldn't have to touch. The junkie caught the move, but she could care less about what Charles thought of her. She snatched the bill with an ashy claw and went back inside to get her house shoes. She hadn't eaten in the last 18 hours, but she definitely wasn't headed to the grocery store.

CHARLES FINALLY FOUND Stacy at her friend Toya's apartment. Toya was a redbone with enough titties to give her back problems. She had a thin waist and nice, juicy lips that were always coated with red lipstick. She had more curves than a motocross track, but Charles was too angry by then to pay her any mind, even though Toya was trying her best to get noticed.

"Damn, Chuck. You put on a lot of muscles while you was locked up."

Toya stood in her doorway wearing a little tee shirt with boxer shorts. Charles could see her big nipples through the fabric. He also couldn't help but notice her cute belly button and thick thighs. He had a thing for skinny girls, but there was no denying Toya had it going on.

"Where Stacy?" he asked.

"She in there sleep," Toya said. She stepped back to allow Charles and his son entry. Her apartment wasn't in great condition, but it was mostly clean. Charles didn't want to leave his son just *any-old-where*, but this place was acceptable.

"You gon' get her, or I can go back there?" Charles asked.

"You can go back there," Toya said. She smiled, still devouring Charles with her eyes. "You got my number?" she asked before he headed down the hallway.

"What I need your number for?"

"In case you looking for Stacy," Toya said. "Or, you know, whatever else you wanna call for."

Charles looked into her eyes, and she parted her lips, and he could imagine sliding his manhood into her mouth. He knew he could have fun with her, but it wasn't worth it. Every since he got out of prison, women had been throwing themselves at him. But he had enough willpower to walk away from even the baddest vixens.

"You ain't finna get me hemmed up like that," he said and headed for the back bedroom.

Stacy was curled under the blankets in a cramped bedroom with no bed. There was just a mattress on the floor. Charles told her, "Wake up, girl," and she looked up at him drowsily. She squinted at the afternoon sunlight sneaking through the blinds.

"What, what you doing here?"

"I came to drop Charles off. I been looking for you for damned near two hours."

Stacy sat up and rubbed her eyes. She reached up and was comforted to find a handkerchief still tied around her hair. "Where he at?"

"In the living room. What you do last night that got you just now getting up at one o'clock?"

"None of yo business," Stacy said. "Don't worry about what I be doing. You didn't wanna do it with me."

She was looking for jealousy, but she didn't find it. Charles wouldn't care if there was another man on the mattress with her right now.

"Yo, why you be taking my son to yo dopefiend ass mama?" he asked. "She don't need to be watching no kids."

"Fuck you," Stacy said. "Don't be talking shit about my mama."

"I seen her today," Charles said. "You know she ain't right. That damned house full of trash. What the fuck wrong with you?"

"Well, you find somebody to keep him then," Stacy said. "I got shit I got to do, and yo ass wasn't around."

"You ain't got shit to do," Charles growled. "You ain't even got no job."

"Get the fuck outta here," Stacy hissed. "Leave me alone."

"Who else you be letting watch my son?" Charles demanded.

"Why, nigga?"

"What the hell you mean *why*? He gon' end up fucked up, that's why! You ever do shit with him? You ever read him a book?

Fuck no! All you ever tell him is '*Mama be back.*' He took me to four places today looking for your ass. He say he done spent the night damned near everywhere!"

"Leave me the fuck alone!" Stacy screamed. She grabbed the closest item, which just happened to be a hardcover bible, and threw it at him.

Charles blocked the book easily, and he advanced on her with a quickness that belied his size. But he stopped himself before he put his hands on her. This was a classic *nigga moment*. The penitentiary was filled with brothers who made the wrong decision at a time like this. Nearly 100% of all nigga moments could be solved by one person humbling himself. This might actually be the key to survival for the entire black race.

"Alright. You right," Charles said as he took a step back. His humble pie tasted like mud and barbed wire cooked at 350 degrees, but he swallowed it down. No one had to go to jail today. It wasn't THE MAN'S decision. It was Charles'.

Stacy was shocked by his discretion. The moment she threw the bible, she knew she was going to get slapped.

"Just call me next time," Charles said. "If you ain't got nobody to watch him, call me first." He turned and left the bedroom while she contemplated the unexpected ending to their argument.

Back in the front room, Charles Jr. was sitting on the couch. Toya was in the kitchen. They were both completely quiet, as was the rest of the house, and Charles knew they had been eavesdropping.

"I'll holler at you later," Charles told his son. He didn't think it was manly to hug the boy, but he did rub his shoulder a little.

Little Charles' eyes started to water before his dad left the apartment, but Big Charles pretended not to see it.

It was better that way.

CHAPTER
22

SINCE HE WAS playing Daddy so much lately, Charles wanted to see his daughter Shanice (generally referred to as Shay) before he headed home. He hadn't seen her in nearly a month. Charles loved his daughter as much as he loved his son, but there were different dynamics at work in their relationship, and his time with her was always somewhat stressful.

Charles met Pamela King when he was 22. She was nineteen. She was a smart girl, a freshman in college at Texas Lutheran. But when it came to men, Pam was very immature. She liked rap music, a Houston rapper named Slim Thug in particular, and none of the preppy guys at her school could even get to first base with her.

She liked men who sold crack and drove old cars, and if they had gang tattoos, that was even better. She met Charles at a Stop N Go not far from the university, and she was hooked from the moment he walked up to her and said, "Damn, baby, you way too skinny to have an ass that fat! What yo name is?"

Charles wasn't too muscular back then, but his dark chocolate skin mixed with his gangster bravado had Pam's panties wet every time Charles lowered his bushy eyebrows and stared at her like he would literally *take* the pussy if she didn't give it up consensually.

But of course Pam always gave it up. The first time they made love, Charles took her to a motel on Miller Street that was so dangerous, the manager kept a .45 in full view, right next to the cash register. Pam saw two crackhead women fighting in the parking lot and a drug dealer threatening to shoot anyone who broke it up. When Charles led her to their room, Pam was so frightened she didn't think she'd take her pants off. But Charles took his off first, and Pam forgot all about those crackheads when she saw what he was packing.

Charles had the biggest dick she had ever seen at the time. She doubted if he would fit in her mouth or between her legs. Pam tried both, and she was right, for the most part. But the parts he could squeeze in filled her with more pleasure than pain. She fell in love with Charles' sex and his lifestyle, and she didn't realize what a bad companion he was until she told him she was pregnant, and he ran away like a little boy.

Looking back on it now, Charles still didn't have a good explanation for his cowardice. He knew Pam was a good woman, but even while they were together, he knew she wasn't the woman for him. They were from opposite sides of the track. He wasn't going to change for her, and he definitely didn't want her to change for him. So he did what he thought was the best thing for her: He got the hell out of her life so he couldn't ruin it any worse than he already had.

What Charles didn't know was the next five years of Pam's life were hellacious because of him. Not only did she have the baby by herself, but she raised Shanice on her own, all while continuing her higher education. When Charles went to prison, his daughter was four, and he hadn't seen her more than a dozen times.

By the time Charles realized what a treasure he had in Pam, it was too late. She hated his guts. She didn't want anything from his sorry ass – not even for him to be a father to his daughter. During his incarceration, Charles was eventually able to gain Pam's forgiveness through the many letters he wrote her. But when he got out, things were still very frosty between them.

He learned that Pam was a RN, and she owned her own home and car. Her boyfriend Kevin was also a registered nurse at Jackson Memorial. Charles' daughter Shay was eight years old and as cute as a button. She was twice as smart as Charles was at her age, and she didn't remember her father at all. She didn't seem to care for Charles much, either. He had absolutely nothing to talk to his daughter about. So far all of their visits seemed forced, but he was determined to stick with it until she loved him as much as he loved her.

NORMALLY PAM WOULDN'T let Charles come over without at least a half-day's notice, but today was a holiday and she and Shay were both free from work and school. Charles felt out of place as he piloted his ugly Bonneville through Pam's middle class neighborhood. The feeling of unease was still with him when he knocked on her door a few minutes later. Kevin answered with the same look of surprise and disappointment he always wore for Charles.

"Can I help you?"

Charles wanted to slap the self-righteous glare right off his face. *Can I help you? You know why I'm here, ho-ass nigga!*

"Where Pam at?"

"Hold on," Kevin said and he closed the door in Charles' face.

Charles simmered, but he did not kick the door in while he waited. *One day at a time*, he told himself. He didn't have to be what these people expected him to be. It was his choice, not a predetermined fate.

Pam opened the door a few moments later, and she was such a vision of beauty, all of Charles' anger vanished in a second.

"Hey," she said and stepped back while pulling the door open.

Charles entered her home, which was decorated much better than any house he had been in since he got out of prison. Pam had a black, leather sofa and a 52" plasma television mounted on the wall. The rest of her furniture was decorated in earthy tones.

But as pleasing as this was, it was nothing compared to the woman of the house. Even wearing a tee shirt and capris, Pam was by far the classiest woman in Charles' life. Her skin was smooth and mellow like champagne. She got her hair done at least twice a month. Today it was long and flowing like Gabrielle Union's.

Pam was *pretty* when Charles dated her ten years ago. Now she was no less than stunning. Her maturity and intelligence deepened this effect. She had big, brown eyes with thin eyebrows and the prettiest pink lips. She didn't have too much going for her in the breast department, but she had a slim waist, and great hips. Charles tried not to get caught staring at her derriere when he visited his daughter, but he always failed. Pam stood no more than five feet two inches. Her ass looked like it belonged on a larger woman.

"What's going on?" he asked her when she closed the door behind him.

"Nothing," she said. She looked him up and down.

Charles wore jeans with a golf shirt that was a little too small. His goal was to show her that he had more clothes in his closet than tee shirts and jerseys, but the outcome was something different. The cotton fabric stretched over his traps and pectorals mercilessly, revealing the sculpted physique of a natural athlete.

"I brought this for Shay," he said, showing her a plush, caramel brown teddy bear. Shay didn't seem too excited about the last two gifts he brought her, but Pam told him she liked to collect stuffed animals.

"That's nice," Pam said. She didn't smile much. She looked anxious, and Charles started to feel that way too. "You can have a seat," she told him, and then she turned and disappeared down the hallway.

As soon as her back was to him, Charles' gaze slipped to the awesome lady lumps squeezed into her capris. His peeping was cut off by Kevin who entered the room from the kitchen. Kevin was wearing the royal blue scrub suit required by his job. He had his keys in hand and an undisguised look of angst for Charles who should've known better than to ogle his old girlfriend while her new man was on the premises.

Kevin stopped short, and the two men stared into each other's eyes. Kevin was good-looking; a light-skinned pretty boy with short, reddish hair and wire-rimmed glasses. His nose was European, but his lips were full. He was a few inches shorter and at least fifty pounds lighter than Charles. Before he initiated their long-awaited confrontation, Pam returned to the room.

"You forgot your lunch," she told her man, offering him a plastic grocery bag filled with good home cooking.

Kevin looked at her and smiled, once again deciding he had nothing at all to fear. Pam was sleeping with him, not Charles. She was cooking for him, not Charles. The lowlife, thuggish ex-con didn't stand a chance with his woman, but Kevin would put an end to Charles' wayward eyes at some point. If he lived with Pam, he would've done so the first time he caught Charles coveting the woman he could no longer have. Kevin wasn't a macho guy at all, but some shit is absolutely intolerable.

"Thanks, babe," he said and kissed Pam deeply. He gave her juicy ass a nice squeeze before he backed away. He didn't do anything stupid like look into Charles' eyes afterwards, but the message was clear.

Pam led Kevin out of the house and turned back to Charles with a bright smile. Even though she was glowing from another man's love, her smile made Charles' heart skip a beat.

"Here's Shay," she said, looking into the hallway.

Charles turned and saw that the pint-sized version of Pam was even more beautiful.

"Hey," Charles said, rising to his feet. "I got this for you."

Shay didn't smile, but at least she reached for the toy this time and looked at it like she wanted it.

"Thank you."

That's progress, Charles told himself. He returned to his seat and smiled at her. Pam left the room so they could have another go at repairing their damaged daddy-daughter relationship.

THE VISIT WENT better this time.

Usually Charles spent thirty minutes or more asking asinine questions, and Shay gave him guarded answers like he was her school principal. This time Charles wisely asked what hobbies she was into, and Shay loosened up as she told him about her teddy bears and hamster family.

Charles asked if he could see her pets, and Shay led him to her bedroom where she had a huge cage mounted on a short dresser. She told him the names of all of the rodents, and she even took one out and let Charles cradle it in his large hands. He didn't dare tell her that he was afraid of mice, and he'd probably crush *Moe* to death if the squeaky critter bit him.

Pam called them to the kitchen for hotdogs afterwards, and she sat down and ate with them. Shay was a lot more comfortable with Charles in her mother's presence. She even initiated a few questions about what jail was like and what Charles currently did for a living.

He told her jail was the worst place imaginable and he was never going back. And, "I'm still looking for a good job right now. Another bad thing about jail is nobody wants to give you a job when you get out. They think you're still the bad person you were before you went in."

Shay accepted this with a maturity that belied her years, and she suggested Charles go to school to become a nurse like her mom. After lunch she gave Charles a quick hug before returning to her room to finish up some chores. Pam put the dishes away and then walked Charles outside.

The weather was getting chilly. Pam shivered a little as she stood on her porch, her backside pressed against the front door. Charles took a few steps towards his car and then turned to face her.

"Shay is so smart," he said. "We getting along better. Can I take her somewhere next time?"

"Where?" Pam asked.

"I don't know." Charles shrugged. "To the movies or the park or something."

He hadn't been alone with Shay since he got out, but Pam said, "That's fine. Just call the day before so I can get her ready for you."

Charles smiled. His whole body felt warm, despite the temperature. "I been spending a lot of time with my son," he said. "I want Shay to meet him. I want her to know who her brother is."

Pam nodded. "Why don't you bring him by here so I can meet him too? How old is he now?"

"Five," Charles said. "Almost six."

"What's his mama up to?" Pam asked.

"I don't even know my damned self," Charles admitted. "I'm moving pretty soon, so he can stay with me more. He don't be wanting to leave, when I drop him off. I kept him all weekend." Charles hoped that would garnish some kudos, maybe Pam would see that he wasn't such a bad father after all. But she was still very protective of Shay.

"Bring him by here first. And I don't want you taking Shay over to that crack house you live in."

"I don't live in no crack house."

"I've seen those apartments you stay in," Pam reminded. "If you're not selling crack out of your place, you're the only one."

"I don't sell crack," Charles insisted.

"I know," Pam said. "You're a stripper now, right?" She didn't smile like she was teasing him. Just stating the cold, ugly facts.

"I won't be doing that for too much longer," Charles said.

"You don't have to tell me that," Pam said. "It's better than everything else you used to do for money. At least it's legal."

"Yeah, but I don't wanna be stripping," Charles told her. "I'ma get a real job, watch."

Pam shrugged.

Nearly a decade had passed since they broke up, but Charles knew she was still upset with him. Her life was going just fine while he was running the streets or locked up. She didn't need him coming by, confusing Shay; getting her used to his presence until he inevitably abandoned her again. She didn't need him waging little wars with Kevin every time he came over, either.

"How's everything with your man?" Charles asked, reading her mind.

"There will never be an opening," Pam said.

"I didn't say–"

"I love Kevin," she said. "But even if we had troubles, there will never be an opening – not for you."

"Who said I was looking for an opening?"

Pam grinned at him. Her smile set Charles' heart on fire. "Yeah right. If I told you to bring all of your stuff over here and live with us, you wouldn't come?"

Charles grinned too. "I don't need none of that shit at my apartment. It wouldn't even look right in your house. I can come right now."

He took a step towards her, and Pam opened her door and quickly stepped inside.

"There will never be an opening," she repeated before closing the door.

Charles chuckled and turned back to his car. Whoever thought God didn't have a sense of humor needed to check out his story: One of his baby-mamas would cut off her foot to get back with him, but he despised her. The woman he wanted to be with would cut off her foot *and* give up a kidney before she succumbed to a creep like Charles.

That was cool. There's always more fish in the sea. Only a sucker would get love-sick over a woman who already had a man and was quite happy with him. Moving on was the thing Charles did best of all.

CHAPTER 23

APEX TELESERVICES WAS closed on New Year's Day, so Nicole got to spend a nice, relaxing day at home – except the twins weren't in daycare, so relaxation was at an all-time low. Nicole often complained about her high daycare fees, but after spending her day off cooking, cleaning, bathing, dressing, and chasing Kevin and Keisha around the house, she thought the daycare center probably deserved a little *more* money.

She got a call from the twins' father around noon, but Cliff could offer no relief on this day. He was calling from the Tarrant County Jail. Nicole had to spend four dollars just to accept his call, and the bastard had the nerve to ask her to help find a bondsman for his new drug charge.

"You ain't gotta do nothing but look up a number," Cliff instructed her. "I'ma give you my homeboy Pookie's number. Call him when you find out how much they want. If he say he ain't got it, call my sister and see if she can put in on my bail money. If it's still too much, you prolly have to find another bondsman. Pookie and Yolanda gon' give you the money, and you can take it–"

"What the?" Nicole knew she hadn't heard him right. "Boy, I'm not bailing you out of jail."

"I didn't ask you to bail me out," Cliff said. "I just need you to make some calls and take the money down there."

"I'm not even doing that," Nicole said, frown wrinkles furrowing her brow. "I got these kids to look after. I don't have time for that."

"See how niggas do you when you can't do for yourself..."

"You got some nerve, you no-child-support-paying..."

"Damn, girl! I'ma pay you!"

Nicole kicked herself for volunteering for this harassment. A recording stating, "YOU HAVE A COLLECT CALL FROM [*YO, THIS CLIFF!*], AN INMATE IN THE TARRANT COUNTY JAIL..." should've been her cue to hang up the phone.

"I gotta go," she told him.

"So you not gon' help me? It's like that? You know I ain't gon' be down forever..."

Nicole thought about his threat. Cliff wasn't a good father to his children, but his drug dealing was generally lucrative. Whenever Nicole *really* needed something for the twins, Cliff would give her the money. And every now and then he surprised her with a few hundred dollars she didn't have to ask for. If she didn't help him today, he might cut her off completely.

With that in mind, she still told him, "Alright, talk to you later." She wasn't going to play secretary in return for the child support he rightfully owed her. If that meant her family had to buckle down a little more and be more thrifty, so be it.

"A'ight," Cliff said. "But don't think it ain't gon' come back to you. Karma's a bitch."

"I can't believe you got the audacity to say some mess like that," Nicole replied, but Cliff hung up midway through her sentence.

AT EIGHT P.M., Nicole left her house for a family outing that might make the day feel like an official holiday. She met a couple of her friends for dinner at McDonalds. Afterwards they planned to go downtown to watch a second New Year's celebration at LaGrave field. The official fireworks show last night was always filled with drunks and rowdy revelers. Tonight's event offered just as many fireworks with more of a family atmosphere. Plus no one had to stay up until midnight, which made it perfect for working moms.

Shawn started to act moody as soon as he heard about Nicole's plans, but he never said he didn't want to go. Blanca and Stella met Nicole at McDonalds, and Blanca was the first to notice Shawn wasn't as excited as her kids or the twins who played together in the restaurant's playpen.

"It's his dad," Nicole told her.

She and her friends sat at a table littered with burger wrappers and empty French fry containers. Blanca's children were still young enough to have fun in the play area, but Stella's kids thought they were too old to even watch fireworks. Both of them stayed home.

"He died around New Years, right?" Blanca remembered.

"On New Year's Eve, but it was after midnight," Nicole confirmed. "Got hit by a drunk driver. That guy walked away from the accident just fine. He only did six months in prison."

"That's messed up," Blanca said.

Nicole nodded. "Some celebrities only get thirty days for killing people while they're drunk."

"How old was Shawn when his father died?" Stella asked.

"He wasn't even a year," Nicole said. "He didn't used to be like this. One year my mama told him he could see his dad in the fireworks on New Year's, and, I don't know why, but it freaked him out. He hated New Year's and fireworks ever since."

"You gotta talk to him," Stella said. "You gotta talk to him when those fireworks are in the sky. You gotta undo whatever his grandmamma told him; teach him there's nothing to be scared of. When I was little, my mama told me my late grandfather was watching over us, and it scared the shit out of me. I would try to cover my breast when I took a bath and everything."

Blanca chuckled and then frowned, thinking of how awkward that must have been.

"That's why I don't believe in people looking down on us from heaven," Stella went on.

Nicole was surprised by that. Stella was the most religious of all her friends. "Really?"

"It don't say nowhere in the bible that dead people be watching us from heaven," Stella explained. "I don't think there's any ghost floating around the earth in limbo either. I think once you dead, you get cut off from the physical world. At least I hope it's like that. I know I don't wanna check on my son after I die and catch him in the bathroom with his magazines and his lotion. *Ugh!*" She shuddered at the thought.

Nicole giggled nervously, still not sure what to think or what to tell Shawn about his father. Initially she wanted to let him develop his own beliefs about the afterworld. But if he continued to get upset around this time every year, then she had to intervene somehow.

"Has Byron been by again?" Blanca asked, eager to change the subject.

"No," Nicole said. "But I did run into somebody interesting at Walmart last week."

"Who?" Blanca asked.

"You'll never guess," Nicole said, chuckling.

"Then quit trying to make us guess and tell us!" Stella demanded.

"*Dripping Chocolate*," Nicole said.

Her friends recognized the name immediately, and they were shocked and amused at the same time.

"What?!"

"Are you for real?" Blanca asked.

"He came up to me and asked for my number," Nicole confirmed.

"He recognized you?" Stella asked.

"Not 'til he got close," Nicole said. "When he did, we was both tripping. But he had his son with him, and I had Shawn with me, so we kinda played it off, like we didn't know each other."

"You gave him your number?" Blanca asked, her eyes wide, her cheeks crimson.

"What the hell he doing at Walmart with a kid?" Stella wondered.

"I did give it to him," Nicole said. "And what's wrong with him having a son?" she asked Stella.

"Strippers shouldn't have no kids," Stella said. "Why you give him your number?"

"What's wrong with him having a kid?" Nicole wondered. "He just a regular person."

"He a freak!" Stella said. "You said so yourself."

"Did he call you?" Blanca asked.

"He did," Nicole said, now regretting bringing this up.

"You didn't talk to him, did you?" Stella asked.

"Um, he um..."

"Lawd, have mercy!" Stella said.

Nicole laughed. "Are you serious?"

"I know you don't wanna have sex with that man," Stella said.

"What did he say about you coming to his club?" Blanca wondered.

"Nothing really," Nicole said.

"So, do you like him?" Blanca asked. "Are you gonna go out with him?"

"Well, I was," Nicole admitted. "But now y'all making me feel like I'm making a mistake."

"Girl, I know your last boyfriend turned out to be crazy," Stella said, "but you're not getting *desperate*, are you?"

"*No*," Nicole said, frowning now. Stella's *desperate* remark put her on the defensive. "What's wrong with Charles? Y'all don't know nothing about him."

"*Charles*, is that his name?" Blanca asked. Her smile was adorable.

"Yes," Nicole said. "He's cute and y'all know he's fine. And he seemed like a good father to his son. He been to prison, but he–"

"*Oh Lawd!*" Stella said.

"What?" Nicole said.

"Girl, what he done did to get in your head like that?" Stella asked. "You still thinking about that dance, ain't you? I know he got you all hot and heated, but–"

"No, I'm not thinking about that dance," Nicole said. Her face flushed with embarrassment. "That dance is probably the one reason I *wouldn't* go out with him. I don't wanna think about the stuff he does at that club."

"But you know he doing it *every night*, with a *bunch* of women," Stella said.

Nicole's stomach rolled. What the hell was she thinking?

"What did he say to make you wanna go out with him?" Blanca asked.

Nicole thought about it and felt like an even bigger fool. "He said he came looking for me after we left Peeping Jane's. And when he found me again at Walmart, he felt like he was a prince, and I was Cinderella."

Thankfully, her friends had the decency not to laugh in her face.

"You know that's game, don't you, baby?" Stella asked.

"I do now," Nicole said. "But no, when he said it, I didn't think it was."

"Well, at least we caught you before it's too late," Stella said. "You don't wanna go out with nobody like that, Nicole. You gots to remember that man manipulates women *for a living*. That's how he gets paid. Ain't no turn-off switch when he leaves the club. It don't matter if he talking to his landlord, a cashier or the police; if it's a woman, best believe he manipulating them."

"Thanks," Nicole said, and she meant it. Her friend just saved her some unnecessary drama.

"I don't think you should judge him by what he does for a living," Blanca countered, but it was too late.

"No, Stella's right," Nicole said. "I don't wanna go out with nobody who be rubbing up on women all night. If he'll let me touch him, he'll let anybody do it. I ain't cool with that."

The crisis averted, Nicole checked her watch and saw that it was time to go. "Y'all ready?"

"Yeah, let's get it," Stella said.

The ladies gathered their kids and got into three separate vehicles for the short trip to LaGrave field.

CHAPTER 24

THE NEW YEAR'S celebration wasn't that special – definitely less edgy than the New Year's *Eve* show last night – but it provided Nicole an excellent opportunity to talk to her oldest child about his father's untimely passing. Shawn was usually against sharing his feelings, but he didn't put up a fuss when Nicole led him to an isolated section of the bleachers, away from the racket Blanca's kids and the twins were making.

"How you feeling tonight?" Nicole asked him. "You thinking about your dad?"

It was chilly that night, hovering around 49 degrees. Nicole and Shawn both had jackets on, but they huddled closer to one another for more warmth.

"Why he have to die?" Shawn asked. He rested his head on his mother's shoulder, a lone tear rolling down his cheek.

"I asked myself that a million times," Nicole said. She sniffled and put her arm around him. "Some people told me God needed him at home, in heaven. Some other people told me it was just his time. But no answer will make the pain go away."

"I wish I still had a dad," Shawn confided. "Sometimes, when people at school talk about their dads... Sometimes I get mad at them, because I don't have one."

"I know," Nicole said. "But I'm always here for you, ain't I?"

Shawn nodded. "Yeah, but we read this book that said your mama will teach you how to do *some* stuff, but your dad has to teach you some other stuff, like how to shave and how to talk to girls and stuff."

"Who read that book?"

"We did at school."

Nicole frowned. Why would his teacher introduce a book like that – especially at a school full of minorities who were less likely to have a father figure at home?

"That's *kinda* true," Nicole said, "but you don't really need a father to teach you all that stuff. If you ever have a question about something like that, you can call your uncle Wally."

"It's not the same," Shawn said.

Nicole agreed that it wasn't, so she diverted the conversation to something she might actually be able to help him with. "What about the fireworks," she said. "How do you feel about that?"

There were a few bright explosions overhead at that moment. Shawn looked up at them. Nicole watched the fiery colors dance in his watery eyes.

"Do you think my dad's up there?" Shawn asked.

Nicole sighed. "I think, when you're talking about death, there's a lot of confusion in the world. People feel like there has to be something, but nobody knows what really happens until they die. It's like a deep, dark cave that everyone's afraid to go into. Some people say there's gold and all of your pain goes away in there. Others think it's just a dark cave, and once you go in, you get lost forever."

"What do you think?" Shawn asked.

"I think you have to believe whatever makes you happy," Nicole said. "If you get sad every time you think about it, then you need to believe something else. Why does, why do the fireworks make you sad?"

Shawn closed his eyes and looked into the sky again. The crowd cheered at each new explosion, but Nicole felt her son shiver.

"Because, I know when cars hit each other, they blow up," Shawn said. His voice was so slight, Nicole had to strain her ears to pick up every word. "When those things go up in the sky, they explode too," Shawn said. "I think, I think my daddy, he keep blowing up, over and over again, up there…"

Nicole put a hand to her mouth, and her tears flowed as well. After all these years she finally understood her son's thinking. It was heartbreaking, to know that he'd been imagining his father's car accident countless times in his mind.

But at least it was all out in the open now, and hopefully she could change his thinking.

"Shawn…" She wiped her face with her coat sleeve. "Shawn, your father didn't die in any explosion. It was just a regular wreck. There wasn't a fire at all."

Shawn looked into her eyes. He was surprised by this.

Nicole shook her head. She never felt the need to discuss the specifics of his father's death, but she failed to consider how wild a child's imagination can be.

"And God would never want to hurt your feelings, by putting explosions in the sky to make you think about how your father died. That's, you shouldn't ever think like that. I think what your grandmother was telling you was that if you want to think your dad's looking down on you, you can look into the sky on New Year's and see all the pretty colors. You can see the people smiling and laughing all around you. And it should make you feel *good*, to know that your dad still loves you enough to put on this show every year, just for you."

Shawn thought about that and decided he liked this alternative view of death much better than the twisted visions he'd been imagining for the past few years. He smiled, and for the first time he could remember, he did think the fireworks were beautiful.

After a while Nicole took his hand and led him to the rest of their group. For the remainder of the night Shawn enjoyed the New Year's festivities like a regular kid.

CHAPTER 25

AFTER SUCH AN emotional night, Nicole felt drained when she returned to the house and got everyone ready for bed. The last thing she wanted was to have a flirty phone chat with some man who only wanted her for the wrong reasons, but she was happy when she saw that Charles called while she was in the shower.

The talk with Shawn had done more to make up her mind than anything Stella or Blanca had to say about Mr. Dripping Chocolate. The fact of the matter was Nicole had three young children to raise. She didn't think it was wise to entertain a fling with some exotic dancer while her son was desperately seeking a father figure. Shawn was likely to cling to any man she started dating, so she had to be extra careful about the decisions she made.

Charles was finishing up his pushups for the night when Nicole called him back. He sat on the corner of his bed topless, his dark skin glistening with sweat. In the front room MikeyMike completed a transaction with one of the local dopefiends and escorted her out of the apartment.

"Hey," Charles said when he answered the phone. He was only slightly winded. "What you doing? How'd that show go tonight?"

"It was fine," Nicole said.

"I saw some of it on the news," Charles stated. "Looked like they had a pretty big crowd."

"Yeah," Nicole said vaguely.

"What's up?" Charles asked. "You didn't have fun on your day off? The twins run you ragged?"

"Look, um, I changed my mind about going out with you."

"Why?" he asked, not sounding surprised at all. "'Cause I'm a stripper?"

"You uh, huh?"

"Or is it 'cause I been to the pen?"

"It's, I don't know, both..."

"You don't even know me," he said. "You don't know what kind of man I am."

"I know. But, it's just..." She shook her head. "I got kids to look after. I don't got time for–"

"I know you got kids."

After a pause, she said, "Okay."

"I knew that before I walked up to you at Walmart."

"So, you see what I'm saying..."

"Yeah, but I don't think you see what *I'm* saying."

She was confused.

"When I first seen you, I didn't see your boy," he explained. "But when I started walking up to you, I saw your son. And I was like, *Damn, she got a kid.*"

"*Damn she got a kid*? Yeah, that makes me feel *real* good."

He chuckled. "It wasn't *damn* like you saying it."

"I said it just like you said it."

"I didn't say it at all," Charles said. "I thought it. I'm trying to tell you about my thought process."

"I don't think I like your thought process."

"That's 'cause you won't let me finish."

Against better judgment, she piped down and listened to what he had to say.

"All I'm saying is I knew you had at least one kid before I walked up to you. When I first saw you, yeah, I might've had one thing on my mind. But when I saw your son, I had to change my way of thinking. I had to re-work everything in my head. I wouldn't approach a woman with kids the same way I would if she didn't have none. I wouldn't treat her the same either. I had the choice of turning around when I saw your son, but I kept going."

Nicole expected a lot of things, but not this level of honesty. "So, how do you treat a woman who got kids?" she wondered.

"Different," Charles replied.

"Different how?"

"Just *different*," he said. "It's hard to explain. I wouldn't dog no woman who got kids, I can tell you that."

His words made Nicole feel special. Being a single mother with three kids was a problem for most guys. This was the first man who ever said Nicole deserved more respect because of her children.

Wait. She stopped herself and listened to Stella's voice in the back of her mind.

This is game, game, game.

"How do I know when you're telling the truth?" she wondered. "You con women for a living, Charles. That's how you get paid."

"You don't have to believe nothing I say," he said, growing a little irritated with her doubt. He had to prove himself to Pam. He had to prove himself to his children. And he had to prove himself to everyone else who expected him to go back to prison within the next six months. He longed for someone who could accept him at face value.

"I done put it all out there," he said. "If you wanna go out with me, that's cool. If you don't, that's cool too. I know who I am. If you don't wanna find out for yourself, tell me now, and I won't call you no more."

Nicole's heart beat quickly, filling her veins with both hope and fear. She liked how he stood up to her, wouldn't let her break him down. But behind the strength, she also saw his sensitivity. She felt the pain of a man who was constantly trying to get people to believe in him. Or was this all part of his master plan to get the booty?

She decided that one date wouldn't hurt anything. And she could judge his bullshit level a lot better if they were face to face.

"Okay," she said. "Where you wanna take me?"

CHAPTER 26

CHARLES VISITED HIS son that Friday, but he had to turn him down when Charles Jr. asked to stay the weekend again.

"I gotta go to work, man. Ain't got nobody to watch you."

"I can watch myself," Little Charles replied. "Mama let me watch myself all the time."

Charles cringed, but didn't respond to that. He didn't even ask Stacy about it when he dropped his son off. Complaining was for women and children. A real man put his nose to the grindstone and took care of business. Every visit with his son made Charles more focused on his money and his long-term goals.

He already found an apartment complex on the south side of town that would rent him a unit despite his felony convictions. Usually the only apartments that would do that were rundown and crime-infested, but Windham Pointe was in a good neighborhood. Charles would have no problem letting his son play outside there, and he couldn't wait to keep his daughter over night.

So far all of his visits with Shay had been supervised. Charles didn't think they would ever develop a real bond until she was fully his responsibility for a couple of days. He wanted to tuck her in at night and wake her the next morning with the smell of bacon and waffles. He wanted Shay to call him sometimes, just to shoot the shit, like Little Charles was starting to do.

To make it to Windham Pointe, Charles needed money for new furniture and utility deposits. To get this money, Charles increased his marijuana sales and shook his ass for cash at Peeping Jane's. He didn't think he'd ever get used to being a stripper, but he did learn a few more dance moves that drove the women crazy. He left Peeping Jane's with $350 on Friday night and almost four hundred on Saturday.

With the weed money stacking up and MikeyMike's rent money still rolling in, Charles believed his new life was only weeks away, rather than months.

ON SUNDAY, HE woke up at eleven and got dressed for his first date with a pretty young thing named Nicole. He didn't have any slacks or Dockers in his wardrobe, but he did have a few long-sleeved Polo's that were crisp and clean, fresh out of the cleaners. He wore a solid white one with faded jeans and new Chuck Taylors. He left the house at 12:30 and met his date at the Olive Garden on Hulen Street.

Nicole had on straight-leg jeans with a V-neck tee and a short leather jacket. She had her hair styled in a short bob. Charles thought she looked a lot better than she did when they met at Walmart, and she was still skinny-girl-fine. She offered a bright smile when they locked eyes in the parking lot.

"Hey."

"Hey. How you doing?" he asked her.

"I'm fine," Nicole said. She checked him out openly, liking his outfit and his thick eyebrows. She liked how he was always well-groomed. Charles had a fresh-from-the-barbershop vibe.

"You hungry?" he asked. "You go to church today?"

Nicole liked his voice too. It was deep and commanding, like her brother's.

"Yes and yes," she said. "And I didn't eat breakfast this morning, so don't think I'm gonna pick at my food."

He grinned. His lips were full and pink. "I know you not gon' eat *that* much. You too little."

"Watch me," Nicole said and led the way to the restaurant.

Charles' eyes instinctively rolled down to her booty for a second before he caught up and walked beside her.

"You sho' look good today," he told her.

"Thank you."

"Naw, thank you for coming," Charles said. "I know you had your doubts." He opened the restaurant's door for her.

"I still do," Nicole said as she stepped inside.

"That's cool," Charles replied. "As long as you give me a chance to prove you wrong."

THEY DINED ON chicken Marsala and shrimp Alfredo, and true to her word, Nicole didn't pick at her food at all. She ate her whole appetizer and salad and more than half of her main course. Charles watched her curiously when she finally pushed her plate away and reapplied a coat of cherry red lipstick.

"What?" she said, noticing his stare.

"You wasn't kidding, was you, about your appetite?"

"They keep saying it will catch up with me one day."

"Who said that?"

"My family, friends. They think I'm gonna blow up."

"Maybe they just jealous," Charles offered, "'cause you so much finer than them."

"I ain't fine," Nicole said with a smirk.

"Yes you is," Charles said right away. "I'd choose you over any of them girls you was at the club with."

Thinking about the club made Nicole blush. "Just for the record, I had never been to a strip club before."

"That's cool," Charles said. "I hadn't either. That was my first day."

"For real?"

"Yeah, you couldn't tell?"

"I thought you couldn't dance," Nicole admitted. "But your stripper moves was okay."

"Damn," Charles said and chuckled. "I thought was really doing something up there."

"It didn't matter if you could dance or not," she said, "'cause you was definitely the finest brother there that night."

"You think so?"

"*Definitely*. Or maybe it was the way you danced for me..." She had to look away as visions of his dark, glistening body filled her head. "Whew!" She fanned herself with a dainty hand. "And just for the record *again*, I didn't touch no other dancers that night."

Charles lowered his eyes and smiled. Nicole hoped he'd say no other women touched him, either, but no such luck. Her smile slipped a little as jealously began to rear its ugly head.

"Why are you stripping?" she asked. "I mean, you got the body for it, but how did you get into that?"

"I don't wanna strip," Charles said honestly. "It's just, something that happened. I was willing to do anything I could to stay out the joint. Selling crack was the only thing I was good at, but that's one thing I ain't *never* doing again. Niggas is stupid, getting out the pen and going right back. Not me though."

"You was locked up for crack?"

"I was into a lot of mess," Charles confided. "But yeah, crack is what they got me for."

"What else was you into?"

"Gangbanging, mostly," he said. "Me and my brother Blacc used to be some straight up *nightmares*. Robbing, stealing cars, beating fools down, drivebys. You name it, we done it. He went to the pen two years before me. He should be coming up for parole this year."

"I know you miss him," Nicole said.

"I do," Charles said. "But at the same time, I kinda don't. I know that sounds messed up, but you gotta understand what kind of person my big brother is. He hardheaded. He don't take no for an answer, and he don't put up with no shit – 'scuse me."

"It's alright," Nicole said.

"My brother was our OG," Charles went on. "He started a lot of beef all across the city. He used to have us busting at niggas just 'cause we was bored. It got to the point where we had so many enemies, we wasn't safe nowhere but our own neighborhood. Blacc didn't care though. He figured the more people hated us, the more famous we was. If we wasn't warring with nobody, then we wasn't about nothing."

"What happened?" Nicole asked, totally engrossed in his story.

"The district attorney got on our ass," Charles said. "They started putting cases together on all our leaders. And then one day they came through and took 'em all down. They gutted our gang, did the same to most of our rivals. The homies that was left couldn't hold it together, not with everybody trying take over the top spot at the same time. Jesse Jackson couldn't have stopped our gangs from beefing, but the white man took care of the problem in less than six months.

"By the time I got locked up, people was still claiming different gangs, but we wasn't shooting nobody. And when I got out, I saw that the whole city was basically cool with each other. I got a homey at my house right now who prolly would'a tried to kill me six years ago – if I didn't try to kill him first."

"What's gonna happen when your brother gets out?" Nicole wondered. "Does he know about how things are now?"

"He do," Charles said. "And he already told me he don't like it. He wanna get the gang started again. I told him I ain't with that no more."

"But that's your big brother," Nicole reasoned. "I know you not gon' turn your back on him if he needs help."

"I'll help him all I can," Charles confirmed. "*Unless* he want me to shoot somebody or sell dope. I will turn my back on him then – him and anybody else that try to keep me down."

Nicole stared into his eyes, and despite all of the warning signs, she believed him. She respected him and applauded him as a *thinking* black man. Charles probably didn't have the brains to write a coherent essay, but he was smart just the same.

"Tell me about your kids," she said.

Charles shook his head slightly. "What about you, Miss Thang. When you gon' tell me some of your stories?"

"My life is boring," Nicole said. "Yours could be a movie."

"Tell me anyway," Charles said, leaning back in his chair. "I like watching you talk."

Nicole blushed again. "What that mean?"

"Just what I said," Charles replied. "I like watching your lips move, your teeth, your tongue, your eyes. I think you're beautiful."

"Wow," Nicole said. She felt a flock of goose bumps sprout on her arms and neck. "Now I'm too nervous to talk. Too much pressure."

"I took off my clothes for you," Charles said. "That's pressure."

Nicole giggled. "You didn't do that for me."

"Yeah I did. And you didn't even tip me or nothing."

"I'm sorry," she said. "I meant to. I can give it to you now, if you want."

She actually reached for her purse, which made Charles laugh.

"Naw, that's alright," he said. "Just tell me more about you, and we'll call it even."

CHAPTER 27

NICOLE TOLD HIM about the rowdy twins and their deadbeat father Cliff, who would probably never have half the drive and focus Charles seemed to have. She told him about her oldest child and a little about Shawn's father Elliott, who died in a New Year's Eve car accident before his son could walk.

Charles in turn told Nicole about his two children and the recent friction between him and Charles Junior's mother. He told her that one of his biggest challenges, besides not going back to the pen, was establishing a relationship with his daughter Shay.

"I thought I'd get out, and she'd all of a sudden be Daddy's little girl. But she don't know me at all. The first time I went over there, she wouldn't even look me in the eyes."

Despite all of his obvious baggage, Nicole thought Charles was a good catch – with the exception of the indecent happenings at Peeping Jane's. No matter how she looked at it, she didn't think she could have a serious relationship with a man who took off his clothes and grinded on women every weekend. The opportunity for sex on the side was enormous.

"I know. Everybody thinks like that," Charles told her as they exited the restaurant. "But I ain't like those other guys. If I don't wanna sleep with somebody, ain't nothing they can say or do to me make me change my mind."

"What if they offer you a lot of money?" Nicole asked. "What if they're real pretty *and* they offer you a lot of money?"

"It still don't matter," he said. "Matter of fact, last night some girl came up to me in the parking lot after the club closed. She had took everything off, except her heels and her coat. She was fine; a cute little redbone. She asked if she could roll with me. She opened her coat and showed me what I could have."

Nicole didn't have serious feelings for Charles, but her jealousy kicked in strong.

"If that's supposed to make me feel better about your stripping, it's not working."

"You ain't let me finish," he said with a grin. "I told her it wasn't happening. Sent her on her way. Anybody else try to come at me like that get told the same thing."

"But you met me at the club, and now we're at a restaurant," Nicole said as she approached her Honda. "What's the difference between me and her?"

"The difference is I want you, and I didn't want her," Charles said bluntly.

Nicole stopped at her car and turned to check his eyes for bullshit, but she didn't get a chance to. Charles took her small hand in his and drew her close, and Nicole barely had time to close her eyes before their lips touched. She was startled, but not totally against the move. Her date was so tall, she had to crane her neck almost all the way back. Charles moved his other hand to the small of her back and pulled her even closer, until their hips touched.

He kissed her again, which was good because Nicole wasn't prepared for the first one. This time she kissed him back, taking time to briefly suck his bottom lip before they separated. She'd been staring at that juicy lip throughout their meal. It tasted just as good as she thought it would.

Her head was spinning when he let her go, but she managed to maintain her balance without his strong hands on her frame.

"I'm sorry," he said. "I should've asked you first."

He didn't look sorry at all, and even with her red lipstick glistening on his mouth, Nicole thought he might be the most handsome man she ever kissed.

At a loss for words, she simply said, "Okay."

"I'll call you later," he said. He took a few steps back before turning and heading to his own vehicle.

Nicole let out a pent up breath as she unlocked her car. Kissing on the first date was not cool. Dating an ex-con with two baby-mamas was not cool. And going out with a stripper was definitely not cool.

But Dripping Chocolate was the essence of cool, and his comment was still ringing in her ears.

The difference is I want you, and I didn't want her.

There was still a strong chance he was full of shit, but it felt good to have a fine man like Charles tell her that. So Nicole chose to believe him.

For now.

CHAPTER 28

NICOLE'S HEAD WAS still in the clouds when she got home. She was so distracted, she didn't notice a black and gray Buick pull to a stop in front of her house until she was out of her car and Byron was getting out of his.

Fear slapped her hard in the face when their eyes met, and Nicole froze, caught in one of those dreaded fight or flight scenarios. As her brain raced, her eyes captured everything. She saw her brother's truck parked in her driveway. He was inside the house babysitting. A loud enough scream would bring him to her rescue, and Nicole knew Wally always had a weapon nearby. He would retrieve it before he even thought about confronting the stalker.

Nicole also thought about her own gun. It was a nickel-plated .25, semi-automatic. Wally picked it for her because it was small, it didn't have much recoil, and it was relatively easy to use; just cock it and point at whatever you want dead.

Nicole was still carrying the .25 in her purse. She had plenty of time to reach for it, but when she studied Byron more carefully she saw that he didn't have a weapon, and he wasn't threatening. The worst he could do was hit her with the vase of roses he toted in one hand. Or maybe he could give her a paper cut with the greeting card he had in his other hand.

"What the hell you doing here?" Nicole hissed. She kept her voice low because despite this harassment, she really didn't want Byron to get hurt. He ruined their relationship with his insecurities, but before that he was a nice guy. He loved Nicole, and she thought he grew to love her children as well.

"I just wanted to give you this," Byron said, offering the flowers. "I don't mean no harm, Nicole. I swear to God I don't."

Byron wore a black, New York style bomber jacket. His jeans were new, and his sneakers were too. He looked a lot like his old self.

"Are you following me?" Nicole wondered. "I'm calling the police."

"Please, Nicole. Don't be like that," he whined. He looked like he might hold it together, but his face contorted in agony, and fresh tears squirted from his eyes. "I just wanna talk to you. *Please*. Can't we talk?"

"No, Byron. We can't talk." She kept her features stern, but it was getting harder and harder to treat him this way. She didn't have the heart to sic Wally on him, and she knew she could never shoot him herself.

"Will you at least read my card?" he begged. The Hallmark was trembling in his hand. The vase was too. "*Please*. I got you some, some flowers. Just take them, and I'll go."

Nicole's eyes darted back to her house. Her heart was knocking so loudly, she couldn't think straight. She sensed something bad was going to happen. Either Wally would look out of the window and put an end to this once and for all, or Byron wanted her to get closer so he could grab hold of her again. Nicole cursed herself for still having compassion for this man, after all that happened.

"Leave it," she said in a hushed voice. "My brother's in there right now, Byron. He gon' hurt you. Please, just leave it and go."

"Okay, I'll leave. Here. I'll, I'll go." He took another step towards her, and Nicole tensed up again.

"Put it on the ground, right there!" she nearly shouted. Her eyes darted back to her home, but she didn't see any of the front curtains move. "Hurry up and go! He gon' shoot you, Byron. Just, just leave it and go."

Byron didn't appear to be concerned with his personal safety. He stared into her eyes and shook his head slowly. "I never meant to hurt you," he said as he crouched and set the vase upright on the lawn. "It was just that one time, Nicole. Why you can't forgive me?"

He placed the card on the ground next to the vase and stood again. He pleaded one last time, with just his eyes, and then he turned and returned to his vehicle when Nicole didn't loosen up. His engine sounded like a lion roaring when he started it, but a few second later he was gone. Wally still hadn't emerged from the house.

Nicole raced to hide the evidence of her weakness. She grabbed the card and jammed it in her purse. She hefted the vase and hurried to the side of the house where her shrubbery was barren of leaves but still pretty thick. She dumped the roses behind the bushes and tossed the vase over the fence that enclosed her back yard.

She rushed back to the front of the house and took a couple of deep breaths as she mounted the porch. She wiped the sweat from her forehead and used her key to open the door. Inside she found the living room deserted, which explained why no one heard the slight commotion outside.

She found her family at the kitchen table, waiting patiently for a ravioli meal Uncle Wally had prepared. He turned away from the stove and asked Nicole, "How'd it go?"

"Great," she said, barely remembering that she just had a nice date with a very handsome man. She thought about Charles' kiss and forced a smile that didn't look forced at all. "I had a real good time."

SHE DIDN'T READ Byron's card until she had the kids in bed for the night, and she was ready to crawl under the sheets herself. The front had *Thinking of You* printed in pretty calligraphy. Nicole skipped the poem inside and went straight to the sloppy handwriting Byron added underneath:

Baby, I can't stop thinking about you. I know I hurt you and Shawn. I understand that now. I know I was too jealous of you. I been to counseling. I know about my problems. Please call me. You are the best girl I ever had. If we can't work it out, I still want us to be friends. I miss you so much. I will never hurt you again. Call me. Please.

Nicole read the message a second time before she tucked the card in her nightstand drawer. She knew this would not end well. Byron was going to end up in jail again. But Nicole didn't think he deserved to get locked up for what he did today.

No! You need to take that card to the police first thing in the morning!

Nicole knew the voice in her head was telling her right, but she simply didn't have the heart to get Byron arrested – not for bringing her flowers. Or maybe she was a fool.

Next time, she told herself. *If he comes again, I promise I'll call the police then.*

Her mind made up, she went to sleep hoping she'd dream about something sweet, like candy rain or dripping chocolate.

167

PART FOUR
THE OPENING

CHAPTER 29

THE NEXT COUPLE of weeks passed rather quickly.

With New Year's out of the way, Shawn's demeanor changed for the better, at school and at home. One of his teachers called to sing his praises. She asked if Nicole finally found a counselor that could reach her child. Nicole told her Shawn's depression was seasonal, but hopefully they nipped it in the bud for good. They wouldn't know for sure until New Year's Eve rolled around again, but Nicole was optimistic that Shawn wouldn't go back to the way he was.

The other good news in Nicole's life was her budding relationship with Charles Hester, who really didn't like to be called *Dripping Chocolate*. Since their first date at the Olive Garden, Nicole had the pleasure of seeing Charles two more times, once at the Red Lobster near University and again at the AMC theatre downtown. The movie they saw was a predictable and mostly ridiculous drama, but Nicole didn't complain. She always liked the intimacy of dark theatres.

On Wednesday, January 23rd, Charles dropped Nicole off at work after a quick meal during her lunch hour. Nicole thought she was keeping things pretty discreet, but her friends hovered like vultures as soon as she returned to her desk.

"Mmm, hmm. I seen you," Stella said. She peered around Nicole's cubicle wall with a *tsk tsk* look on her face.

"Was that that stripper?"

That voice came from Nicole's right side. She looked that way and saw Twyla staring at her with a totally different expression. Twyla looked like she had a dirty secret to tell, or she was eager to hear one.

"What are you talking about?" Nicole asked.

"That man you was kissing in the car," Twyla said.

"We saw you," Stella said. "That was that stripper, wasn't it?"

Nicole blushed. "How'd you see me?"

"Me and Stella went to Subway," Twyla said. "When we came back, we saw you in the car with some *man*. His tongue was all down your throat!"

Nicole felt cornered, looking from one friend to the other. And Twyla's comment was downright embarrassing.

"I was not kissing that man like that," she said. "And be quiet! I don't want everybody hearing that."

"I seen you," Twyla said. "I seen you with my own eyes. Why you didn't tell me you was going out with a stripper?"

"We just started," Nicole said. She couldn't wipe the smile off her face, despite her unease.

"That's the same one who was all up on you at Peeping Jane's?" Twyla asked.

"Yeah, that's him," Stella said. "*Dripping Chocolate.*"

Twyla laughed and then licked her lips. "Damn, Nicole. How you hook up with *that*?"

"I thought you was gonna leave *that* alone," Stella said. She didn't look like she was happy about any of this.

"I met him at Walmart," Nicole told Twyla. "And I was gonna leave him alone," she said to Stella. "But when I tried to tell him, he talked me out of it. He told me I shouldn't judge him, and I don't think I should."

"How you meet him at *Walmart*?" Twyla wondered. "What's the odds of that?"

"He said Nicole was his Cinderella," Stella mocked. "He said she ran away from the party, and he'd been looking everywhere, to see if she fit the glass slipper."

"What?" Twyla said.

"He didn't say all that," Nicole said, not liking the facetious way Stella told the story.

"But he said he was looking for you?" Twyla asked. Her eyes were big, and her smile was bigger.

"He said he looked for me *that night*," Nicole corrected, "at the club. But when he saw me at Walmart, that was totally coincidental."

"*God damn*," Twyla said. "How you do that?"

"How I do what?" Nicole asked.

"That was the finest one at the club that night. Why he want *you*?"

"Uh, excuse me?"

"Naw, I don't mean it like that," Twyla said, but she didn't offer a better explanation.

"What I wanna know is what you want with *him*?" Stella said. "You said he had two baby-mamas, he been to the pen, and we know he get butt-nekkid every night."

"He don't get *butt-nekkid*," Nicole said.

"Close enough," Stella said. "What happened to all that stuff you was saying about strippers before we went to that club?"

"She found out how good they can fuck," Twyla said with a slick grin.

"No I haven't," Nicole said. She was in pure defense mode now, not smiling at all. "We haven't did nothing."

"So what happened to all that mess you was talking?" Stella asked again. She wasn't smiling either.

"I just, I don't know," Nicole said with a sigh. "I guess, you know, it ain't right to be judging people. That's stereotyping, when I said all strippers was one way just because some of them are."

"You sound like that boy got you brainwashed," Stella said, her look of disapproval growing meaner by the second.

"Naw, she sound like she want him to drip some chocolate on her," Twyla said with a laugh.

"What's going on over here?"

The new voice was Blanca. She rounded the corner grinning, though she was supposed to be reprimanding.

"Nicole's still going out with that *nasty stripper*," Stella told her.

"He not nasty," Nicole said.

"He sho' ain't," Twyla said. "Dripping Chocolate got it going on! You remember his chest – and his *ass*? I say *goddamn*!"

Twyla had to fan herself. Nicole felt very uncomfortable about this whole conversation – especially the way Twyla was talking about her possible future boyfriend.

"Mmm hmm. You might as well get used to it," Stella said, noticing Nicole's disposition. "Damn near every woman in the city done seen him naked. Everywhere you go will prolly have somebody talking about his body. And if he as freaky as *I* think he is, they'll be talking about more than that."

Nicole knew "*every woman in the city*" was a huge exaggeration, but she couldn't deny there were quite a few ladies who had seen Charles' goodies (and who could continue to see them any Friday or Saturday night they pleased). This was somehow worse than being with a whore like Cliff because Charles' whoring was wide open, come one, come all.

"I don't think there's anything wrong with it," Blanca said. "It's not like he's in porn. It's just a job."

"*Whatever*," Stella said. "He got hard when he was on the stage, and he got hard when he came and danced for Nicole. If your job makes you horny, then you're a freak! And if you think a man can get horny without doing something about it," she said to Nicole, "then you just got your blinders on. It's fifty women in that club every night who would love to help Mr. *Dripping Chocolate* out with his hard-on."

Nicole already knew that, but her stomach tightened anyway.

"He don't have to sleep with any of them if he can be with Nicole when he leaves," Blanca offered.

"Do he be horny when he get off work?" Twyla asked. "I bet that be some *good* sex!"

"We never had sex," Nicole said again.

"Why not?" Twyla wondered.

"'Cause we just started dating," Nicole said. "We haven't got to that point yet."

"Good," Stella said. "Now you need to drop him before you catch one of his diseases."

Nicole's stomach rolled again. Jeez, this was Cliff all over again.

"Don't listen to her," Twyla said. "If you break up with him before you see how good he work it in bed, you a fool for real."

"No, don't listen to *her*," Blanca said, referring to Twyla. "If you wanna be with him, it shouldn't be all about sex. Just because he's a stripper doesn't mean you can't have a regular relationship. If you trust him and he stays true to you, after awhile you'll see that it's just a job."

"Fuck all that," Twyla said. "You need to hurry up and see how good he can work that *stick*."

"Naw, what you *need* to do is lose his phone number," Stella advised.

"I need to take a call," Nicole replied and rolled her chair back under her desk. She grabbed her headphones and stared at her computer screen until a new caller popped up.

After a few moments, her friends made their way back to their workstations as well.

CHAPTER 30

LATER THAT AFTERNOON, Charles made his way to Pam's house to spend time with the prettiest little angel on earth. His visit had been planned since yesterday, but Pam's boyfriend Kevin acted like he had no idea who this big hoodlum on his woman's porch was. He answered the door with a look of disgust that made Charles want to punch him in the mouth and collect Kevin's teeth when he spat them out. In prison, they called these trophies.

Charles was an insatiable Tooth Fairy a couple of years ago. If he wasn't positive Kevin would call the police, he would've touched him up a month ago.

"What do you want?" The male nurse was shorter than Charles, but he somehow managed to look down his nose at him.

"Nigga, you know why I'm here," Charles said. He was all for being respectful, but he wasn't going to keep giving if he wasn't getting any back.

"Excuse me."

"I'm here to see Shanice. Get out my way." Charles took a step forward, but Kevin held his ground.

"You're not going to barge up in here. This isn't your house."

"It ain't yours either!" Charles snapped. "Why you always over here anyway? Don't you got your own house?"

"I got a key, boy. And you know what me and Pam do up in here."

Charles could care less about the sexual innuendo. It was Kevin's arrogant nature that made his blood boil. Kevin reminded him of one of the prison guards that used to harass him during his stay on the Ferguson Unit. Those guards could pull you out of line anytime they felt like it. They could search you on a whim, make you strip totally nude and bend over in front of everybody.

The guards were rarely attacked because the consequences were devastating. Like them, Kevin was banking on the free-world laws to protect him from Charles. But what Kevin didn't know was Charles wasn't on parole or probation. He did all of his time so he wouldn't have to worry about THE MAN keeping up with his address and work history when he got out. One assault might get Charles arrested, but it wouldn't send him back to prison.

With that in mind, he looked Kevin dead in the eyes and said, "Call me *boy* again, and I'll break every bone in your face."

Kevin's eyes widened with terror, but only for a moment. Luckily for him, his woman intervened.

"What's going on?"

Pam appeared behind Kevin, and then she stepped between the men when no one answered.

"What are y'all doing?" she asked again.

"Nothing," Charles said. He kept his eyes glued on Kevin's. The nurse was the first to look away.

"I'm getting sick of this shit," Kevin said and then he turned and walked out of the room.

"What happened?" Pam asked Charles. She was wearing a tee shirt and canvas shorts, and she looked as good as ever.

"I don't know why he don't like me," Charles said honestly. "You gon' let me in, or what? I been standing here for a minute."

Pam stepped aside and allowed him entry. She looked over her shoulder, in the direction Kevin had gone, and said, "You can go back to Shay's room. I'll..."

She headed towards the dining room without finishing her sentence. Charles went down a different hallway that led to his daughter's room.

THE VISIT WITH Shanice might have been Charles' best ever. He and Shay listened to the other adults argue for awhile, and then Charles discovered there was at least one thing he and his daughter had in common: Neither of them liked Kevin.

Pam's house was fairly large. Charles couldn't make out every word of the argument with her boyfriend, but he did hear one verbal exchange very clearly:

"Why he got to come over here all the goddamned time?"

"That's his daughter! What am I supposed to do?"

"It ain't even the weekend. He ain't supposed to see her but every other week!"

"We don't have no child support papers drawn up, Kevin."

"Then you don't have to let him see her at all!"

"Why would I stop him from seeing his daughter?"

"'Cause he's coming too damned much, Pam! Shit. Too damned much!"

There were a few more comments Charles couldn't hear, and then there was some stomping, and then a door slammed. Seconds later another door slammed in the living room. Charles and Shay looked at each other, and Shay finally broke the silence.

"He's gone."

"Sounds like it," Charles agreed.

"I hope he don't come back."

Charles was surprised to hear that. "Why? You don't like Kevin?"

"He always telling Mama what to do," Shay informed.

Charles couldn't believe she was confiding in him, but he wanted to keep it going. He went and sat on the floor next to her bed.

"Maybe he loves her," he offered.

"He's jealous, of *you*," Shay said.

Wow. Charles had to fight hard to keep from grinning. Shay was a treasure trove of information. "You don't know that."

"They didn't start arguing 'til you got out of jail," she told him. "The first time you came over here, when you left, they started arguing."

"But before I got out, you used to like him?" Charles asked.

Shay shook her head.

"Why not?" Charles asked.

"He eats all the food," Shay said, and Charles couldn't help but laugh.

HE VISITED WITH his daughter for an hour, and then he went to the kitchen, lured by the smell of fresh pasta. Pam was at the stove preparing a spaghetti meal. Charles thought she might still be upset about the argument with Kevin, but she was bright-eyed and upbeat.

"You staying for dinner?"

"Uh, naw. I wasn't planning on it." He took a seat at the kitchen table and watched her from behind. Pam's curves weren't all that flattering in her canvas shorts, but that was okay because Charles was trying to stop staring at every big booty he came across. He and Nicole weren't an official couple, but they were dating. If things became serious, Charles planned to be true to her.

Pam dropped two fistfuls of raw pasta in a boiling pot and wiped her hands with a kitchen towel. She came and sat across from her baby's father. She didn't have on any makeup, but she had a natural beauty that was destined to shine. She rested her forearms on the table and sighed.

He didn't think he was lucky enough to get two women in this house to confide in him on the same day, but he'd be damned if he wouldn't try.

"Man problems?"

"Why y'all so immature?" she asked.

"Who me? I'm not immature," Charles said.

"You didn't threaten to break all his facial bones?" Pam asked.

"He started it," Charles said.

Pam gave him a funny look, and he laughed. She did too. It felt good to laugh with her again.

"Why he got a problem with me anyway?" Charles wondered.

"You're asking *me* why two roosters can't be in the same pen?" Pam said.

"It ain't even like that," Charles said. "I know that's your man, and I ain't trying to get at you."

"Yeah, but we been together," Pam said. "And you get out of prison all tall, dark and handsome, muscles everywhere. I'm sure Kevin is starting to feel a little inadequate."

"You think I'm handsome?" he asked with a grin.

"Your flirting doesn't help," Pam said. "Kevin seen you looking at my butt a couple of times."

"I don't be trying," Charles said with a chuckle. "It's your fault for wearing jeans and shit."

"You full of shit," Pam said, but she was still smiling.

"You see I didn't look at it today," he said, "'cause you got them baggy shorts on."

"That was Kevin's idea," Pam admitted.

"No shit?"

"I thought he was going overboard, but I guess he knew what he was talking about."

"Yeah, but ain't that a little too controlling?" Charles asked. "You got that nigga telling you what to wear..."

"Try to look at it from his side," Pam suggested. "It's been just him, me and Shay for the last year and a half. And then I tell him you're getting out of jail. At first it's no big deal. We all figure you'll come by a couple of times and then disappear again. Next thing you know we'll find out you went back to the pen."

"Good to know you had such high hopes," Charles said.

Pam smiled again. Charles was falling for another woman, but *this* woman's smile still gave him goose bumps.

"But then you get out and you wanna be all *Super Dad*," Pam said. "No one expected you to come around this much – especially not Kevin."

"Alright, I feel you," Charles said. "But if you let me take Shay away from here when I come by, then I won't be all up in his face no more."

"Where do you want to take her?" Pam asked. "I know you're not going to let anything happen to her."

Charles didn't show it, but her trust meant the world to him. Little by little he was repairing every relationship he damaged.

"I'm moving to my new place next week," he said. "You can come by and check it out when I get everything set up. I want Shay to stay the night with me sometimes."

"You're moving out of your *dope house*?"

"I told you I don't sell dope," Charles said. "But yeah, I'm moving out of those cracked-out apartments."

"In a week?"

"Yeah."

"Really?"

"Yeah, girl. What, you don't believe me?"

"No, I believe you. I just, didn't expect you to get on your feet this fast."

"I got people depending on me," Charles said. "Like my son. If it was up to him, I woulda moved out two weeks ago."

Pam brought a hand to her face and rubbed her chin. She watched Charles, for a long time it seemed.

"What?"

"How can you afford a new apartment if you're not hustling? You still selling weed?"

Charles shook his head. "Not after I move. I make good money at the club, and I'm trying to get me a job working on AC's and heating units."

"You did that before?" Pam asked.

"Naw, but I got a certificate for it when I was locked up."

Pam stared at him a little longer.

"Girl, what you looking at me like that for?" he wondered.

"Nothing," she said and rose to her feet.

"It must be something," Charles said. He wiped at his face. "I got something in my nose, or what?"

Pam chuckled. She turned back to the stove and stirred the softening pasta. "I was just thinking," she said. "If I had known you were serious about getting your life together, I might have responded to some of those letters you sent from prison."

Charles' heart rate increased. This was the opening he'd been looking for. Or was it? There was only one way to know for sure. "You was with somebody anyway. And you still with somebody now…"

"Kevin? *Hmph.*" Pam made a sound like he wasn't worth the dust on the bottom of his nursing shoes. "Things weren't going all that good before you got out. And now they even worse…"

Oh shit. Charles' heart beat even faster, and he felt a warm tingling in his underwear. This *was* it! He'd been trying to get back with Pam for so long. She didn't come right out and say she was interested, but Charles knew she would give in if he made the first move.

He imagined himself standing and walking slowly to the stove. He would put both hands on her hips and kiss the side of her neck. She'd turn, probably asking, *What are you doing?*, and he would kiss her again, on the lips this time. His hands would slide to her backside, and he'd pull her hips close to his. And she'd feel his erection. And she'd drop her wooden spoon and kiss him back.

His erection grew a little more, just thinking about it. But he thought about the other woman in his life, and his butt remained glued to the chair. Nicole took a big gamble with him, and he couldn't hurt her like that. His feelings for Pam might have been a little stronger at that moment, but when Charles was with Nicole, he didn't think about Pam at all.

"You sure you not staying for dinner?" Pam asked.

"Yeah, I'll stay," Charles said, mainly because he didn't want to stand and reveal his semi-erect state. "You a good cook?" he asked.

"I handles my business," Pam said. "You should see how mad Shay gets when Kevin eats the leftovers..."

CHAPTER 31

EIGHT DAYS LATER, on Thursday January 31st, Charles accomplished his goal of moving to Windham Pointe Apartments, which was in the same city, but felt a world away from the drug-ravaged lands he left behind.

There was nothing flashy about Windham Pointe, but at the same time, everything felt fresh and brand new. Most of the cars in the new apartment's lot were less than five years old, and there were no loiterers lurching about, looking for an unfamiliar face to prey upon. The worst Charles had at Windham Pointe was noisy skateboarders and an elderly woman who, for some odd reason, looked through all of the dumpsters during her daily walk around the property.

Charles purchased the bulk of his furniture brand new from one of the discount stores on Seminary, but there were a few items he did bring from his old place. He and MikeyMike loaded his recliner and a few other essentials onto a borrowed truck and took them to his new home early in the afternoon. When they were done unloading, Charles laughed at his friend's exhaustion.

"Damn, nigga. You act like we really did some work."

"We did," Mike said, sweating profusely. He plopped down on the sofa and checked out his homey's fresh digs. Charles wanted to tell him to get his sweaty butt off the new furniture, but he bit his tongue. "You got some water?" Mike asked.

Charles went to the fridge and found a bottle of Gatorade. He handed it to Mike and sat across from him on his favorite recliner.

"Yo shit look nice," Mike said, looking around. "But why you move way over here, with these white folks?"

"It's mostly Mexicans over here," Charles informed him.

"That's even worse," Mike said. "Mexicans hate niggas."

"I ain't worried about all that," Charles said. "I just didn't want to be in the hood no more."

"The hood is where it's good," Mike said, quoting one of his favorite rappers.

"It's good for hustling," Charles acknowledged, "and for getting shot. That's about it."

"I tried to get them to let me keep your old apartment," Mike said. "They said naw."

"That's 'cause you ain't got no job."

"You didn't have no job, either," Mike said, "when you first moved over there. Why they rent you a unit?"

"I took Stacy with me," Charles said. "She co-signed for me. Plus they made me give 'em two month's rent and a deposit."

"I told them I'd give 'em two month's rent, too," Mike said. "They still told me no."

"That's 'cause you look like a criminal," Charles said with a chuckle.

"I ain't no different than you," Mike said. "Matter of fact, you been to the pen, my nigga. I ain't never been to no pen."

"Sometimes it ain't about what people see on paper," Charles said. "It's about how you talk to them. People know when you really trying to do right or when you trying to get over."

"Fuck them ho's," Mike said, taking a swig of his drink. "I'll find somewhere to hustle. I don't need nobody, ya heard me?"

Charles nodded, though it was clear Mike was upset about losing his crack spot. He'd been riding Charles' coattails for five months. But it was all over now. Charles moved on to bigger and better things.

"So I guess you ain't coming by the hood no more," Mike said.

What for? Charles wondered. What did the hood have to offer him except heartache and pain? The people in Charles' old circle were unmotivated, but they were hungry, which was a dangerous combination.

If you've never been to prison, you might think it's hard to get there; you'd have to do something really, really bad. But for a guy like Charles, getting locked up was fairly easy. It could be as simple as getting in the car when one of his old homey's said, "Hey, come ride with me, Chuck."

"I'll be around," he told Mike. "I'll swing through every now and then."

"You know your brother getting out pretty soon," Mike said and Charles' chest tightened – not from fear, rather the expectancy of new stress in his life.

Charles loved his brother dearly, but Fred (aka Blacc), was one of the most ignorant people he knew. Blacc was the kind of brother most Republicans thought about when they explained why their tax money *should not* be spent in the hood. Charles learned a lot from his big brother when they were young, but as they grew into adulthood, most of what Charles learned from Blacc was what *not* to do, how *not* to be.

"He been talking about getting it cracking again," Mike went on. "He say it's been a lot of set-tripping going on while he was locked up, and he gon' straighten everything out when he get back."

"I know he didn't tell *you* that," Charles said. "Blacc was beefing with y'all HoovaLand niggas before he got locked up."

"I ain't talked to him," Mike confirmed. "But that's all over, Chuck. We ain't beefing no more."

"You sure?" Charles asked. "I heard Blacc was gon' settle up with HoovaLand *first*." He was kidding, but Mike looked a little spooked.

"Nah, man. It ain't even like that. What you think, I'ma get into it with your brother?"

"Nah, I'm just messing with you," Charles said.

Mike couldn't hide his relief. "Yo, that ain't cool, man."

Charles laughed.

"So, you ain't gon' be down with Blacc when he get out?" Mike wondered. "I know he gon' need help getting back on his feet. I got his back, if he ask me. But you his brother. I know he gon' come to you first."

"Yeah, I know," Charles said, and he became contemplative. "You know I got my brother's back, through thick and thin. But I can't do *everything* that nigga wants. He got his own life to live just like I do. I hope when he gets out this time, he'll see that his old way wasn't working, and he needs to try something different. But I don't think so. You right about him wanting to get the old gang tight again."

"If he do, I know you gots to get back down with the set," Mike predicted. "You still got them tats. This Crip shit is for life."

Charles shook his head and actually got a smile out of that. "We not in L.A., Mike. A nigga can leave the gang whenever he wants around here. All he got to do is stop coming to the block."

Mike frowned, but he knew Charles was right. Overbrook Meadows could be a rough place at times, but no one was going to get murdered for leaving a gang. They might get beat up a couple of times, but that was about it.

"Well, I'ma be down with yo brother," Mike concluded, "even if you ain't."

"More power to you," Charles said and leaned back in his recliner. "But you better make sure he cool with y'all HoovaLand niggas first. Or you might catch a beat down."

Charles tried to keep a straight face, but he started laughing again.

"Fuck you nigga," Mike said and gulped down more Gatorade. "Say, I don't like it over here, man. It's too quiet. When you gon' take me home?"

CHAPTER 32

CHARLES LET HIS son spend the night with him on Thursday, but Friday he had something totally different in mind. He invited Nicole over for a home cooked meal. Charles chose to cook for her because it would give him an opportunity to show off his new place. He knew that if there was one thing women found absolutely irresistible, it was a single man with his own pad – especially if it was clean and brand new like Charles' apartment.

When Mr. Dripping Chocolate invited her over for dinner, Nicole knew what was up right away. A grown man doesn't want pretty gal to come to his house to play pinochle. Nicole weighed the pros and cons of their inevitable intimacy, and she felt tingles in her stomach when she agreed to come over. They'd been dating for nearly a month. So far Charles didn't exhibit any of the player tendencies her friends warned her about.

Nicole showed up at Charles' apartment at 7:30 on Friday evening. She wore a sleeveless black dress that wasn't too tight. It flowed perfectly with the natural contours of her body. The skirt stopped a few inches above her knees. Her hair was straight and layered, flowing down to her shoulders.

Charles answered the door wearing black Dockers with a dark blue collar shirt that had a sateen shine. His sleeves were rolled midway up his forearms, and he had a spatula in hand. He stared at Nicole like she was the most beautiful thing he'd seen in a long time.

"Hey. Welcome. You look real nice."

"Thank you," she said. She stepped inside the apartment, and (as Charles predicted) she was immediately impressed.

His couch and loveseat were tan colored, slightly darker than the carpet. His entertainment center was filled with expensive electronics. Charles even bought curtains to match the color scheme, and he had an artificial ficus standing tall in one corner. His coffee table had a glistening glass top. The only thing out of place was an old recliner that was in need of reupholstering.

"That's my favorite chair," Charles said, following her eyes.

"I didn't say nothing," Nicole said. "Your apartment looks good. I wish my house was this nice."

"I always wanted a place like this," Charles said. He closed the door behind her and gave her a brief kiss on the lips. Nicole got a whiff of his cologne, and she liked it, though she couldn't say what brand it was.

"What are you cooking," she asked, noticing another pleasing aroma.

"Baked chicken," Charles said with a grin. "I was going to make meatloaf, but I don't think you ready for my *best* meal. It would probably blow your mind."

Nicole was skeptical. "Can you cook?"

"Of course I can cook," he said. "You think I'd invite you over for a home-cooked meal if I can't do no home-cooking?"

She giggled. "Alright. We'll see."

"I'm almost done," he replied. "You just sit your pretty self right there, and I'll let you know when it's ready." He motioned for her to take a seat on his sofa. "The remotes over there, if you want it."

"Okay. You sure you don't need no help in there?"

"Naw, I got this," he said. "I'm the man."

"Alright," Nicole said. She chuckled as she eased down on the soft cushions. "Handle your business then, Mr. Man."

CHARLES' "HOME COOKING" turned out to be a bigger bust than Michael Jordan as a baseball player. Nicole suspected he was having trouble when she didn't hear a peep out of him for a full fifteen minutes. By the time she got up to check on him, there was a thin layer of smoke rising to the ceiling, and the fire alarm went off. Charles rushed to open the front and patio door. He fanned the smoke with a spiral notebook while Nicole checked the oven to see how bad her dinner looked.

It was really bad.

He had a whole chicken in there, and it was crispy black. Charles thought they should try to cut into it, to see if there was any salvageable meat inside, but Nicole convinced him to put the poor bird out on the patio so the burnt smell wouldn't linger in the apartment.

"You could've told me you can't cook," she teased.

"I can cook," he said. "You shoulda seen some of the spreads I made when I was locked up. This stove, it just cooks too fast." He stared at the appliance with disdain.

Nicole laughed and wrapped her arms around his torso. This was the first time she initiated contact, and she was surprised by the sheer bulk of her man. Charles was solid, like a mighty oak.

"At least you tried."

He looked down at her, and a sheepish grin spread across his face. "I can make you something else."

"No, that's alright."

"It won't take that long. I got some–"

"*No,*" Nicole said, a little more forcibly than she meant. "I mean, we don't really have time for that. I'm hungry *now.*"

"Alright," he said. "I'll order some Chinese. It'll be here in thirty minutes."

"That sounds perfect."

"But next time, I'm gonna cook again. I can't have you thinking I can't cook."

"Okay," Nicole said. "Remind me though, so I can make sure I bring some sandwiches. Just in case."

THEY WENT TO the living room and cuddled like teenagers while they waited for the food to arrive. Nicole told him about her long-term goal to go back to school and study radiology, if she couldn't reach a supervisor or manager position at her current job.

Their dinner was delivered in just twenty minutes. Charles told Nicole about his plans to get a job in A/C and heating repair as they ate. He said the certificate he got in the penitentiary was as good as a degree from ATI. He just had to find an employer who was willing to give him a chance.

"Is that why people go back to prison?" Nicole asked. "They get tired of trying?"

"Yeah, but not really," he said. "From what I see, most niggas go back to the pen because they lazy. Yeah it's hard to get a job when you got felonies, but it ain't impossible. When niggas get out, they'll try to do right at first. They'll fill out a couple of applications. But they give up too easy when don't nobody call them back, or if it's too hot outside, or they don't have a ride. Or they feel like the only job they can get is mopping floors.

"But me, before I made it home I decided I would do anything I could to not go back. I will mop floors, clean horse stables, walk some rich lady's dogs – It don't make no difference."

"But you ended up stripping," Nicole said.

Charles looked down at his half-empty to-go box and said, "You through?"

"Yeah." she handed him her leftovers.

Charles took the food to the kitchen and came back and sat next to her on the couch. Nicole still couldn't figure out what fragrance he was wearing, but she was growing more and more fond of it. She was growing more fond of Charles as well.

"Stripping pays good," he said. "But it's not something I wanna be doing for a long time."

"Why not?" she asked.

"It's degrading."

Nicole was taken aback. She never thought she'd hear a man say something like that.

"And it's not cool if you got a woman," he went on. "I know I couldn't be with no female stripper, no matter what she told me."

Nicole couldn't agree with him more, but she remained silent.

"And then when you really start to like somebody," he said, "it gets even harder to go work, as a stripper. I'm not no sorry ass dude, and I ain't no prostitute neither. I don't want no woman touching me unless I like her. But being a stripper, I got to keep my mouth shut and take it. One of the dudes I work with is married. I don't see how he do it."

"I try not to think about it," Nicole admitted. "I hate strip clubs."

"So that mean you ain't gon' come see me dance no more?" he kidded.

"No," Nicole said with a smirk. "I won't be doing that."

"But how you gon' see my new moves?" he asked. "I got a lot better since the last time you saw me."

Nicole looked into his eyes, and they both smiled.

"You got some pretty lips," he told her.

"I like your eyes," she said.

As she spoke, his beautiful orbs closed as he leaned in for a soft kiss. His lips were both electric and magnetic. Pulses of energy flowed from Nicole's chest and quivered in her stomach before coming to a rest between her legs.

Charles brought a hand up and lightly brushed the hair away from her cheek. With his fingers behind her neck, he urged her forward, ever so gently, and she gave in to another kiss. This one was slower and smoother and more electric than the first.

Charles backed away with her lipstick on his mouth. Nicole reached to brush it off. Charles kissed her thin finger, sucking lightly. Nicole withdrew her hand and kissed him again, makeup be damned.

She placed a hand on his chest and sighed inwardly when she felt how firm his pectorals were. She didn't mean to grope him, but the contours of his muscles were unreal. Surely he was more sculpture than flesh and blood.

"Do you wanna see the rest of my apartment?" he asked. He spoke softly. His breath was warm and sweet.

"Yes," Nicole said, her voice almost a whisper. She knew he was talking about the bedroom, but she wasn't nervous or self conscious.

Charles took her hand and rose to his feet. He helped her up, and as she stood, she glimpsed a huge bulge in his pants that looked as big as a child's femur bone.

She was nervous then. And also curious. But mostly nervous.

CHAPTER 33

ALL OF THE furniture in the bedroom was just a couple of days old, and the color scheme matched the living room perfectly. Charles led Nicole to the bed and motioned for her to have a seat. He stood before her and removed his shirt. It wasn't a strip tease, but Nicole couldn't have been more excited about the show.

She saw him topless at the club already, but Nicole was drunk that night, and the lighting was far too inadequate for a man as fine as Charles Hester. He'd been out of prison for nearly six months, but his stomach was still flat and rigid with a solid six pack. Charles had arms and shoulders like a heavyweight boxer.

But his chest...

Nicole wasn't aware that her mouth hung open.

His chest was nothing less than *outstanding*. His creases were deep. The definition was perfect. His nipples were beautiful, slightly darker than the rest of his chocolaty skin. Nicole thought each of his pectorals was as big as her head. Her mouth salivated at the thought of sucking one of those nipples. She wanted to climb him like a set of monkey bars.

She bit her bottom lip as he slowly approached her. Charles eased between her thighs, much as he did when they first met at Peeping Jane's, except this time Nicole spread her legs willingly, and she didn't object when his erection brushed her dampening panties. She put her hands on his chest, still not believing he was real. Her hand skated across his frame like ice cream dripping down a cone, finding more succulent flesh at every turn.

She planted kisses on his neck and traps. She sucked his lips and licked from his ear to his collar bone, loving the taste of his dark brown skin, his cologne. Charles ran his large hands from her rib cage to her hips. He squeezed her ass, and the throbbing in his boxers became too much to bear. He released her so he could unbutton his pants and relieve some of the pressure. Nicole watched him closely, and she swallowed hard when she looked between her legs again.

It's too big.

This wasn't a matter of speculation, it was simple mathematics. She reached to touch it, just to be sure. She pealed his boxers down and stared at his bare penis, her eyes growing larger by degrees. It appeared to be staring right back at her, with its one eye. It taunted her, with its fat head, long, thick shaft. Perfect dimensions, but it was definitely *too big*. But it was so beautiful! Nicole grabbed it with both hands. She gasped at the heat and sheer power she felt beneath her fingers. A rivulet loosened in her panties – but she knew this wasn't going to work.

He was *too freaking big*.

Charles' chest began to rise and fall and a quicker pace. He took Nicole by the shoulders and gently lowered her onto the bed. He lifted her knees and reached to snag her panties. He pealed them off slowly, staring between her legs the whole time.

Nicole stared at the ceiling, her head spinning. When he got her panties off, he pulled her to a sitting position again. He kissed her while he unzipped her dress. His hands were huge, nearly twice the size of hers, but his touch couldn't have been more tender. He eased the straps off her shoulders, and she helped slide her arms out of the dress. He licked her lips as he undid her bra. He suckled her breasts as soon as they were free.

He broke away and said, "Let me get a condom."

Nicole watched as he turned towards his dresser. His back fanned out like a deck of cards. The way his muscles flexed was hypnotic. His bubble butt was the best Nicole had ever seen – in real life or in the movies. But when he faced her again, Nicole's eyes fluttered like she saw a ghost. She had to voice her concerns.

"It won't fit."

"It will," he promised.

Nicole shook her head slowly as he torn the condom open and rolled it the length of his shaft. She was still doubtful when he approached her again and laid her down so he could remove her dress completely.

She lay flat on her back, her heart pounding. She scooted back until her legs were no longer dangling off the side of the bed. She felt like she had never been more wet, but when Charles crawled on top of her, he encountered heavy resistance. He reached down and tried to guide himself in, but Nicole inhaled sharply and winced. He pulled out, though he hadn't even gotten the head in yet.

"Need, need some lube," Nicole breathed.

He continued to back away until his feet were on the floor. He stared between her legs longingly and then reached and caressed her labia. He inserted his middle finger and smiled.

"I don't got no lube, baby. But you got some..."

Nicole had no idea what he meant until his face disappeared from sight, and she felt his hot breath between thighs. Her legs started to close reflexively, but he held them apart and delivered what had to be the most mind-numbing lick Nicole ever experienced.

She stared at the ceiling at first, totally in shock, but when her legs started to shiver, her eyes and hands returned to the bobbing afro between her thighs. Charles sucked and licked like a clitoris connoisseur, and Nicole fought the urge to buck and maybe fuck his face. She did place a hand on each side of his head, though. She held on for dear life, but she didn't have to guide him. Charles knew exactly what he was doing down there.

Her heart thundered. She felt like she was 100% wetter in a matter of minutes, but he didn't stop until her clitoris became hard and rigid and her vaginal walls began to contract, squeezing his tongue and lips at the same rate of her heartbeats.

When he stopped, his face was slick with her essence, and Nicole wanted him inside her more than she wanted anything else in recent memory. She wanted to *feel* him, all of him. Her emotions went way past the physical. She longed for him heart and soul. When he mounted a second time, the head slid in almost all the way before the pain came back. He looked into her eyes, and she held her breath and nodded.

He pushed a little harder, and the fat head squeezed through, followed by seven inches of delicious shaft that was almost as thick. Nicole exhaled and gasped again, but the pain was already receding, giving way to a pleasure so intense she almost cried.

Charles' tongue action put her on the verge of a climax, and his pipe work took her the rest of the way in less than ninety seconds. But even with the extra lubrication, he couldn't plunge *balls deep* in her love. There was about an inch and a half of rock hard man meat that was left out in the cold.

Never one to give up, he tried again a couple of hours later after they ate their leftover Chinese food and sipped some wine he forgot he had chilling in the fridge.

Nicole thought he was finally able to submerge fully when he rolled her to the doggy style position, but she was sexed nearly out of her mind by then, and she was too overwhelmed to ask.

CHAPTER 34

AT WORK THE following Monday, Nicole wasn't eager to tell her friends about her night with Charles. She had a great time, and she felt they were developing a real bond, but Stella warned Nicole (multiple times) to leave him alone. Nicole knew Stella wouldn't approve when she found out they were intimate.

But keeping a secret of this magnitude from the rat pack was mission impossible. Nicole failed before she even got started. At 9:20 am, less than thirty minutes after she clocked in for the day, Blanca approached her desk. After a little small talk, Blanca commented that there was something different about Nicole today.

"Did you get your hair done?"

"No," Nicole said. She hadn't taken any calls yet, but she didn't mind starting off her day with some good, old-fashioned slacking. Better still, her supervisor initiated the slacking, so she couldn't get in trouble for it.

"You trying some new makeup?" Blanca asked. She looked Nicole over once and then twice trying to figure it out.

Twyla got off the phone with a customer and peered around the cubicle wall. She too began to stare at Nicole.

"You look like you got some *good* sleep," Twyla remarked. "You usually look all messed up in the morning."

"What?" Nicole frowned at that. "I don't never look *messed up*."

Blanca laughed.

"I don't mean *messed up*," Twyla said. "You just be looking like you was in a rush to get out the house, and you didn't have time to do your hair right or get your makeup and your outfit together."

Nicole shook her head, and then she had to laugh herself. "That still sounds like you saying I look messed up."

"Yeah," Twyla agreed. "You do be looking messed up some of the time."

"Whatever," Nicole said.

"But you get yourself together by lunchtime," Twyla offered.

"Yeah, you do," Blanca agreed. "You were sitting over here with a curling iron one day, weren't you?"

"Hell no," Nicole said with a chuckle. "Those were just some hot rollers."

Everyone laughed – except one person. Nicole didn't know the fourth member of their clique was in on the conversation until Stella spoke up.

"That ain't no damned makeup. That heifer's glowing. You slept with that stripper, didn't you?"

Blanca, Twyla and Nicole's eyes widened at the same time. Nicole wanted to deny it, but Stella was staring at her with a mean look that reminded Nicole of her mother. This was the kind of look that said, *I got a built in lie-detector, so don't even try to feed me a bunch of bull.*

Caught between lying and not lying, Nicole's mouth opened and closed a couple of times without any words coming out. And then they knew for sure.

"*Bitch!*" Twyla was so loud half a dozen people turned to glare at her. "Why you didn't tell me you slept with that man?"

"*Be quiet!*" Nicole urged. "Damn, Blanca, do your job," she told her other friend. "Make her be quiet."

"You gotta keep it down," Blanca said, but she didn't even look Twyla in the eyes. She had to be the most non-confrontational supervisor ever.

"You did!" Twyla said. "You did, didn't you?"

"Yeah, she did," Stella said. She sighed and rubbed her forehead, like this was causing her emotional distress. "Dammit, Nicole, why'd you do that?"

"It's not what you think," Nicole said.

"You didn't sleep with him?" Blanca asked.

"Yes I slept with him," Nicole admitted, "but–"

"How was it?" Twyla asked. "Did he have some moves? Was he really as big as he looked?" Her smile was big and toothy, from ear to ear. "Damn, girl, all that chocolate all up on you! I know he can do it *good*, right? I know he can!"

Stella shook her head some more, but Blanca was eager for this scoop.

"I don't wanna talk about all that," Nicole said. She was still happy and excited, but Stella's disposition was a big downer. Nicole couldn't tell her friends what they wanted to hear with Mother Goose sitting right there.

"You *gotta* talk about it!" Twyla demanded. "What kind of shit is that? *You not gon' talk about it.* What the hell?"

"You really need to calm yourself," Nicole told her. "It's embarrassing enough as it is. I don't want the whole department to know about it."

"You shouldn't have did it if you knew you were gonna be embarrassed about it later," Stella said.

"I'm not embarrassed about what I did," Nicole clarified. "I'm embarrassed about the way y'all reacting. Twyla, you know I'm not gonna give you no dirty details. And Stella, you acting like I slept with Jeffrey Dahmer or something. Charles ain't that bad."

"He ain't *that* bad?" Stella said, her brow furrowed. "What does that mean?"

"He's not bad at all," Nicole said. "Charles is a good man."

"You got three kids," Stella said.

"I know that," Nicole said. "What's that supposed to mean?"

"You need an *honest* man," Stella said. "Somebody you don't have to be embarrassed about."

"I'm not embarrassed about Charles," Nicole reasoned. "You're the one who keeps giving me a hard time."

"What are you gonna tell your son?" Stella wondered. "*Hey, here's my new boyfriend, Dripping Chocolate. He shakes his ass for nickels at a nudie bar?*"

Nicole was trying to keep it lighthearted, but Stella's attacks were getting too personal.

"No. Why would I tell my son something like that?"

"Well what are you gonna tell him?" Stella asked.

"I don't know," Nicole said, "but it don't have to be nothing like that. You don't even know Charles. You need to watch your mouth."

Stella's eyes widened. "You're the one who said you don't like strippers."

"I know," Nicole said. "And I still feel that way. I don't think what they're doing is good, but that doesn't mean all strippers are bad. Charles is a good man. He takes care of his kids, and he's doing his best to get his life back together."

"And he's fine," Twyla added.

"Yeah, he's that too," Nicole agreed. "But this ain't about his looks."

"You don't think he's doing drugs?" Stella asked.

"No," Nicole said. "I know he's not."

"He's not selling them either?" Stella queried.

Nicole shook her head. "No. That's the main reason he's stripping; he don't want to get caught up in his old lifestyle."

"And I guess he told you he ain't sleeping with none of them girls that come to the club, either," Stella said. "You believe that too, huh?"

"What am I supposed to do?" Nicole wondered. "Any man I meet could be doing all of that stuff. I treat Charles the same way

I would treat anybody else I date: Until he gives me reason not to, I have to trust him."

"But why can't you trust a *regular* man?" Stella asked. "Why it got to be a stripper?"

"Regular like who?" Nicole asked. "Like Byron? Regular like my twins' daddy?"

"No, not like them."

"Alright then," Nicole said. "So you have to admit that *anybody* could do *anything* at *anytime*. You never know how trustworthy somebody is until you give them a chance."

"Damn, look at Nicole defending her man," Twyla said.

"He's your man?" Blanca asked. "Charles is your boyfriend now?"

Nicole hadn't asked Charles specifically if they were in a relationship, but some things were a given. "I wouldn't sleep with nobody I wasn't gonna be with," she said.

"So was he good or not?" Twyla asked. "Forget all this arguing."

Nicole was still a little frazzled, but she couldn't stop a grin from spreading across her face as she nodded. "Yes, Twyla. He was very, very nice."

"That's awesome," Blanca said.

"Whatever," Stella said and scooted her chair back to her desk.

"Did he eat you?" Twyla asked, and Nicole figured that was a great place to end the conversation.

"You know I'm not going there," she said and returned her attention to her computer.

"He did, didn't he?" Twyla said. "This my last question, Nicole. Just tell me!"

"Blanca, make her do some work," Nicole told her other friend.

"Yeah, we do need to get back to work," Blanca said to no one in particular, and then she turned and headed back to her office.

"Did you suck his d—"

"Twyla!" Nicole cut her friend off and burst into laughter. "You going too far, girl. I'm not talking about none of that!"

"I'll take that as a *yes*," Twyla said. She grinned. "You go girl. Defend yo man. I hope it works out for y'all. But if it don't, tell him you got a friend who ain't go *no* problem with strippers."

Nicole rolled her eyes. "Bitch, get to work."

CHAPTER 35

AROUND THE SAME time APEX's rat pack was trying to pry personal information from Nicole, Charles was twenty-six miles away in the city of Burleson; interviewing for an AC and heating job with a little company called Climate Kings.

The manager didn't seem impressed with Charles' resume, which he gave verbally, but he did say that he liked the cut of Charles' jib – whatever the hell that meant. There was just one hang-up...

"It's, we normally don't hire anyone with felonies," the portly manager said.

The two men sat in a small room that didn't have much furniture and nothing at all on the walls. But Climate Kings wasn't a big operation to begin with. They had less than ten employees and only three trucks roaming the metroplex at any given time. Charles thought they'd be happy to have a strong buck like him, but even these small-timers were picky.

"I guess it'll depend on what it was for," the manager said. A small name plate on his desk said his name was Michael Cochran. He looked like what Chris Farley might have looked like if he made it to his fifties.

"It was for drugs," Charles said. He sat uncomfortably in a small plastic chair that didn't seem very sturdy. Charles feared the chair would break if he leaned back too much, so he sat with his elbows on his thighs. He wore black slacks with a white shirt tucked in neatly. He even wore shiny shoes with black socks, a combo he hadn't worn since he graduated high school.

"Drugs," Mr. Cochran said with a hint of exasperation. He sounded like every black man that came into this office had a rap sheet for the same thing. "Have you ever been arrested for anything violent?" he asked.

"No, sir," Charles said. "I never hurt nobody." That was a huge lie, but a background check couldn't prove otherwise.

"Were you selling or using drugs?" Mr. Cochran asked.

"Selling," Charles said. "I made some mistakes when I was a kid. I thought the fast life was for me, but it wasn't."

"When'd you get out of prison?" the manager asked.

"Almost six months ago. I did four years."

The fat man frowned. "How old are you?"

"Thirty-two," Charles said.

"That doesn't sound like you made these mistakes when you were a *kid*," Mr. Cochran deduced. "Sounds like you were a grown man..."

"The mistakes started when I was a child, and I was stuck in the same pattern as an adult," Charles said. He tried to sound intelligent, like some of the educated inmates he met when he was locked up.

"What kind of work you doing now?" Mr. Cochran asked.

"I work at a club," Charles said. "I'm a dancer."

The big man frowned. "What, you mean like a *stripper*?"

"Yessir," Charles said. "Just 'til I can find a good job."

The manager shook his head and sighed. "I don't know. I was thinking that if you worked like, a regular job, I could tell the boss how long you been there. And if you been clocking-in on time every day, that would help a lot. But he's not gonna care about a stripping job."

Charles nodded. "Yessir." His heart sank deep in his chest as his hopes and dreams came crashing down again, but you couldn't tell by looking at him.

"Alrighty." Mr. Cochran stood and offered a hand to shake. "I'll talk to the owner and see what he has to say about it. If it was up to me, I'd give you a shot. But I just do the interviewing. The boss man makes all the decisions."

"Yessir," Charles said, shaking his hand. "Thank you, sir. I sure hope to hear from you guys."

Thirty seconds later he was back in his old Bonneville. He figured his chances of getting this job were only about 10%, but that was a better chance than he had before he left the house this morning. He never realized it before, but optimism is very important, especially to a black man with few positive options and a shitload of ways to get paid illegally.

SIX HOURS LATER he was in a better mood when he picked up his son from Castleberry Elementary. Lil Charles was in a good mood too. Starting today he'd get to spend a full week at his dad's new apartment. But even more importantly, Lil Charles was going to meet his big sister for the first time.

He had plenty of questions as his father drove to Pam's side of town. Charles finally told him, "Hey, settle down, man." He looked into his son's bright eyes and chuckled. "All these questions will be answered when we get there, in about ten minutes."

"I just wanna know if she's pretty," Charles Jr. said. "That's my last question."

"She's beautiful," Charles said. "But that's your *sister*. I don't want you to be getting no crush on her or nothing like that."

"I'm not, Dad."

Charles returned his eyes to the road to hide the euphoria his son just gave him.

Dad.

It felt good for someone to call him that. He couldn't wait to hear it from Shay. So far she just looked at him and started talking, but at some point she'd have to call him *something*. *Dad* or *Daddy* was probably pushing it, but Charles definitely didn't want her to yell, *Hey Mister*, or something impersonal like that.

At a quarter till four Charles pulled into Pam's driveway and told his son to wait in the car. Pam answered the door after a few knocks. Charles thought she looked stressed, but still attractive.

Pam wore her blue scrub suit, and she had her hair pulled back in a ponytail. She told Charles, "Hold on a minute," and disappeared down the hallway. She came back a moment later with two backpacks in hand, one large and one a little smaller.

"This is for school," she said, referring to the smaller one.

"This one has her clothes for tomorrow and her hair stuff."

Charles rushed to lighten her load.

"I braided her hair last night," Pam said, "so you shouldn't have to do anything to it in the morning. But I got her combs and gel and stuff in there just in case. She has to wear a uniform at school. You'll have to iron it when you get it out the bag. She has to be at school at 7:45. Where is she gonna sleep? How many bedrooms you have?"

"I got two bedrooms," Charles said. "She'll either sleep in my room or the other one. I'm sleeping on the couch."

"You got your son out there?" Pam asked.

"Yeah." Charles nodded. "You wanna meet him."

"I do," Pam said. "You got some money for dinner tonight?" She looked around the living room and then headed for the coffee table where her purse was lying. Charles grabbed her hand.

"Wait. I don't need no money, Pam. I got money to feed them."

"You know where her school is, right?"

"Yes, I know where the school is. I been living in this city nearly all my life. Why you so worried? You looked stressed out."

Sh pulled her hand away and rubbed her hair back. She sighed. "I'm not worried."

"What's your problem then?" Charles asked. "You starting to change your mind?"

"No, it's not you," she said, shaking her head.

"What is it then? Where yo boyfriend at?"

"He left," Pam said. She looked Charles in the eyes. "He said he didn't wanna be here when you got here, so he left. We were supposed to ride to work together. We get off at the same time. It doesn't make sense, taking separate cars. He just..." She waved a hand in dismissal. "Never mind."

"He still tripping about me?" Charles asked. "Y'all had another argument?"

"It's nothing," Pam said. "I'm not worried about him. I have a daughter, and you're her father. I'm not going to stop you from seeing Shay, so if Kevin can't get used to you coming around, that's his problem. I don't think you're doing anything wrong."

Charles felt a tingling in his gut. He couldn't believe Pam was taking up for him. Even though it was causing friction in her love life, she was defending Charles. A couple of months ago she told Charles he had no chance with her, there was never going to be an opening. Now he wasn't so sure.

"I did do something wrong," Charles said. "I wanted to get back with you. I told you so myself. I didn't tell Kevin, but he could see it in my eyes. He could tell by the way I was looking at you."

"But he should still trust me," Pam countered. "I told him I didn't want you back, but he won't believe me. I can't tell you how many arguments we had, about how I was leading you on. Every time I didn't come home from work on time, he swore up and down I was somewhere with you."

Charles' eyes dilated. "Damn, I didn't know it was that bad."

"Jealousy is something I can't put up with," Pam said. "I was listening to that Keyshia Cole song the other day, *I Should've*

Cheated. It made me think of you. Made me think I might as well go out with you, if Kevin's going to treat me like I am anyway."

Charles felt his pulse increase. He felt something stirring below the waist too, but this wasn't right. He and Nicole made love. That didn't necessarily make them a couple, but, yeah, it kinda did. This was the most conflicting predicament Charles had been in since he got out of prison. Not selling drugs and not committing crimes with MikeyMike was easy, but not jumping on an opportunity to get Pam back was extremely difficult. She was intrigued by his hesitance.

"Hmm. I can't believe you're not going to start talking noise about Kevin..." She smiled, and that made it even worse. Charles wanted to kiss her so badly his mouth watered.

"He just going through some shit," he said. "I can't blame him. If I was some skinny ass nerd, and my woman's baby-daddy got out of prison, and he was way bigger and finer and more good-looking than me..."

Pam's smile grew bigger. The little devil on Charles' shoulder told him to snatch her up. *Hug her. Grab her ass right now! She wants you to take charge.* But Charles stuck to his guns.

"If I was that nerd ass nigga," he continued, "I'd be pissed too. I'd probably start arguing with my woman since I sure as hell can't say nothing to that big motherfucker who keep knocking on my door."

Pam laughed. She put a hand on Charles' chest while she laughed. It may have been flirty. Maybe not. Luckily a little ray of sunshine appeared in the hallway and cut the encounter short.

"I'm ready."

The adults turned and smiled at the life they created.

"Alright, I got all your stuff packed up," Pam told her daughter.

"You nervous?" Charles asked her.

"A little," Shay said. But she was smiling, so Charles hoped it was a happy nervousness.

"Let's go meet Charles Jr.," Pam said and headed for the front door. "Is he as handsome as his daddy?"

"No doubt," Charles said. "I got the best-looking son in the state. I got the best-looking daughter, too."

He put an arm around Shay's shoulders as they exited the house, and she didn't pull away. Charles sighed silently. Next to his son calling him Dad, his daughter letting him hold her was the best thing that happened to him all day.

CHAPTER 36

THE NEXT COUPLE of weeks seemed to fly by.

On Valentine's Day Charles surprised Nicole with two dozen roses and a box a chocolates sent to her job. That was the first time she ever had anything delivered to her at work. The flowers were nice, but the best part was the way her coworkers reacted when the deliveryman brought the gifts to her cubicle. Every eye was on Nicole. She felt like the luckiest girl in the office.

As their relationship blossomed, Charles took Nicole somewhere special at least once a week. She even let him strip for her one night. Nicole changed her cellphone's ringtone to *I'm in Love with a Stripper* because it made light of Charles' glaring imperfection. She and Charles didn't argue a lot, but when they did, it usually had something to do with Peeping Jane's.

His stripping was like a big elephant in the room. Nicole tried to get used to it. She rearranged her furniture around it and even hung pretty curtains on its tusks so it wouldn't look so ugly. But sometimes it took a huge shit, and there was no way to deny that there was a big ass elephant in the room.

And it was stinky.

And Nicole hated it.

BUT WHEN THAT elephant wasn't on her mind, Nicole had a great time with her man. On Friday, February 22nd Charles took her to Sushi Express because Nicole told him she never had sushi before.

"How'd you make it this far in life without trying sushi?" he asked as they dined in the dimly lit restaurant.

"I don't know," she replied. "They don't sell it at any grocery stores I go to. Or if they do, I never thought about buying it. I think everything I eat should be cooked."

"What if I felt that way," Charles asked. He lowered his eyebrows and gave her one of his sexiest looks. "I eat you raw all the time."

Nicole's eyes widened. Her whole body grew warm. She looked around uneasily. "What are you doing?"

Her nervous smile made Charles want to make love to her, right there.

"Just talking about licking you," he said. "I thought you liked it when I put my mouth on you."

He licked his lips, on purpose, and Nicole's clitoris quivered.

"You're not even whispering," she said in a hushed tone.

"Nobody's listening to us," Charles said. He leaned back in his seat, still speaking rather loudly.

"You don't know that," Nicole said.

"Pussy," Charles said and then smiled.

Nicole put a hand over her face and looked down at the table. "Oh my God," she said, but she was still smiling.

"I can't believe you're so embarrassed."

"I can't believe you're not."

"You know what I do for a living," Charles said. "Anything I do with my clothes *on* is way easy, compared to that."

Nicole felt a brief stab in her gut, but she didn't let his comment about Peeping Jane's get her down.

"You wearing panties?" he asked.

"Yes," Nicole said, still blushing. "I always wear panties."

"G-string?"

She shook her head. "No."

"Do you mind if I lick you up and down, when we leave here?"

Nicole was getting into the groove of his mild exhibitionism, and she was able to look him in the eyes again. "Do you mind if I suck on you when we leave here?" she asked. She lowered her eyes like he did and licked her lips, her grown-woman-sexy on full blast.

Charles tried to keep his cool, but Nicole knew she surprised him. She wasn't totally against fellatio, but she would never do that for someone she wasn't seriously involved with. So far Charles had yet to feel her hot tongue or her sweet lips on his manhood. He was starting to think Nicole didn't get down like that.

"Uh, yeah, I mean *no*. I wouldn't mind," he said.

"Do you want me to cup your balls while I'm sucking?" she asked.

Charles looked around comically and then met her eyes again. He was blinking quickly, like she might be a dream.

"Uh..."

"What's wrong?" she asked. "Cat got your tongue?"

"Naw," Charles said. He smiled. "But you shouldn't play around like that."

"It's okay for you to do it?"

"It's different," he said. "Because I will do everything I said I would."

"Me too."

"You ain't did it before."

"I didn't feel like it," Nicole said. "But since I'm trying something new tonight..." She scooped a sushi roll up with her fork, having given up on the chopsticks long ago. "I figured I could try something new with you, too," she said. "Unless you don't like the idea of your dick in my mouth..."

She devoured the whole sushi roll. Charles' mouth fell open. It was fun to watch him try not to squirm. Nicole waited five... four... three... two... *Ah. There it is.* He scooted in his chair, trying to readjust his erection without touching it. She laughed.

Charles looked around for their waiter. "You ready to go?"

"No," she said. "We just got here." They'd actually been there for forty-five minutes, and she was quite full, but she enjoyed teasing him. "Aren't you still eating?"

"Uh uhn." He shook his head. "I'm done."

"What about your wine?"

He grabbed his glass and swallowed the rest with one gulp. "Mmm," he said as he returned the glass to the table. "That was great. You ready?"

"Um, not yet," she said. "I was gonna ask the waiter to teach me to use my chopsticks again."

"I'll teach you," Charles said.

Nicole laughed again because she knew he was as amateurish as she was.

"You grab that motherfucker like this," Charles said, holding one of his chopsticks like a spear. "And then you *jab it*," he said, demonstrating as he spoke. "You jab it in there." He stabbed the dull chopstick into one of his sushi rolls. "And then you pick it up and eat it." When he lifted his chopstick, the mangled sushi roll somehow remained on the stick until he brought it to his mouth. Charles chomped on the food roughly and nodded. "See, ain't nothing to it."

Nicole was cracking up. "Okay, Charles let's go."

CHAPTER 37

SHE THOUGHT ABOUT teasing him a while longer when they got to his apartment but decided against it. Charles was a good man, and he deserved some oral stimulation. Nicole had been with him for nearly three months, and Charles pleased her with his tongue almost every time they made love. Never once did he ask Nicole to reciprocate.

She followed him into the kitchen when he went to drop off their doggy bag. When Charles turned and saw her standing there, he was confused.

"What's up?"

Nicole dropped to her knees and unbuckled his pants. "It's time."

Charles was skeptical, so he didn't help her undress him. But he was nearly fully erect by the time his pants and boxers fell to his ankles. Nicole squeezed his manhood with both hands (it was that big), and then she wrapped her lips around the fat head before her inhibitions could stop her.

She took him in as far as possible with the first gulp. She only made it halfway down his shaft before he was pushing against her tonsils, but that was just fine with Charles. He moaned and shuddered, looking down at her with his mouth ajar, his eyes still not totally believing.

But the warm sensations of Nicole's tongue and jaws as she began to slowly bob her head brought everything into reality very quickly. Charles grew steadily in her mouth, and he was at full mast within seconds. He didn't pump his hips, unsure of how she would react, but he did reach and tentatively touch her shoulder. His hand gradually made it behind her neck, but he didn't have to urge her forward. Nicole's pace was already perfect.

The physical stimulation she gave him was enough to induce a heart attack, but the visual aspect was just as good. The sight of her lips wrapped around his meat and the thin layer of saliva she left as she worked her neck made Charles weak in the knees. He watched her jaws go concave as she sucked with increased pressure. He felt her breaths on his pubic hair each time she exhaled through her nostrils.

And as promised, she cupped his balls with one hand while she stroked his long shaft with the other. She was even skilled enough to use her own saliva as a lubricant to jack him off while she sucked.

Two minutes hadn't passed before Charles felt an eruption brewing. He held out until the last moment and then pulled out, not sure how Nicole wanted to handle his climax. She didn't resist his withdrawal, and she didn't stop stroking either. She licked her lips as she pumped her fist. She watched his penis closely, almost in awe, and that turned Charles on even more.

He said, "Oh shit," and Nicole felt the pulsation working its way up. She turned to the side at the last second and narrowly avoided a face full of his hot semen. She watched it squirt past her instead (the first blast travelled all the way to the sink!) and she continued to milk him until he was totally spent.

His kitchen floor was a mess, and Nicole's panties were wetter than they had ever been.

"I never watched nobody cum before," she said.

"I can go, again," Charles said, his breathing slightly labored.

"Are you sure?" she asked. His dick was still like a lead pipe in her hand, but considering all of the semen on the floor, she didn't think there was anything left in his balls.

"Yeah," Charles said. "I'm sure, baby."

MUCH TO NICOLE'S gratitude (and pleasure), Charles wasn't lying about his sexual prowess that night. He took a short break to mop up the mess they made in the kitchen, and then it was off to the races again. As repayment for Nicole's job well done, he sucked on her clit and labia for so long she came in his face twice and caught a cramp in her left booty cheek.

She still had enough energy to ride him like a cowgirl afterwards, and she nearly passed out from an ecstasy overload when Charles rolled her into doggystyle, which was his all-time favorite position. Nicole was so content when they got done, she nearly forgot that this was a Friday night, and Charles had to leave soon to go to his stripping job.

She didn't complain often, but she didn't want to share her man with all of the freaky girls in Overbrook Meadows, Dallas and Arlington. She wanted him all to herself.

"When you gonna find a new job?" she asked as they spooned on the soft mattress, Marsha Ambrosius playing softly on his bedroom stereo.

Charles wasn't surprised by the question, but he was surprised that it took this long for Nicole to bring it up. "I'm working on it," he said vaguely.

"Are you still filling out applications, for an AC job?"

"I haven't in a couple of weeks," he admitted. "I had an interview. I thought it was going somewhere. I gave them time to call back, but they never did."

"Have you looked for a job doing something else?" Nicole asked.

"Like what?"

"I don't know. Anything."

"Most McDonald's won't even let me flip burgers with a felony," Charles informed her. "Even if they would, I can't go from what I'm making now to ten dollars an hour. I know I ain't got a lot going for me, but I'm worth more than that."

"You're not going to find *any* job that pays what you're making now," Nicole said. "Unless you go to school and get a degree."

"I don't need the same as I'm making now, but I do need better than minimum wage," Charles reasoned. "I told you; I don't wanna be stripping. But I don't got no problem paying my bills right now. I can't quit my job and end up struggling."

Nicole didn't want him to struggle. And she knew it wasn't fair to ask him to quit his job. He was a stripper when she met him. She knew it would become harder to accept as they grew closer, and she let the relationship develop anyway.

"I just don't want you to get comfortable," she said. "If the money's too good, and you wanna keep working there, I need to know."

"Why?" he asked. "What if I told you that is how I feel?"

Nicole's heartbeats slowed, almost to the point of not beating at all. She was in love with this man, but it was still early. If she waited, it would be harder to lose him later.

"Then we'd have to make some decisions," she said, her eyes wide and fearful. "Or, I know I would."

Charles waited a few moments before responding. "Nicole, I don't wanna strip. I told you that when we first started talking. I told you I was gon' find another job. If I don't do it, then you *should* leave me, for lying to you."

She stared into the darkness, hanging on his every word. Charles always seemed to know exactly what she was thinking. It was beautiful, but also kind of scary.

"But I wasn't lying to you," he went on. "I haven't lied about nothing I told you. And you my woman now, so I know I gots to do what's right for you."

He spoke into the back of her neck. He had his arm and one leg draped over her. His body was warm, but his words made Nicole feel even warmer. She knew they were in a relationship, but there was something altogether wonderful about him saying *you my woman.*

"So if I gotta quit my job and make ten dollars an hour," he said, "I'll do that, for you. If it's to that point now, let me know. Otherwise, I got to go to Peeping Jane's tonight."

She blinked quickly, not sure how to respond. She wanted Charles to quit stripping, that was a no-brainer. But she didn't like the idea of being responsible for his financial well-being. It's true what they say: With great power comes great responsibility. She had to look at it from all angles before she made a decision of this magnitude.

"You can't stop stripping until you have another job," she said, though it assured her man would leave her arms soon and drift into the lust-filled arms of another. "And you can't settle for no minimum wage. I guess I'll be okay with you stripping, for now."

"Alright," Charles said. He kissed the back of her neck and lingered there, enjoying her scents. "I'll fill out some more applications next week. I'm jumping on the first job I get, as long as it's at least ten dollars an hour."

Nicole nodded. She wanted to offer encouragement, but the cold reality of what Charles had to do tonight began to sink in. A few weeks ago he told her that although the rules at Peeping Jane's explicitly forbade patrons from touching the dancers' genitalia, the dancers generally ignored this rule, especially in the "Champagne Room." He told her he didn't want to, but his tips would suffer heavily if he didn't get down with the program too.

"What you doing tomorrow?" he asked. "I'm taking my kids to the movies. You think you might want to come with us, with your kids?"

That caught Nicole totally off guard. She had to roll over and look him in the eyes for this one. In the scant lighting, she thought she saw her man grinning.

"You can tell me when to quit my job, but I can't meet your kids?" Charles asked.

Nicole smiled too. "I knew there was a catch."

"Am I your man or not?" he asked her.

"Yeah," she breathed. "I like the way that sounds."

"So, you don't want them seeing me, or you don't want me to see them?"

"No, I think it's cool," she said. "It's definitely you I'm more worried about. The twins, they, they're um..."

Charles chuckled. "They just kids. How bad can they be?"

She raised an eyebrow. "Um... Very."

"Well then I got a right to see them," he joked. "You done spent a lot of time worrying about what *you* getting into. But maybe I'm the one who should be worried. What y'all doing tomorrow? You wanna get the kids together, or not?"

"Yeah," Nicole said, though she really was worried about what Charles would think of the terrible twosome. "That sounds cool."

"Cool," Charles said. He kissed her and then sat up in the bed.

She giggled.

"What?"

"Just thinking about what's gonna happen when your two kids meet up with my three."

"It'll be sweet," Charles predicted. "Just like the Brady Bunch."

Nicole was thinking it'd be more like The *Crazy* Bunch, but she didn't say anything. Sometimes it's best to wait and see for yourself.

CHAPTER 38

THE FOLLOWING AFTERNOON Charles arrived at her house at 2:00 pm sharp. He had Shay in the car already, but he had to pick up Charles Jr. on the way to the movies. Nicole borrowed her friend Angie's SUV for the day because neither her nor Charles' car was big enough to fit seven people comfortably.

She had her whole family waiting in the living room when Charles knocked on the door. She wore jeans with sneakers because Charles mentioned taking them out to eat after the movie. Nicole knew the twins would take off running at least once, and she didn't plan on pursuing them in heels. Nicole even had her hair pulled back in a ponytail, in anticipation of the hectic outing.

Charles still thought she looked beautiful. He felt the same way about the twins the moment he laid eyes on them. They didn't look *terrible* at all, with their matching Nike sneakers and windbreakers. And Charles hadn't noticed how much Shawn resembled his mom. He knew Shawn would be his toughest critic.

"Hey, y'all. Come on in," Nicole told him. "This is the twins, Kevin and Keisha. And you met Shawn at Walmart."

"Hey, how y'all doing?" Charles asked. He wore jeans with a pristine white tee shirt. His size was almost alarming. His deep voice was equally intimidating. He immediately had the full attention of everyone in the room. "I'm Charles, but y'all can call me Chuck if you want."

"*Mr. Charles* is fine," Nicole interjected.

"Alright, I answer to Mr. Charles too," he said. "This is my daughter Shay. I told her a lot about y'all, and she's happy to – well, I don't have to talk for her. Introduce yourself," he said, urging his daughter forward.

"Hi, I'm Shanice." The girl was nervous, but not nearly as nervous as Shawn. He stared at her like an angel walked right out of his dreams and into his living room. "I'm eight," she said. "Everybody calls me Shay."

"Wow, you're so beautiful," Nicole said, and you could tell by her smile that she meant it. "My son's almost your age," she went on, oblivious to the slight heart attack Shawn was having. "Go on, Shawn. Introduce yourself."

The boy was stunned silent for an awkward moment, but he cleared his throat and looked down at the floor. "I'm, I'm, I mean, my name is Shawn. I'm nine, almost ten."

"And apparently he's feeling shy today," Nicole said, finally picking up on her son's unease. "But that's cool. We'll have plenty of time to get to know each other. Where's CJ?" she asked Charles. "I thought you were bringing him, too."

"I went to pick him up, but he wasn't there," he said. "I wanna try one more place on our way to the movies."

"Oh. Okay," Nicole said. "Well, we're ready to go if you are. I borrowed my friend's Explorer, so we'll all have room."

"Cool," Charles said. "Let's get it."

He and Nicole exchanged a glance. He was confident, as usual. Nicole, not so much.

"We gon' have a good time," he assured her.

"Yeah," Nicole said, and then she looked down at the twins' car seats leaning against the couch. She hoped he knew how much hard work he signed up for. "I guess the first thing we need to do is get these loaded up..."

CHARLES TOOK BOTH of the car seats by himself. Nicole offered to tote one of them, but her man wouldn't hear of it. The kids were so nervous, no one talked while Nicole helped get the twins strapped in. Shawn and Shay sat together in the back and tried their best not to look at each other. Nicole touched Charles' hand for the first time when they were seated up front and ready to embark on their outing. She wanted to kiss him, but she didn't want to freak anyone out more than they already were.

"Thanks," she said, "for offering to take everybody."

"It's all good," he said and gave her a flirty wink.

"I just hope the twins don't get to acting a fool," Nicole said as she buckled her seat belt.

Charles turned in his seat and smiled at the pint-size menaces. "They don't look like they could do too much," he stated. "I think you be over exaggerating."

Nicole actually got a laugh out of that. "You think so, huh?"

"Yeah," he said. "What could possibly go wrong?"

"Famous last words," Nicole said as she got the SUV moving.

CHAPTER 39

STACY ANSWERED THE phone when Charles called her again, and he didn't question why she hadn't answered his previous five calls this morning. She told him she was at Toya's house, and she'd have Charles Jr. ready in ten minutes.

When Charles got there, Stacy tried her usual seductive game. Once again she got pissed off when he wouldn't yield to her advances. Stacy got even more belligerent when he told her, "Damn, girl, I don't got time for this. I got somebody waiting on me downstairs."

"Who?" Stacy asked, primed for a confrontation.

"Her name's Nicole," he said. "And you bet not fuck with her."

"Who said I was gon' fuck with her?"

"I know you," Charles said. He helped his son find his shoes, and then he sat CJ on the couch and fretted while the boy hurriedly tied them.

"Where that ho parked at?" Stacy asked. She stepped into a pair of flip flops and brushed her hair back with her hands. Charles didn't think Stacy would attack Nicole for no reason, but he couldn't put anything past the hellcat.

"It don't matter where she parked. You ain't got no business going down there."

"How come I don't?" Stacy said. "You finna put my son in the car with her – I got a right to see who she is."

"Whatever. As many places as you drop him off at, I know you don't care."

"Well I care today," she spat.

Charles sneered at her. He grabbed CJ's hand when the boy had his shoes tied, and the threesome left the apartment together.

Nicole saw Stacy descending the stairs with her man, and she had time to size up his baby-mama before they made it to the car. She sensed bullshit was on the horizon, so she didn't bat an eye when Stacy came to her side of the vehicle and folded her arms under her chest. Stacy struck a pose that would've made certain women, like Angie or Twyla, get out of the car and kick their shoes off.

"Who is you?"

"I'm Nicole."

"Them yo kids?" Stacy asked, peering into the backseat.

"Most of them are."

Stacy's frown intensified. "What that mean?"

"The twins are mine," Nicole said. "And the oldest boy is mine too."

"Why you didn't just say that then?" Stacy wanted to know.

"Hey, gone on with all that," Charles said as he returned to the passenger seat. "She done answered your question."

"I'm just saying, why she gotta get an attitude, like she better than somebody?" Stacy said.

"Ain't nobody getting no attitude but *you*," Charles barked. "I'll call you when we on our way back."

"Come *by yourself* when you bring CJ back," Stacy said. "I need to talk to you when you get here."

"Whatever," Charles said. He shook his head and told Nicole, "Come on, let's go."

She got the SUV rolling again.

When they exited the parking lot, Charles sighed and told her, "Sorry about that."

"Sorry for what?" Nicole said. "If my baby-daddy was as awesome as you, I'd be jealous too."

Charles grinned, relieved she was taking it so well. "You don't have to drop me off at my car first, on the way home…"

Nicole smacked her lips. "Boy, please. I'm definitely going to bring you back over here *first*. If she got something to tell you, I'll wait."

He laughed. "I see know what you're doing."

"Always," Nicole said. "Do you?"

He nodded. "Yeah. I think so."

"We'll see," Nicole said. She looked up at the ten expectant eyes in the rearview mirror. "We will see."

THEIR FIRST TIME at the movies was as awful as Nicole expected. She remembered her mom taking her to the movies when she was a child, and it never seemed like a life-altering event. Nowadays, to take a group of seven, you had to stand in line and really contemplate whether your finances could survive the hit. Gas money or 3D glasses? The concession stand or next-week's groceries? It was no wonder Netflix was doing so well during the recession.

But Charles planned for the gouging, and he had a pocket full of twenty dollar bills. He parted with five of them at the admissions booth. He parted with two more for popcorn, soda and candy. Nicole started to feel guilty before they took their seats. She hoped the twins would show their appreciation by being good, but no such luck.

About thirty minutes into the show, they felt comfortable enough to talk to Charles. That wouldn't have been so bad except Kevin and Keisha only had one volume, which was LOUD. And then they spilled a whole bucket of popcorn. And then they had to go to the bathroom. And then they drank their soda and got to talking again, this time to each other. And then they spilled the soda and had to go to the bathroom again.

By the time the movie was over, Nicole knew Charles would break up with her. But he put an arm around her and even carried one of the twins back to the car, smiling the whole time.

"Y'all wanna get something to eat?" he asked when everyone was buckled in.

Shawn and Shay were still tight-lipped (Nicole hoped they weren't developing a mutual crush), but the younger kids were excited and full of sugar. "Yeah!"

"Y'all wanna go to Chuck E Cheese's?" Charles asked, and the twins actually screamed their approval. "Alright, let's get it!" Charles said and hopped in the passenger seat.

"I wanna give you the money back for those tickets," Nicole told him as she started the car. "I don't think nobody watched that movie."

"You'll do no such thing," Charles said. "If you wanna pay me back, you can give me a kiss."

Nicole laughed, but that was an offer she couldn't refuse.

The car erupted in a chorus of "*Ooooh's!*" and giggles when she leaned over for the smooch.

THE TWO HOURS at Chuck E Cheese's didn't go as badly as Nicole predicted. The twins exploded like dogs chasing a squirrel as soon as they got a few tokens in hand, but Charles didn't have a problem with their antics. He even chased them down and monitored their gaming, making sure they didn't get ripped off by any of the broken arcades.

And in an environment where they could actually talk to each other, Nicole liked the interactions between the older kids. CJ already met and developed a friendship with Shay, and he was eager to do the same with Shawn. Out of the three, CJ was by far the most talkative. He didn't notice the way Shawn and Shay were watching each other, with an intensity that could almost be described as flirting.

Nicole observed all of this carefully. She didn't want to interfere with her son getting along with Charles' daughter, but she knew that at some point she'd have to give their relationship a little direction.

After an hour of free time, Charles gathered the crew together for pizza. He didn't get upset with the kids the whole afternoon, but he did get a little stern when they wouldn't quiet down for a short prayer.

"Alright, y'all need to calm down now, so we can pray for our food. It's a time for playing around, but this ain't it. If y'all don't wanna pray, ain't *nobody* eating."

Everyone piped down, and (at their table at least) you could hear a pin drop while Charles blessed the food. He didn't normally pray for his own meals, but whenever he and Nicole dined together, he noticed she did it.

"God, bless this food we about to eat. And bless our families too. It's hard to get different people together like this, but, you know, it's a good thing..."

Charles hesitated, feeling like his prayer was missing something. But Nicole took his hand and squeezed it softly and said, "Amen."

Everyone else followed with their own "Amen," and Charles smiled, like he had really done something special.

"Alright, y'all. Let's eat!"

THE DAY ENDED as their dates always did; with Nicole in Charles' arms and her head high in the clouds. There were so many reasons their relationship shouldn't work, but they were defying the odds, and it felt great. They kissed deeply under her porch light – but not too passionately because Shay was waiting (and watching) in Charles' car.

"So, you did it," Nicole said, her arms wrapped around him. "You got all of us together. How does it feel?"

"It feels, *right*," Charles said. He was brimming with pride. "You should let me pick Shawn up sometimes, take him to play hoops or something."

That caught Nicole off guard, though she wasn't sure why. Charles had already done everything he could to prove himself. She should've known he would want to bond with Shawn.

"I don't have to," he said, reading her expression. "I just thought..."

"No, I think it'll be okay," she said. "Let me talk to him, see what he thinks."

"It don't have to be no time soon," Charles said. "Maybe in a week or two."

Nicole nodded. Her eyes were glossy, but Charles didn't notice.

"Alright," he said. He kissed her again before backing away. "I'll call you when I get home. I had a good time. Those twins are something else."

He chuckled as he headed for his car. Nicole watched until he climbed behind the wheel. When she went inside Shawn was waiting for her in the living room. He asked if Mr. Charles was her boyfriend.

"Yeah," Nicole said. "You like him?"

Shawn nodded and said, "He big."

"He is," Nicole said with a grin.

"He can take care of you," Shawn decided, "if somebody mess with you."

"Yeah," Nicole said. She wiped her eye before the tear had a chance to fall. "Yeah, I'm sure he can..."

PART FIVE
A NIGGA MOMENT

CHAPTER 40

"YOU DID WHAT?"

Stella looked like Nicole told her she sold her car for gas money. It was lunchtime at APEX Teleservices. All four members of the rat pack were outside, chilling in the smoking area. Twyla was the only one who smoked, but it was a bright, sunny day, and her friends didn't mind accompanying her.

Nicole was glad they were outside, because her latest news about Mr. Dripping Chocolate was stirring up some strong emotions.

"Calm down," she told Stella. "It's getting to the point where I don't wanna tell you nothing about him."

"Why?" Stella stood with her back against the concrete building. She wore a long skirt and a hard look of frustration. Nicole knew Stella was at her wits' end.

"Because you hate him, and you don't know nothing about him," Nicole said. She sat on a bench next to Twyla. She didn't care for the smoke from her friend's Black & Mild, but the wind was blowing the other way, so it wasn't that bad.

"I don't have to know him," Stella said. "I found out everything I need to know about him at that *club*. What is wrong with you, girl? Why would you want your kids hanging around a man like that?"

Stella was vexed about Nicole's decision to let Charles meet her family. Nicole expected dissent, but she was hoping her mother-figure would get over it already.

"What movie did y'all see?" Blanca asked.

"What difference does that make?" Stella said.

"The new Charlotte's Web," Nicole said. "It was good, I think. I had to take the twins to the bathroom so much, it felt like–"

"So I guess this is your man now?" Stella said.

"I wouldn't let him meet my kids if he wasn't," Nicole replied.

Stella shook her head. She felt like one of her children decided to shoot-up heroin, right in front of her. "You *just* met him," she reasoned. "There's no way you know what he's all about this fast."

"I met him almost three months ago," Nicole countered. "How long am I supposed to keep him in the dark? Shawn knew I was dating somebody."

"Does he like him?" Blanca asked.

"Who?" Nicole said.

"Shawn. Does he like Charles?"

Nicole nodded. "Yeah. They get along great."

"How do you know he's not using you?" Stella asked.

"Using me for what?" Nicole wondered. "I ain't got nothing. He makes way more money than I do."

"The sex," Stella guessed. "He's using you for sex."

Nicole rolled her eyes. "He can get sex from *anybody*."

"I didn't say you were the only one," Stella said. "He probably has a whole *flock* of women, all around the city."

Nicole laughed at that.

"What's funny?" Stella said.

"You," Nicole said. "You not even thinking about anything I said. You're so full of hate, all you see is what you want to see."

"I don't hate nobody," Stella said. "But I know a *dog* when I see one. And I know when you *shouldn't* bring a boy home to mama – or to meet your kids."

"I'm not gonna keep defending myself," Nicole told her. "If you wanna hate on Charles, that's your problem. But I don't wanna hear about it no more. Can't you say something constructive?"

Stella was stunned and somewhat offended by that comment. She and her friend didn't always see eye to eye, but Nicole never shut her down completely. "Do you love that man?" Stella asked, with a more subdued tone.

"Maybe," Nicole said.

"And it's not about the sex?"

Nicole shook her head. "I'm too old to fall for somebody just 'cause they got good sex."

"He do got good sex though, don't he?" Twyla asked.

Nicole grinned but didn't respond to that.

"So he met your kids," Stella said, reluctantly giving up her fight. "That makes it official, don't it?"

Nicole nodded. "It can't get no more official than that."

Stella pursed her lips and closed her eyes while she sighed.

"Do you remember that alcoholic they took out of the homeless shelter?" Nicole asked her.

Stella frowned and shook her head.

"He was a math genius," Nicole recalled. "They cleaned him up and gave him a scholarship to Texas Lutheran. He graduated, too."

Stella was still confused. "So? What about him?"

"It just goes to show," Nicole said, "that you never know what people can do until you give them a chance. If a homeless man can be a math wizard, why can't I find a stripper who's a good man?"

Stella considered the analogy and shook her head again. "I just don't want you coming to work next week crying about this fool. I don't think he gon' do you right, Nicole. That's my honest-to-God *gut feeling*. When I get feelings like this, they ain't hardly never wrong."

"I love you," Nicole told her. "You're like a play-mama to me. You know that. But I done thought about this way more than you have, and my gut feeling's telling me something different. I don't need no man, but I wanna be with Charles."

"That's awesome," Blanca said.

Stella didn't agree, but she kept her mouth shut.

"What about the *dick*?" Twyla asked. She sucked her mini-cigar and blew the smoke out of her nose. "Why you won't tell us how good he fuck?"

Blanca grinned, growing red about the face.

Nicole smiled too, but she shook her head. "I'm not adding fuel to Stella's fire. If I tell you that, she'll think it *is* all about the sex."

"Forget her," Twyla said.

"I don't even care no more," Stella announced. As proof, she gave Nicole one more look of disappointment before pushing off the wall and walking away. Her friends watched in silence until she was out of sight.

"Okay, she gone," Twyla said with a twisted smile. "Now tell us."

"I'm not," Nicole said. She looked down and kicked a few pebbles around. She knew she hadn't done anything wrong, but Stella made her feel guilty. And stupid. "I don't see why she gotta act like that."

"Forget her," Twyla said. "You know she stuck up."

"She's just being protective," Blanca said, "because she cares about you. She knows you're not close with your mom. Maybe she thinks you don't have nobody else giving you good advice."

"Maybe she need to mind her own damn business," Twyla suggested.

"Do, do you think she's right?" Nicole asked.

Blanca was surprised by the question. "What do you mean? I thought you said you were sure."

"Yeah," Twyla said. "What about that crackhead Einstein you was talking about?"

Nicole chuckled, but the humor never made it to her eyes. "I am sure," she told them. "I was just, I'm just saying..."

CHAPTER 41

BY THE TIME she left work, Nicole was once again confident about her decisions regarding her stripper beau. But Shawn threw another monkey wrench in the works when she picked him up from school. His feelings about Charles were completely opposite Stella's, but it still gave Nicole pause, to hear him rattle on about Mama's new boyfriend.

"I made a hundred on my journal today," Shawn announced. His smile was big and bright. Nicole couldn't remember the last time he was so animated after a long day of school.

"You did?"

"Yeah." He dug through his backpack until he found a red spiral notebook. He opened it to the last page he wrote on and showed Nicole a full sheet of his chicken scratch. At the top, there was a smiley face and a big "100" written in red ink.

"You wrote all of that today?" Nicole asked.

"Mmm hmm." Shawn nodded. "Our journals only have to be half a page, but I wasn't done, so I kept writing, and this is how much I had done when time was up." He turned the page, and Nicole saw two more sentences on the back.

"You must've had a lot to say..."

"Today the topic was *What did You do This Weekend?*"
Shawn informed. "We always get that topic on Monday. Usually I
don't have nothing to talk about, but today I did, because we did so
much on Saturday. I talked about Mr. Charles and CJ and Shay
and the movies and Chuck E Cheese's too. Want me to read it to
you? I had to read it to the whole class. Teacher said it was the
best journal I ever wrote."

He was talking so fast, Nicole struggled to keep up. She
loved to see him excited about his schoolwork, but she felt uneasy
about this particular assignment. "Yeah, read it to me," she said.

Shawn read his whole journal entry as Nicole made her
way to the twins' daycare center. He was smiling the whole time.
His writing wasn't very creative, but he did get a good description
of everyone and every place they visited during Charles' outing.
The points Nicole keyed in on was how he thought Shay was
"pretty," and how he described Charles as "big," "strong,"
"muscular" and "nice."

"Wow," Nicole said when he was done. "I guess you had a
pretty good time."

"Mmm hmm," Shawn said, putting his notebook away.
"Are we going out with Mr. Charles again this weekend?"

"I don't know," Nicole said. "I doubt it. That whole day
was pretty expensive. I don't think Charles can afford to do that
again, not right away at least."

"That's okay," Shawn said, not too disappointed. "When is
he coming back again?"

"You wanna see him?"

"Yeah."

"You didn't talk to him that much," Nicole said. "I didn't
know y'all got along so well..."

"He said we're going to play basketball," Shawn said.

Nicole frowned, her sense of dread growing stronger.
"When'd he say that?"

"At Chuck E Cheese's. We was playing that hoop game. He said he wanted to take me to a real court. I told him I would still win, but he said he would. Do you think he could beat me?"

"Um, I don't know," Nicole said. "I never seen him play."

"He missed a lot of his shots on that game," Shawn said. "He said the rim was too little. I don't think he could beat me – not unless he blocked all of my shots. But when you play with big people, they not supposed to block your shots, right?"

Nicole was still listening, but everything seemed to be moving too fast around her. She felt like she was breaking into a cold sweat. But when she reached to wipe her forehead, it was completely dry.

Charles told her he wanted to play ball with her son, but Nicole didn't know he told Shawn as well. She never saw Charles talking to Shawn for any extended period of time. She didn't mind, but it felt like her worst fear had come true. She suspected Shawn would cling to the first man she started dating. But she never thought it would happen so quickly, and so thoroughly.

This wasn't a problem if Charles was everything he said he was, but what if Stella was right about him? Personally, Nicole could handle the heartbreak, but Shawn didn't deserve to have his dreams smashed again. Why didn't she wait – at least until Charles quit his stripper job and held down a regular lifestyle for a little while? Why wasn't she around to hear this stupid basketball conversation? Why was Charles so damned likeable?

"Did you hear me, Mama?"

She nodded. "Yeah, baby."

"What I say?"

Nicole looked over at him and grinned. "What's this, a pop quiz?"

The boy giggled. His smile was like a fog lamp, brightening every crevice of Nicole's soul. If the world was right with him, then it was right with his mama too. Nicole smiled. This time it reached her eyes as well as her heart.

"You said big people shouldn't block shots when they're playing against little people."

"Oh. So that's true, ain't it?"

"I think so, baby."

"Are you going to tell Mr. Charles, so he'll know too, for whenever we get to play?"

"Sounds like you're worried about losing," Nicole noticed.

"No, I'm not."

"That's what it sounds like to me."

"Will you just tell him? *Please*?"

"Yeah, baby. I'll tell him," Nicole promised.

CHAPTER 42

WHEN SHE GOT home, Nicole went through her regular routine of cooking dinner, making sure Shawn got all of his homework done, and providing the twins with at least one educational activity before she got them ready for bed. As she went about her motherly duties, the conversation with Stella and the talk with Shawn kept swirling through her mind, creating a twister of worry that threatened to grow into a full blown hurricane if left unchecked.

Relationships are tricky things. She felt like she had at least partial control over every other aspect of her life, but there's no way to control what someone else does. That can be both a blessing and a curse.

She called Charles at nine o'clock. He said he was visiting his daughter.

"I need to talk to you," she said, nibbling her thumbnail.

"Can I stop by when I leave here?" he asked.

"Yeah. That'd be fine."

He knocked on her door an hour later. Nicole was surprised to see that he cut his hair. It was all shaved close to his head now, the same length all around. His edge-up was still perfect, and the lack of an afro made his bushy eyebrows seem even thicker.

She stepped out onto her porch rather than invite him inside. Nicole was barefoot, wearing basketball shorts and a tee shirt. She didn't have any extensions in her hair today. It was pulled back in an easy ponytail.

Charles smiled as he reached to hug her. He kissed her on the lips and frowned when she barely kissed him back.

"What's wrong?"

She shook her head. "I wanted to ask you about Shawn. You told him you were going to take him to play basketball?"

Charles was puzzled. "Yeah. I think so. I told you that, too. Why?"

"I didn't know y'all had talked that much," she said. "Where was I at?"

He shrugged. "I don't know. Probably chasing Keisha or Kevin." He chuckled. "Why? What's the problem?"

She sighed. "I just, I don't like for people to tell him stuff, if they not gon' do it. He gets all, worked up about it."

Charles cocked his head slowly. "What you mean? You didn't want me to talk to him? You shoulda told me that before I came to your hou–"

"No, I didn't say I don't want you to talk to him."

"But you don't want me to play basketball with him?"

"No. I didn't say that either."

"Then I don't get what you saying."

"I don't know what I'm saying, either," Nicole admitted. "I just don't like for people to tell him they're gonna do something–"

"If they not gon' do it," Charles said.

Nicole looked into his eyes. "Yeah."

"Why you think I wasn't gon' do it?"

She sighed again. She wrung her hands together. He took hold of them to stop her.

"I don't know what you're going to do," she said honestly. "I think, maybe I had a bad day. It wasn't really bad, but something happened at work that made me, nervous."

"What happened?" Charles asked.

Nicole debated whether she should tell him and decided to go ahead. If someone in Charles' life had strong feelings about her, she'd want to know about it. "Some of my friends think I'm stupid, for going out with a stripper. They think I shouldn't have brought my kids around you."

Her words were like a punch in the gut. But it wasn't a total shock. Charles had been taking heat from all angles, every since he started taking off his clothes for money. Nicole's friends weren't really downing him. They were trying to protect her. And that was something he could respect.

"What do *you* think?" he asked.

"I thought it was a good idea," Nicole said. "Or else I wouldn't have done it."

He thought for a second. "You know, I ain't even mad at your friends for talking noise about me."

"Actually, it was just one of them."

"Well I ain't mad at that *one*. Obviously she loves you and don't want you to get hurt."

Nicole nodded. She held her breath as she waited for him to promise there was nothing to fear.

"But you talking to *me* about it..." Charles smiled and shook his head. "Can I really say something to make you feel better? 'Cause if I'm a liar, and I ain't who I said I was, what difference does it make what I tell you right now? I could be lying again."

That wasn't what Nicole expected at all. And as she thought about it, she realized he was right.

"For the record," he went on, "I wouldn't never lie to no little boy, not about something like that. I told you I wanted to take Shawn to play ball, same as I told him. I ain't never told you I was gon' do something that I didn't do. Have I?"

Nicole couldn't think of anything.

"But on the real," Charles said, "it ain't what I say that matters. It's what I do. If I say I wouldn't dog no woman who got kids, and you see that I ain't dogging you, then you know I was

telling the truth. If I take Shawn to play some ball this weekend –
or whenever you want – then you'll know I wasn't lying about that
either. Would it really make you feel better right now if I told you
I ain't no liar?"

Nicole understood what he was getting at, but she nodded.
It was silly but, "Yeah. It would."

He chuckled. "A'ight, shorty. I ain't no liar. You believe
me?"

She grinned. Rather than answer, she wrapped her arms
around him and laid her head on his massive chest. He held her
back. He kissed the top of her head, still smiling.

"I don't think I'm ever gon' understand women," he said.
"But y'all sho' do feel good." His hands slipped to her rump, and
he squeezed tenderly.

"I hope you just talking about *me*," Nicole said with a
giggle.

"Yes'm. Just you," Charles assured her.

CHAPTER 43

THE NEXT FEW weeks were picture perfect for Nicole and Charles. As February gave way to March, the beautiful flowers of spring blossomed across the city, creating a colorful backdrop for their unlikely love affair.

Nicole learned to obey her heart rather than the varied of opinions about her black stallion, and that alleviated 90% of the stress she was experiencing. When Charles wanted to pick Shawn up one Saturday afternoon, Nicole sent her son away with a smile. When Shawn returned later that day with dried sweat stains on his tee shirt, a brand new basketball Mr. Charles bought him and a huge grin on his face, Nicole embraced his happiness and didn't let her worries spoil the scene.

Because when you think about it, tomorrow's not promised to anyone. Every day is a gift. Rather than worry about all of the things that could go wrong, Nicole cherished the here and now. Sometimes it felt like she was freefalling, but that was okay too because Charles was always there to catch her.

He really was a knight in shining armor, to Nicole at least. His stripping was still a problem, but Nicole began to pray for her man, and she knew God would open a door for him soon. Until then, Nicole waited patiently, and Charles rewarded her by being everything she ever wanted in a man, and then some.

ON TUESDAY, MARCH 19th, Charles was visiting with Shay when he got an unexpected call from MikeyMike.

"Hello?"

"Yo. I got somebody here wanna talk to you."

"Who?" Charles asked, but Mike was already handing the phone over. "Hello?"

"Yo. This Chuck?"

Charles' eyes widened as he recognized the husky voice on the other end of the line. Something hard and heavy flipped over in his stomach. "Fred?"

"Yup yup, nigga! You know who it is! Just touched down a couple of hours ago. Where you at, kinfolk? What you doing today? I'm trying to kick it with my little brother, man!"

Charles chuckled. A grin spread across his face. "I'm with my daughter, on the west side. Where you at?"

"I'm on the south, my nigga. On Davis Street. Same spot. Ain't nothing changed."

Charles felt another squeeze of apprehension, but he shook it off. Overall, he was happy his brother was finally free.

"Alright. I'ma come by there," he said.

"Heard you got your own place. You living high on the hog," Fred said.

"Naw," Charles said, still smiling. "I do alright, but it ain't all that."

"When you gon' get here?" Fred asked. "You need to take me out to eat. Nigga hungry than a motherfucker. I need you to take me to get some clothes too. I ain't got shit to wear, my nig. And I *know* you got some freaks lined up for your big bro. You gon' hook me up with a couple of dollars, or what? What's up, man? When you gon' be here?"

Fred was going a mile a minute, which was his norm. Charles remembered back in the day when Fred used to bark orders to the gang at the same fevered pace: *A'ight, first thing we got to do is go see that nigga Pablo. He got the AR-15's, MAC-11's, a gang of 9's. Yup yup. We gon' take them guns to my lil homeys on Avenue C. P-Loc already waiting; got the goon squad on standby. We come back here and get our own shit, then we roll out at midnight. We gon' hit all four of them cats at the same time. Yup yup. Laws can't say we did all that shit at the same time. Ya heard me? Come on, nigga. Let's go. You ready? Get in the car, cuz! You ready? Get in the car, nigga! Let's go!*

Charles laughed and told him, "I'm on my way."

When he put his phone back in his pocket, he noticed Shay was watching him.

"What's up, little one?"

"Where you going?" she asked. She was at her computer desk, finishing up some homework.

Charles was sitting on her bed, watching her hamster family go about their daily business. He generally didn't like rodents, but he had to admit that Shay's hamsters were cute. And if you sat there and watched them for awhile, you'd see that they weren't filthy animals at all.

"That was your Uncle Fred," Charles said. "He just got out of jail today. I got to go see him."

"You just got here," Shay noted.

Charles was surprised by her comment. "You gon' miss me?" He stood and approached her computer desk.

"You said you were going to take me to get some ice cream when I finished my homework."

"I can take you tomorrow," Charles offered.

"I'll be so hungry by then, you'll have to get a double-scoop. *With* sprinkles."

"Alright," he said, chuckling. "But now I'm wondering if it's me you miss or my ice cream money..."

"I already got some ice cream in the freezer," Shay informed.

"Alright. True that. True that," Charles said. "But I'ma make it up to you tomorrow anyway. Can I get a hug?"

Shay turned away from her computer and grinned at him. She gave him a big hug and a kiss on the cheek.

Charles put a hand to his face when he backed away. "Wow. I get some sugar too! And it ain't even my birthday!"

Shay giggled.

"Love you," Charles said. "I'll see you tomorrow."

He left the bedroom and encountered Pam in the living room. She was lounging on her couch with a bowl of grapes. She wore pink leggings with a long tee shirt. Her bare feet had a pedicure recently. Her cute little toenails were candy apple red.

She looked up at Charles and then checked the clock. "Where you going?"

"To see my brother. He just got out."

"Really? Where's he at?"

"On the south," Charles said. "Where else?"

"You just got here," Pam said. "Shay not tripping."

"A little," Charles admitted. "I had to bribe her with some ice cream."

"I thought you were already taking her for ice cream."

"I gotta get her a double-scoop tomorrow."

Pam smiled. She got up to see him out. Charles checked out her sexy legs a little bit, but he was nowhere near as wolfish as he used to be.

"So is this how it starts?" she asked when they stepped outside.

"How what starts?" Charles asked her.

It was a little after four pm, and the sun was still bright in the sky. The March weather was pleasant, about 78 degrees. Charles stretched his arms big and wide as he turned back to face her.

"Your brother has only been out one day, and you're already kicking your daughter to the curb."

Charles would've been offended by that if Pam wasn't smiling.

"That's a low blow."

"I'm just kidding," she said. "But I am worried about what's going to happen now. You been doing so good."

"You worried about me, huh?"

"I just want you to stay out of trouble."

"'Cause you like me, right?" he joked.

"Boy, stop," Pam said. She hit him on the arm playfully. Charles noticed she'd been doing a lot of that lately; touching him when the situation really didn't warrant it. He thought some of it might be flirting. Or maybe Pam was just a touchy-feely kind of person.

"How come yo man ain't been by?" he asked her.

"Kevin? Please." Pam waved a hand in dismissal. "Ain't nobody worried about him."

"He not still tripping 'cause of me, is he?"

"Kevin trips just to trip," Pam confided. "He don't have to have no reason."

"But he ain't jealous of me no more, is he?" Charles wanted to know.

She shook her head. "No. He's mad at me now – 'cause I haven't sued you for child support."

"So he is still jealous," Charles said with a smirk.

"I guess that's what it all boils down to," Pam confirmed.

"You told him I was giving you money?"

"It ain't about the money," Pam said. "He only wants you to come over every other weekend. And he don't want you to visit Shay over *here*. He wants you to pick her up."

"I can take her every time I come," Charles offered. "I don't have to stay here."

"You can take her if you want to, but I don't have no problem with you seeing her over here," Pam said. "This is my house, not Kevin's. He can't tell me who can and cannot come over."

Charles chuckled. "Look at you."

"What?"

"Look how you treating him. Sound like y'all could work this out, if you really wanted to."

Pam shrugged.

"That nigga's a mark," Charles decided. "You wouldn't be acting like that if you was *my* woman."

Pam frowned. "What you mean?"

"I'd tell you to let that man pick up his child and take her *somewhere else* for their visit. I don't care where, but he ain't finna be sitting up in my house *or* my woman's house. He damned sure ain't finna be sitting up in there while I'm at work. And if I caught him eyeballing my woman *one time*, I'd stretch his ass out *right then*. I wouldn't roll my eyes and go on about my business."

Pam stared at him for what felt like an eternity before she spoke. "Is that what you'd tell me?"

"Damn skippy."

She stared at him some more. "I guess Kevin ain't got it like you."

"I tried to tell you that the first time I came over here," he replied.

"I guess I shoulda listened." She continued to stare, all the way into his soul it seemed, and Charles finally recognized the expression on her face as *longing*.

Oh shit.

He wasn't flirting or coming on to her intentionally, but his remarks triggered something that had been dormant inside Pam for many years. When he first met her, more than a decade ago, she would only go out with rough necks. Her preference changed after Charles knocked her up and left her with a baby to raise on her own.

Pam started dating smart guys; the kind who had nothing but Dockers and collar shirts in their closet. But deep down she longed for a thug to tell her what she could and could not do. And she would never forget how big Charles' manhood was. A big dick nigga who could talk a lot of shit *and* back it up was like her birthday and Christmas all rolled into one.

Unfortunately Charles was taken. He had feelings for Pam, probably always would, but he wasn't the dog he used to be.

"Alright, girl. You take it easy."

He turned and hurried to his car, and Pam stood there wondering what more she had to do to get the reaction she desired. She told him he'd never have a chance with her, but for the past month and a half, she'd been giving him nothing but green lights. The air traffic controller was signaling for a smooth landing, right between her legs.

She didn't know if she should up the ante or let it go entirely, but something had to give. Soon. This cat and mouse game was fun, but it was also getting a little frustrating.

CHAPTER 44

"THE BLOCK" WAS the corner of Evans and Davis Street. Charles saw his old crew hanging out as soon as he turned the corner. It brought a smile to his face, to see that some of his childhood buddies were still alive. But he also felt a strong sense of *impending doom* on that street.

The neighborhood he and his brother used to lord over was depressing, like snap shots of a third world country. It was filled with dilapidated homes, corner stores, liquor stores and violent teens and twenty year olds who didn't realize they were already in the golden years of their lives.

The graffiti near Davis Street was still familiar to Charles, even though he hadn't been in this area in years. The faces on the corner were familiar too, but Charles was apprehensive when he pulled over and exited his vehicle. Just by getting out of his car on this block, Charles left himself susceptible to a driveby, a police shakedown or a spur of the moment act of ghetto violence.

Two weeks ago a man was killed on this street when he refused to move his car, which was parked in front of a "gangster's" dope house. Charles parked less than two feet from where they sprayed the victim's blood with a water hose, washing it down the drain.

"Goddammit! If it ain't fucking *Chuck D!*"

A tall brother with a noticeable limp approached with a hideous smile on his face. He reached for a handshake, but Charles pulled him close for a brief hug.

"Oh shit. What up Skee?"

Skee wore khaki Dickeys with a black tee shirt. His hair was short. His skin caramel brown. He would've been handsome if not for a shotgun blast to the face ten years ago. Skee's wounds were healed, but he would always resemble Harvey Dent from the Batman comics.

"What you been up to?" Skee asked. A lot of people couldn't look directly at him when they talked to him, but Skee was like another brother to Charles.

"Nothing," he said. "Maintaining."

"How come you ain't been by?" Skee asked. "I heard you got out a year ago."

"It's only been seven months," Charles said. He walked with Skee to the rest of the crew hanging out in front of two abandoned homes and a crack house.

There were mostly new faces among the eleven men wasting their lives on that street, but there were some old faces too. Charles gave dap to long lost comrades, like P-Loc, Scoota Mac and Murda Man, and he made the acquaintance of some of the new members of the clique. Everyone was pleased to see him, and a party atmosphere quickly ensued. Charles was offered weed, liquor and even a couple of pills of heroin to snort. He graciously declined all of this.

Some of the youngsters didn't know what all of the fuss was about. P-Loc was quick to educate them: "Man, this is Blacc's brother Chuck D. These niggas is OG's to the fullest. You better recognize. Blacc and Chuck built this shit from the ground up. Everything you know about Davis Street came from them. They got locked up around the same time, and now they both out. These niggas finna regulate this shit. All these crisscrossing ass niggas finna get put in check."

"Yo, Chuck," Skee said, "I got whatever you need, big homey. Pistols, dope, whatever. Just holler."

"I ain't even down with that shit no more," Charles said. "Yo, where Blacc at?" he asked before anyone had time to question his loyalty.

"There he go right there," P-Loc said. He pointed to a corner store across the street.

Charles looked and saw MikeyMike walking with one of the meanest pit bulls ever to break his leash and stand on two legs. A genuine smile exposed most of his pearly whites as Charles crossed the street and gave his big brother a hug.

Blacc was older than Charles by two years, but he was shorter and smaller. Not that that would ever take away from his legend and notoriety on the streets. What Blacc lacked in size, he made up for with his lightening quick hands and his always dangerous *I don't give a fuck* attitude. Blacc could box better than anyone on the block, Charles included, but he rarely fought with just his hands. When they were younger, Charles watched his brother beat people with anything handy, from a chili brick to a liquor bottle or a ragged piece of rebar.

Blacc earned his nickname from his coal black skin and equally dark soul. His hair was short, and he wore no beard or moustache. He had thick eyebrows like Charles, and they were naturally angled, giving Blacc an evil expression even when he was in a good mood.

Blacc was a beast before he went to prison, and everything he learned behind those penitentiary walls made him even more demonic. He was easily the most dangerous man on the south side. But to Charles, he was just a big brother; the same guy who used to steal candy bars from the store and split them with Charles until Charles was old enough to pilfer his own.

"Man! What's going on?" Blacc asked. The siblings held each other for a long time. They hadn't laid eyes on each other in more than six years.

When they separated, their eyes were bright, their smiles genuine. Mike looked on with obvious envy. He could pal around as many gangsters as he wanted for as long as he wanted, but he would never find the real love Charles and Fred had for each other.

"Nothing," Charles said. "Chilling." He and Blacc looked each other up and down.

"You done got big!" Blacc noticed.

"You put on some weight, too," Charles said. His brother wore black Dickeys with a blue tee shirt and black Chuck Taylors. He was healthy and robust. He was as muscular as Charles, just a smaller version.

"Why you ain't come see me?" Blacc asked.

"Nigga, I was locked up at the same time as you!" Charles said.

"You got out first," Blacc said. He was still smiling. Charles was too.

"Yeah, but I knew you was getting out in a few months," Charles said. "If you was gon' be in there another year or two, I woulda came."

The brothers made their way back across the street. MikeyMike followed, pushed to the third-leg category. The rest of the gang watched Charles and Blacc with a happiness they probably couldn't explain themselves. There was excitement in the air. Anticipation of something new, something better.

"I heard you ain't been by the block since you got out," Blacc told his little brother. "I heard you on some *other* shit."

Before Charles could speak for himself, MikeyMike said, "Man, *some other shit* ain't even the word for it!" He laughed. A couple of the other homey's snickered, too. Charles shook it off.

"I'm trying to keep it legal," Charles said to Blacc. "I be–"

"Man, that nigga be strutting around in a straight up *thong, tha-thong, thong-thong!*" Mike cackled, referencing Sisqo's *Thong Song* from 2000. He laughed some more, and a few others did too.

Mike was like a court jester. If someone was to get clowned, Mike was usually the one doing the clowning. It had been that way for as long as Charles could remember.

"I swear my nigga on some straight up *gay shit*," Mike added, with more laughter.

Charles' nostrils flared.

And that was it.

AARON MCGRUDER, CREATOR of *The Boondocks*, describes *a nigga moment* as "a moment when ignorance overwhelms the mind of an otherwise logical Negro male, causing him to act in an illogical, self-destructive manner."

Nigga moments are often triggered by small infractions. If anyone cared to do the research, they would find that *nigga moments* are the cause of nearly every young black corpse to visit a morgue.

Charles didn't have any serious beef with Mike. It was most likely the atmosphere that contributed to their nigga moment. This was one of the reasons Charles avoided his old neighborhood. Because when you're surrounded by hoodlums, you find yourself thinking and behaving like one, even if you don't want to.

Charles had a lot of self control, for the most part, but as he looked around and saw the laughing faces, BRAVADO was the only thing on his mind. He didn't really care about these people, but he refused to let them look down on him. He warned MikeyMike about questioning his sexuality, but Mike wasn't getting the picture. And that he would belittle Charles in front of all of the homeys, Blacc in particular, was way more disrespect than Charles could tolerate.

He turned on his old friend, his fists already raised. "Nigga, I told you about coming at me with that gay shit."

Mike recognized his folly right away. He threw his hands up in a defensive gesture and began to backpedal. "Say, hold up, Chuck. I–"

Charles cut him off with a smooth two-piece; a left hook and a right uppercut. They both landed flush.

BOP! POP!

Mike hit the ground and rolled, his head spinning. Everything happened so fast, most of the homies were still laughing at Mike's joke. Now their mouths hung open, frozen with the same awkward smiles.

Charles was content with the slight whooping he administered, but Blacc never saw a fight he didn't want to be a part of – especially one involving his flesh and blood brother. Before anyone had fully digested what just happened, Blacc rushed the fallen Crip and commenced to kick and stomp the living shit out of him. Mike curled up and tried to protect his face and head, but Blacc sought out these areas specifically with his size ten Chuck Taylors.

"Ho ass HoovaLand nigga!" Blacc berated him as he stomped.

KICK!KICK!KICK!

"This Davis Street, cuz!"

STOMP!STOMP!

"Yup yup! Yup yup, yup yup!"

Charles rushed to stop him. He wrapped his brother up in a bear hug and pulled him off his prey. But the damage was done. Mike struggled to get to his feet. He was only on the ground for fifteen seconds, but he was already completely dusty. His lip was busted, and one of his eyes was starting to swell closed. His braids hung in every direction.

"Fuck y'all niggas!" Mike spat blood as he spoke. He stumbled, looking around anxiously. No one came to his defense. "Man, fuck y'all ho ass niggas!"

"Let me get him!" Blacc growled. He was smiling, but it was a twisted smile. Maniacal. He was strong, but Charles was stronger. He wouldn't let him go.

"Forget that nigga," Charles said. "Get in the car, cuz."

"Get off my block!" Blacc yelled at Mike. He shifted his weight suddenly and broke free of Charles' grip – something he no doubt learned and prison – but he didn't try to attack Mike again. He just yelled at him, stripping away any respect Mike might have retained after the beat down: *"Get yo ass off my block, nigga! You ain't welcome here no more! This Davis Street, nigga! You ain't one of us!"*

"Get in the car!" Charles urged. He had his passenger door open now. He pushed Blacc in that direction.

Blacc pushed him back. "Nigga, why?"

"We need to talk," Charles said. His filled Blacc's vision with his own stern disposition. "I need to holler at you."

Blacc allowed his little brother to put him in the car, but he poked his head back up for one last threat while Charles made his way to the driver's side.

"You bet not be here when we get back, bitch nigga!"

Mike didn't respond. He spat blood and turned away from them angrily. He shuffled down the street slowly, his fists balled, his teeth clenched.

Charles hopped behind the wheel of his Bonneville and took off at a normal speed. He shook his head but didn't say anything to his brother until they travelled nearly half a mile.

CHAPTER
45

"MAN, WHAT YOU do that for?" Charles looked meaner than a corned puma, but Fred laughed.

"What you talking 'bout?"

"Fred, you *know* what the fuck I'm talking about!"

His brother laughed harder. He rubbed his hands together. "What you mad at me for, nigga? You the one dropped him."

"Yeah, but you didn't have to stomp him! You shouldn't have done that man like that."

"Fuck him," Fred said, frowning now. "You know I don't cut for them HoovaLand ass niggas no way."

"And that," Charles said, his eyes widening. "Why you talking all that Davis Street shit? Now it's gon' look like Davis Street got beef with HoovaLand."

"So?" Fred said. "We do got beef."

"*No we don't!*" Charles couldn't have been more frustrated. "It was just *me* against *him*. It didn't have nothing to do with no gangs. You shouldn't have got involved."

Fred frowned. "Chuck, you know I wasn't gon' sit there and watch you fight somebody. If you fight, I fight. If I fight, you fight. It's always been like that."

Charles sighed. He blew hot air from his nostrils. "But you shouldn't have said all that shit about HoovaLand," he insisted. "All that gang shit done died down, Fred. Things is different now."

"I heard that when I was locked up," Fred said. "But that don't mean I got to roll with it. What if I liked things better the way they was?"

"Then you going right back to the pen," Charles said bluntly. "You been out one day, and you already got an assault hanging over your head."

"That nigga ain't gon' call the law," Fred guessed.

"He prolly ain't," Charles agreed, "but it's about your *mentality*." He tapped his temple. "You still don't give a fuck, Fred. You got a chance to be free again, to do something positive. But you wanna get right back in the same shit that got you locked up."

Fred shook his head. He looked away from his little brother, out of the passenger window. "Yeah. I heard you was on some *different* shit. You taking off your clothes, tricking in that club..."

Charles eyeballed him. "I see you want me to check that chin."

"I wish you would, freak nigga."

Charles grinned. "You know I can whoop you, Fred."

Fred smiled too. "You a big motherfucker, but I can chop you down, limb by limb."

They both laughed.

"Naw, but on the real," Fred said. "Why you stripping, man? I thought you was just doing that to save up some money for the dope game."

Charles shook his head. "Naw. I'm doing it so I don't have to get in the dope game. I wrote you before I got out. I told you I would do anything I could to keep my black ass out the pen."

"I guess you really meant that shit," Fred noticed.

Charles nodded. "Yeah, but it ain't gon' be forever, man. My woman don't want me stripping, and I don't wanna do that shit either. As soon as I find another job that's paying pretty good, I'm through."

"Where you staying?" Fred asked.

"Windham Pointe," Charles said. "My shit looks nice. I'll take you by there."

"What about Davis Street?"

Charles shook his head. "That's dead, to me at least."

"You ain't gon' come by, support the homies?" Fred asked.

"Can't do it," Charles said. "I was hoping you wouldn't either."

"What I'm gon' do?" Fred asked. "Get a stripping job like you?"

"I can help you find some work."

"Nigga, you can't even find work for yourself," Fred said and laughed. "Nah, man. I gotta get back in pharmaceuticals. I'ma do it right this time though. I ain't never gon' touch the shit, just the money."

"You know how many niggas done said the same thing?" Charles asked. "I met a bunch of 'em, all in the penitentiary."

Fred thought about it and shrugged. "Maybe so, Chuck. But I gotta do what I gotta do, just like you gotta do what's right for you. I may not agree with what you got going on just like you probably don't agree with me. But we still got each other's back, right?"

"For sure," Charles said. "Long as you don't ask me to touch no dope or shoot nobody..."

"I can respect that," Fred said. He reached and Charles gave him some dap.

"So, you wanna see my apartment?" Charles asked.

"Yup yup. I wanna see some ho's too, Chuck. I know you got some honeys you can hook me up with."

Charles thought for a second. "My baby mama got a friend named Toya. She always good to go."

"She fine?"

"Thick red bone. Booty like two basketballs."

"You know what I like," Fred said, sucking his teeth. "Fuck yo apartment, nigga. Take me by Toya's house *first*!"

CHAPTER 46

WITH HIS BROTHER back on the scene, Charles noticed a steep decline in his free time. Fred was constantly calling with requests to "Bring me something to eat, nigga," or "Take me to Davis," or "Let me hold a couple of dollars," or "Can you drop me off at this broad's house? I'ma need you to pick me up too."

This was a daily occurrence. In fact, Fred often needed his little brother's services several times a day. Charles always complied dutifully, even though Fred was more needy than Shay and CJ combined.

The only real negative thing about spending so much time with Fred was the unsavory places Charles found himself visiting. One of Fred's new girlfriends lived in the roughest housing projects in the city. Charles went to pick his brother up one night, and less than five minutes after parking his car, Charles found himself implicated in a recent burglary. Three angry men surrounded his Bonneville with malice in their eyes.

"Where you from?" the one closest to the driver's side asked. He was as dark as night and twice as spooky.

"What you mean where I'm from?" Charles said. He looked right and left and saw that the trio had spread strategically around his vehicle, one in the back, one on the passenger side, and their leader stood boldly next to the driver. "What you got these niggas around my car for?" Charles spat.

"Polo just ran up in my house," their spokesman said. "You brought him over here?"

"Hell naw," Charles said, still looking around uneasily. "I don't even know no *Polo*. Y'all need to get the fuck away from my car." Charles didn't have a weapon on him, but he refused to let the strangers intimidate him.

"Nigga, you *was* with him," their leader declared, and it occurred to Charles that he might actually *die* over this misunderstanding.

The man he was talking to didn't appear to be armed, but the thug on the passenger side kept both of his hands concealed, same as the guy in the back. At the very least Charles figured he'd have to fight his way out of this. Unfortunately they had him outnumbered three to one, and they also had home field advantage.

But before anyone made a move, Charles heard his brother say, "What the hell y'all doing to my little brother?"

Everyone turned and saw the Davis Street leader marching towards them. Fred had only been out of jail a few days, but he was already well known in various parts of the city.

"Aww, my bad, Blacc," the one talking to Charles said. "I didn't know this was yo brother. Polo just ran up in my spot. Somebody said they saw him get out this car."

Blacc approached the group with his features frozen in a sneer. "Chuck ain't got shit to do what that, cuz. I know y'all ain't trying to check my little brother." He looked around, daring anyone to say that was the case.

"Naw," the other man said. "Ain't nothing like that, Blacc. I was just asking where he was from. Didn't nobody know him. My bad, homey," he said to Charles. "We got much love for Blacc. We ain't mean no harm."

With that, the situation diffused without violence. The three men continued their search for the dastardly Polo, and Blacc hopped in the car with Charles.

"It's just that easy," Charles said as he started up his Bonneville.

"What you talking about?" Fred said.

"How easy it is to get in some shit, when you hang around places like this," Charles explained. "You can go from having a regular day to getting jumped or shot just like *that*." He snapped his fingers.

"Didn't nothing happen," Blacc said. "That shit's over."

"It don't even matter to you, does it?" Charles wondered.

"I can't worry about every little thing," Blacc confirmed. "Gotta keep it moving."

"You know, some people don't think like that," Charles said, trying to educate him. "Some people would look at this mess from all angles. They would probably decide that shit like this wouldn't happen to them, if they stayed they ass out the projects."

"I can't worry about every little thing," Blacc repeated. "Gotta keep it moving."

NICOLE DIDN'T KNOW about any dangerous situations Charles might be involved in, but she still disliked his brother Fred, for selfish reasons. She hadn't seen Charles *once* in the past five days, since his brother got home. Every time she called him, Charles told her he was taking Fred somewhere. Sometimes Charles said he was kicking it with his brother "on the block."

Nicole started to comment that Charles never spent time on any "block" before his brother got out, and from what she knew about the hood, hanging out on some street corner was not the safest thing to do. But she didn't complain. She didn't want to be considered a nag – especially where Charles' big brother was concerned.

Nicole knew Charles would never choose her over Fred, and she didn't want Fred to think she was trying to pull Charles away. Even though she didn't like him, she wanted Fred to like her. Charles' mother was deceased, and his father split when he was a toddler. As far as Nicole knew, Fred was the most important person in Charles' life.

So she played it cool, except when she was around her friends.

On Saturday March 23rd, Nicole invited Angie over for dinner. Afterwards they tried to watch a bootleg movie Angie brought with her, but Nicole spent so much time bitching about Charles, Angie eventually ejected the DVD and returned it to her purse.

"What you doing?" Nicole asked her.

"Taking it home," Angie said. "I guess you ain't noticed that I rewinded the first scene three times already."

"I was watching it," Nicole said. She sat on the sofa with her bare feet tucked under her.

Angie lounged on the couch with a nail file in hand. She cleaned her cuticles while she listened to Nicole's sob story about her neglectful stripper friend.

"You can't even tell me who's in this movie," Angie said. She chuckled. "It's alright girl. We don't have to watch it. Gone and tell me about Charles."

"I'm sorry," Nicole said. "It's only been five days. I should give it more time. I knew it was gon' be like this when Fred got out."

"Yeah, but you might be right about him getting in some stuff," Angie said. "It don't take much. One minute you hanging out on the corner. The next minute you got a dope sack in your pocket. It's easy to get caught up."

"I know, right," Nicole said, her eyes widening. "That's what I be thinking. You think he selling drugs again?"

Angie frowned. "How should I know?"

"He told me his brother was getting back in the game," Nicole said. "If Charles is standing there while Fred's selling, they'll probably think Charles is selling too, right?"

Angie shrugged. "Maybe."

"Or what if Charles takes Fred to get some drugs, and they get pulled over? If Fred say the dope ain't his, they'll arrest Charles 'cause it's his car, won't they?"

Angie shook her head. "Girl, I don't know."

"I be thinking about him getting shot too," Nicole confided. "It ain't as bad as it used to be over there, but it's still pretty rough. You think he don't care, about what happens to him?"

Angie sighed. "Girl, I think you need to call your man and ask *him* these questions. I can't speak for him. I don't know what he thinking."

"Naw, I was just saying."

"I hear what you saying perfectly clear," Angie said. "And what *I'm* saying is you need to call your man. Ain't no sense in worrying yourself about all this if you ain't gon' talk to him."

"What should I tell him?" Nicole wondered.

Angie grinned. "Tell him you love him and you worried about him."

"What if he think I'm sweating him?"

"Have you already told him any of this?"

Nicole shook her head.

"Then you ain't sweating him," Angie said. "Girl, I can't believe you acting so scary. This nigga got you wide open for sure!"

Nicole didn't think her love for Charles was turning her into a wuss, so she found her cellphone and called him while Angie watched. Charles answered after a couple of rings.

"Hello?"

"Hey, baby," Nicole said, trying to sound as sweet as possible. "What you doing? You with your brother?"

"Uh, naw. I'm with Shay," Charles said. "We watching a movie."

Nicole checked the clock mounted above her couch. It was almost ten o'clock. She frowned. It was the weekend, but Nicole was surprised that Charles' baby-mama let him stay that late.

"You not working tonight?" she asked.

"I don't know," Charles said. "I'm kinda tired. I really don't want to."

Nicole sat up, her eyes narrowed. Charles rarely missed work. He would even go in after making love to her.

"You sick?"

"Naw. I'm alright. Just got sleepy, watching this movie. Let me give you a call back."

Nicole was worried about him getting shot on some street corner. Now she wondered about the cozy conditions at his baby-mama's house. Her sixth sense told her something was not quite right.

"Are you in your daughter's room?"

"What?"

"Where are you watching the movie," Nicole asked. "Are you in your daughter's room?"

Pause.

"No. We in the living room."

Nicole's breath was hot, but her chest felt cold. Her fingertips did too. "Is it just y'all two?"

"Huh?"

Nicole swallowed hard. She felt every one of her heartbeats. They were so powerful, she was sure Angie could feel them too. "Where's Pam?" she managed.

"Right here," Charles said. "We all in here together."

Nicole's heart stopped beating altogether then. The room went blurry as she realized her fears about Charles might have been misplaced. Instead of fretting about Fred, she should've been worried about the bigger threat at his baby-mama's house. She never batted an eye when Charles said he was going to visit Shay. But if he was still in a relationship with Pam this whole time, then Nicole couldn't have been a bigger fool.

"Where is she sitting?" she asked.

"Who?"

"Pam."

"Huh?"

Nicole put a hand to her mouth. She stared at Angie who also wore a look of concern.

"Where is Pam sitting?" Nicole spoke slowly, hoping her voice wouldn't rattle, but it did anyway.

"She, um... She right here," Charles said.

Nicole shook her head. "That don't even sound right."

"I'll call you back."

"No. You need to tell me what's going on over there."

"Nothing. Just watching a movie."

"Y'all all huddled on the couch together?" Nicole asked. "Like a big, happy family?" She imagined the scene as she spoke. Her fingers began to tremble. Her heart started to beat again, but it pumped two ounces of dread with every one ounce of blood.

Charles sighed. "I gotta call you back."

"Why?" she nearly shouted. "You can tell me *right now*! Why is she in there with y'all? Why you even over there? You got your own apartment!"

"I'll come by there when I leave," he said. He spoke calmly, but Nicole was a fool no longer.

"Why you ain't saying my name?" she asked.

Pause.

"What?"

Nicole squeezed her eyes closed. She quickly wiped away the tears that squirted from each of them. "Why you can't say my name?" she breathed. "You don't want Pam to know who you talking to?"

"You tripping," Charles said. "I gotta go."

"You bet not–"

But Charles did hang up. Nicole stared at her cellphone, not believing what just transpired. Angie was already on her feet. She rushed to her friend's side and tried to catch her before Nicole slipped into a pit of despair.

CHAPTER 47

CHARLES STOPPED BY unexpectedly at a quarter till midnight. Angie was gone and Nicole wasn't crying anymore. Why bother? Tears never solved anything. Either Charles was sleeping with Pam, or he wasn't. Nicole thought she already knew the answer to that, but she figured she'd let Charles tell her himself. She probably wouldn't believe anything he had to say on the subject, but they had been in a relationship for several months. Nicole figured the least she could do was hear him out.

For this reason she wasn't upset when she checked her peephole and saw a muscle-bound stripper standing there. Charles didn't call her back after he hung up on her. Nicole knew he wanted to tell his lies face to face.

She opened the door so he could look upon the raw sorrow in her eyes, the weariness and disappointment. Charles stared into her glistening orbs and then shook his head woefully. He knew he was the cause of her grief, and it was almost too much to bear. He reached for her, but Nicole backed away. Charles knew he wasn't welcome, so he didn't attempt to enter her home.

He sighed. He stuffed his hands in his pockets and looked down at his shoes. He finally said, "I'm sorry."

Nicole didn't know what exactly he was apologizing for. She was almost afraid to ask. She knew it was over between them, and she could accept that. But if he told her their relationship had been a game all along, she didn't think she would ever get over it.

She wiped her nose with the back of her hand. Her eyes were puffy and pinkish. Her lips quivered when she spoke, but they had to get this over with. She had to know the truth.

"You sleeping with her?"

"No." He shook his head fiercely. "No, Nicole. I swear to God, I haven't touched her in ten years."

She watched his eyes. She studied his gestures and his voice intonations, and she believed him. That was a big weight off her shoulders, but it wouldn't change anything. There was still *something* going on.

"Why'd you hang up on me?"

He shook his head. "I, I don't know."

"You didn't want her to know who I was?"

He met her eyes. He didn't want to tell her the truth, but he couldn't stand there and lie to her. He promised he wouldn't dog her. He didn't feel like he had, but the guilt of his transgressions was like a thousand pound weight on his shoulders. He had to come clean, or he could never stand tall again.

"Naw," he said. "I didn't want her to know."

Nicole sniffled and nodded. That admission hurt her more than he would ever know. But that was the part she knew already. She took a slow, deep breath in preparation for the secrets still to come.

"Y'all been talking?"

"No," he said. "When I go over there, I'm there for my daughter. I don't be talking to Pam like that."

"Does she like you?"

He took one second too long to respond to that. Nicole's nostril's flared while she waited. He knew she would see right through any half-truth he tried to feed her.

"I think she do. She been saying stuff, lately. Stuff that make me think she want to get back with me."

That was the first dagger. Nicole winced as it pierced her heart. Her eyes watered. She wiped the tears the moment they fell. Her legs were weak, but she didn't drop to her knees like she wanted to. It would all be over soon. Just a few more questions, and they could put an end to this charade.

"Do you want to get back with her?"

"No." He looked down at his sneakers again, and Nicole knew this was his first lie.

That was the second dagger.

The pain was so intense she wanted to cry out. But she had to remind herself that this was mental rather than physical pain. Charles could kill her emotionally, but tomorrow the sun would rise again, and she would as well.

"Are you in love with her?"

Charles was stunned by that question. He ran through a scenario of how their conversation would play out as he drove to Nicole's house, and *love* was one thing he hadn't accounted for. Yes he flirted with Pam from time to time. Yes he tried to get back with her when he got out of prison. Yes, he continued to flirt with her after he and Nicole became a couple.

But love... He never considered if that was the true force behind his decisions. He was attracted to Pam, true indeed. He longed for her at times. When she smiled, his heart did too. When she touched him, his whole body tingled. But was he in love with her? Had he ever been?

He shook his head slowly, and a look of confusion spread across his face.

"I don't know."

That was the third and final dagger.

Charles watched in horror as Nicole's expression shifted, morphed into something so awful it was like watching a child take its last breath. She put a hand over her face to hide the way agony stretched her mouth, making her ugly, yet tragically beautiful. Charles expected a mighty wail to force itself from her lungs, but she whimpered softly, just once, and then she reached to close the door.

He didn't stop her. He wanted to, but he was a coward. He couldn't bear to look upon the devastation he created. His heart thundered. His soul begged him to make it right, but he remained still because he didn't know what *right* was anymore.

Thirty seconds after Nicole closed the door, physically and spiritually shutting him out of her life, he was still standing there. He was afraid to knock, but also afraid not to. He wanted to tell her it wasn't true; that he didn't love Pam. But he was man enough to know that he couldn't do that – not until he knew for sure.

Against better judgment, he turned and headed for his vehicle.

HE SAW THE gray and black Buick parked on the corner, three houses down from Nicole's. If he hadn't been in the midst of his own soul searching, Charles would've noticed that there was a dark figure partially concealed in the dark confines of the Buick. He might have noticed that the Buick was positioned strategically to spy on Nicole's home, and the man inside the car was suspicious; sitting quietly, watching and waiting.

But Charles had his own troubles to worry about, so he passed right by Byron, never noticing him at all. Byron turned in his seat and watched Charles' car until it turned the corner and was completely out of sight. He didn't get a good look at Nicole's new friend, due to the darkness, but he saw enough to know that he was tall and muscular, and he would probably ruin everything if Byron tried anything while he was around. But Nicole's friend was gone now, maybe for good.

Byron knew he had to make a move soon.

He'd only get one shot, to make things right.

CHAPTER 48

CHARLES DIDN'T CALL on Saturday. Nicole wasn't surprised by that, but she checked her phone often, thinking she missed him.

On Sunday she took her family to church as usual. When it was time to pray at the altar, she thought about going down there. She could ask God to bring her man back to her, ask Him to touch Charles' heart so that he could know for sure that it was Nicole he loved and not Pam.

But when she thought about it, she decided that was a selfish prayer. She remained in her seat, but she did ask God to bless her family, Shawn in particular. He hadn't asked what was wrong with Mama yet, but Shawn knew that she was upset. He knew she hadn't spent a lot of time on the phone with Charles like she usually did. It was only a matter of time before he realized his new basketball buddy and budding mentor was gone.

Charles called Nicole on Sunday night, but she was watching a movie with the kids, and she didn't want them to see her arguing or crying. She checked her voicemail later, but she didn't call Charles back. According to his message, he didn't want her to:

"Nicole. Hey, this is Charles. I was calling to see how you was doing, how your day went. I wanted to tell you that I was sorry, for what happened. I didn't mean to hurt you. I don't wanna hurt nobody. You know how I feel about you. Ain't nothing changed. I wanna be with you, but I gotta deal with these feelings I got for Pam. I gotta be honest with both of y'all. Just give me a minute, to talk to her. I'll call you back."

That night Nicole found it hard to sleep, with those words swirling through her mind. She tried to cling to the positive things he said. *You know how I feel about you. Ain't nothing changed. I wanna be with you.* But she couldn't get over the fact that Charles had feelings for another woman, a woman who would always be in his life because of the child they shared.

The next morning she didn't feel like she slept at all. Mondays were always rough for her, but this was probably going to be the worst *ever*. She left the house with no makeup concealing the bags under her eyes. She didn't want to hear any *I told you so's*, but she decided to tell her friends what happened. Al Green didn't know how to mend a broken heart, but maybe one of the rat pack did.

THE GANG GATHERED outside during their first break. Twyla was the only one smoking, but Nicole was tempted to take a drag of her Black & Mild. She sat on a concrete bench with Stella and told the whole story, from her worries about Fred to the last message Charles left on her phone last night. Nicole didn't cry, but she was on the verge. It wouldn't take much to push her over the edge.

Blanca was the first to comment. "So, what does that mean? He still wants to be with you?"

Nicole shook her head. "I don't know what it means."

Stella cradled Nicole's hand in her lap.

Twyla stood with her arms folded, a thin cigar poking out of her mouth. "That's some bullshit," she said, a mean sneer distorting her soft features. "After all you done been through with him, he a straight up *buster* for that."

"Should I call him?" Nicole asked.

"Hell no," Twyla said. "If he knew he had feelings for his baby-mama, what he trying to get close to your kids for? That nigga know he wrong for that. You don't do that shit; fucking with kids' heads and stuff."

"He's trying to be honest," Blanca reasoned. "He didn't have to tell her anything. He could've slept with both of them while he was trying to figure it out."

"Who said he didn't?" Twyla said. "How you know he ain't sleeping with that other bitch?"

"He told me he didn't," Nicole said.

"And you believe him?" Twyla said.

"Yeah, I do," Nicole said. "I can tell when Charles is lying to me."

Twyla smacked her lips. "Girl, please. You can't tell when he in love with somebody else, but you can tell when he's lying? You been a fool too long, Nicole. It's time to face the facts: That nigga played you. And if you gon' sit around waiting while he *trying to make up his mind...*" She said it like it was the most ridiculous thing she ever heard. "...Then he *still* playing you. Trust me, girl, you need to move on with your life."

"Why you even listening to her?" Blanca asked. "She's the one who told you to go with Charles just for the sex. She don't know nothing about real love."

Everyone was shocked by that, especially Twyla.

"Who you talking about?" Twyla said.

"I'm talking about *you*," Blanca said.

Nicole could see the fear in her eyes, but at least Blanca stood up for herself. The problems with Charles took a back seat while Nicole and Stella watched to see how this would play out.

"I know you ain't talking to me," Twyla said, rolling her eyes.

"Yeah, I am," Blanca said. She was growing red in the face, but she looked Twyla in the eyes. She even took a step towards her – not too close, but close enough to show that she wasn't backing down this time.

But that was still much too close for Twyla. "You better get out my face."

"Or what?" Blanca said. Nicole's eyes widened as their supervisor took *another* step into the danger zone. "What are you gonna do, hit me? I wish you would. I'll have you out of here before that stinky ass cigar hits the ground."

Nicole was stunned silent. Twyla was equally mortified. A slight smile cracked Stella's lips.

"This bitch done bumped her head," Twyla said.

"No. I'm just sick of you trying to bully everybody," Blanca replied. "You barely do any work, and you talk noise all the time. You shoulda got fired a long time ago!"

Twyla's jaw dropped. Nicole's did too.

"Do I be bullying people?" Twyla asked her other two friends.

Nicole cleared her throat. "Um, yeah. You do kinda be–"

"Hell yeah you a bully," Stella said, as indignant as she wanted to be. "Especially with Blanca. I woulda fired you three years ago, if I was her."

Twyla was incredulous. She looked the three Judases in the eyes, one by one. No one took back the mean things they said. Twyla sighed. She looked at Blanca and said something no one at APEX believed was in her vocabulary:

"I'm sorry."

"I accept your apology," Blanca said right away.

An uncomfortable silence ensued. Nicole wanted to comment on what just happened, but she knew both Blanca and Twyla would prefer to drop it. So she turned towards Stella and said, "How come you haven't said nothing about Charles. I know you hated him anyway."

"I never hated him," Stella said. "I love you. So maybe it sounded like I hated him."

Nicole nodded. That was the same thing Charles told her.

"I didn't want you to go out with him," Stella said, "but you did, and it turned out to be a good thing. I didn't want you to sleep with him, but you did that too. I definitely didn't want you to bring him around your kids, but you gotta follow your heart. You did what was best for you, and it worked. I'm not gonna tell you *I told you so* just 'cause y'all having problems right now."

Stella didn't know it, but that was the nicest thing she ever did for her friend.

"As far as what I think about him," Stella continued, "I think Blanca's right about him trying to do the right thing. It's a lot of men out there who find theyself with feelings for two different women. Most of them don't say *nothing*. Why spoil it when you can keep sexing both of them? They'll wait 'til one of the girls finds out – or both of them, and they'll stay with whichever one don't leave them."

Twyla nodded, like that might have happened to her – or more likely she did that to someone before.

"I know it hurts," Stella told Nicole, "but you got to give him a minute to work it out. He obviously cares about you. I know I said he wasn't no good, but I'm not right all the time. If you feel like he's the one for you, then be patient. He prolly feels just as bad as you."

Nicole nodded. She knew her friends loved her, and they were giving the best advice they could, not letting their personal hang-ups get in the way.

"I don't know how long I can be patient," Nicole said.

"You don't have to wait on him," Stella said. "It's your choice."

Nicole nodded again. She checked her watch. "It's time to go back."

Her friends reluctantly agreed.

"So, whatchoo gon' do?" Blanca asked as they headed back inside.

"If I don't hear from him today or tomorrow, I gotta go on with my life," Nicole said. She knew it wouldn't be easy, but she couldn't float around in limbo while Charles tried to solve his dilemma. It hurt too much. "I gotta move on," she said again, and all of her friends knew she meant it.

CHAPTER 49

CHARLES WANTED TO get some closure, too. He hoped to deal with his issues over the weekend, but Pam was unavailable. She went to Houston for a great uncle's funeral and didn't come home until Sunday night. Charles called her Monday afternoon, but she was at work. He left a message on her voicemail:

"Hey, this is Charles. Is it alright if I come see you today? I don't wanna see Shay, just you. I mean, I do wanna see Shay, but..." He sighed. "You know what I'm trying to say."

Pam called him back at two-thirty.

"Hey."

"Hello, Charles?"

"Yeah. This me."

"I got your message," Pam said. "I'm still at work right now. I don't get off until three-thirty."

"Can I come see you?" he asked. "I didn't know if you understood what I said on the message. I ain't saying I *don't* wanna see Shay – just not today..."

"I understand," Pam said. "You can come by at five. I'll take Shay to my mama's house for a little bit."

"Alright. Thanks," Charles said.

"Okay. Bye."

FOUR HOURS LATER, Charles pulled into her driveway. He thought about their conversation during the drive across town. He told Pam he wanted to see her without Shay around, and she didn't question him at all. He didn't find that strange at the time, but now he thought it was very peculiar. It wasn't like Pam, to agree to something that wasn't explained thoroughly.

The mystery was solved a couple of seconds later when Pam answered her door wearing only a bath towel. Her hair was still wet, as was the rest of her body. Charles paused in the doorway, looking from her eyes to her cute little toes.

"I just got out the shower," she stated the obvious. "I didn't wanna be all stinky when you got here."

Charles swallowed hard. The towel was only long enough to *barely* cover her pubic hair. Her thighs were beautiful, glistening with droplets of water. Charles wasn't even a breast man, but the towel squeezed her chest, creating a good deal of cleavage.

"Wha, where yo boyfriend?" he managed.

"Me and Kevin broke up," Pam said. "You coming in or not?"

Charles nodded absently. A whole police squad couldn't stop him from entering her house. He crossed the threshold into what might be a totally new life for him. Pam closed and locked the door behind him.

SHE WENT TO the bedroom to "put some clothes on." But she came back nearly as naked. She wore a tee shirt that was only about an inch longer than the towel. The tee shirt had a V-neck, so Charles had a good view of her smooth, silky chest. Her breasts no longer had the cleavage she had with the towel wrapped around them, but they were still very nice.

Her thighs were even better. This was the first time Charles got a good look at her legs since he got out of prison.

His eyes swam over her body. He thought her tee shirt was the worst tease imaginable. It was long enough to conceal her back and her front, everything Charles wanted to see the most. But when she moved, the fabric did too, giving hope that maybe he could get a peek at her goodies if he watched long and hard enough.

He blinked hard, trying to snap out of it. He wasn't a horn-dog, and it was obvious Pam was open for whatever he had in mind. If he wanted to see her body badly enough, all he had to do was grab hold of the shirt and lift it up. She'd probably let him take it off completely, if he wanted.

But still. Pam sat next to him on the couch, and she crossed her legs, and it drove Charles crazy; imagining what she was hiding between those thighs. Did she have panties on? He sat back and looked her in the eyes, trying to get his mind out of the gutter.

"So, what happened to Kevin?" he asked her.

"I told you we been having problems," she said. Her hair was curly when it got wet. She had it pulled back, secured with a pink scrunchie. Her face was completely clean, no makeup at all, and she was still exceptionally attractive.

"When y'all break up?" Charles asked.

"I don't know." Pam shrugged. "You want the actual date or the day he stopped touching me?"

"Why he stop touching you?" Charles heard some strange things in his time, but a straight man who didn't want to make love to a woman as fine as Pam... That was unnatural.

"I told you why," she said. "He couldn't get used to you being in the picture. He started acting like a punk. I'm not gonna sit there and argue all night long. I don't wanna be with nobody like that. I need a real man."

She looked at him like he was just what the doctor ordered, but Charles didn't know if he was ready to take this plunge.

"The reason I wanted to come over here," he said, "is 'cause I got some things going on in my life right now that I'm trying to get straight. This is hard for me. I don't wanna hurt nobody. But

I got a woman, and I did hurt her, when I told her how I feel about you."

Pam nodded. She knew about his girlfriend already. Shay told her all about the family outing to the movies and Chuck E Cheese's. Shay said Charles looked happy with his new girlfriend, but Pam knew he wasn't.

Shay said his girlfriend had *three* kids; two of them were still toddlers. Pam knew Charles didn't want to raise three kids that weren't his – not if he didn't have to. With Pam, there was only Shay. If Charles got back with her, they could raise their daughter together, like they should've been doing all along. Hell, Pam wouldn't even mind if Charles brought his son with him. From what she heard, the boy needed a stable mother-figure in his life.

"You haven't even told *me* how you feel," she said, trying to push him along. He was indecisive, but she knew what he needed. She always knew.

"I don't know," he said. "Every since I got home, you know I wanted to get back with you."

She nodded. "Yeah..."

"But you was with somebody," he said. "You said I didn't have no chance, so I had to move on. I found somebody else. We been together since January."

Pam nodded some more. "Yeah..."

"But every time I come over here, I be feeling real conflicted," he said. "I got a woman, but it's just something about you, that I can't get over. I feel like my feelings for you are just as strong as my feelings for her."

"I got feelings for you, too," she said.

Charles had been playing dumb with her for so long, he didn't know any other way. "You do?"

"You know I do." She smiled. "I been practically throwing myself at you ever week."

"I didn't, I wasn't for sure," he said. "I didn't want to think nothing like that, if it wasn't really happening."

"It is happening," Pam said. She took his hand and brought it to her lap. "It can happen right now."

She guided his hand until it slipped under her tee shirt and came in contact with a small patch of pubic hair. She moved his hand lower, until his fingers brushed her labia. Charles felt lightening shoot through every one of his limbs. His penis began to respond immediately, but he jerked his hand away. He stared at Pam like he was afraid. Her tee shirt came up a little when he withdrew his hand, and she didn't reach to pull it back down.

Charles stared between her legs, his eyes wide, his mouth slightly ajar. Pam was shaved, but not completely bare. Her juice box was just as tempting as it used to be – even more so. Charles brought a hand to his mouth subconsciously and began to nibble the nail on his pointer finger. He didn't realize this was the same hand Pam pulled into her lap until he caught a whiff of her essence. The scent was tantalizing. Charles manhood nearly burst through his britches.

He frowned. He shook his head slowly. Pam knew she was losing him, so she leaned in quickly and kissed him. It was a slow, passionate kiss. But it takes two to tango, and Charles didn't kiss her back. In fact, he gently pushed her away.

He stood. His erection was massive. It made Pam's heart sigh, just to look at the bulge in his jeans.

But Charles said, "I gotta go."

Pam couldn't believe it. She was more than shocked.

Charles hesitated. He now had the answer he sought, but he didn't want to hurt Pam's feelings. He came to her because he was confused. His feelings for Pam had become an overwhelming desire. He thought he was in love with her. He thought his love for Pam was stronger than what he felt for Nicole.

He came to sort out his feelings, but Pam only wanted sex. She wanted him to think with his dick rather than with his brain – but that was exactly what got him in trouble in the first place. He wasn't in love with Pam. He wanted to have sex with her. And while that was enough to keep their relationship strong ten years ago, Charles knew he needed something with more substance now.

He was one hundred percent in love with Nicole – whether they had sex or not – and *that* was the difference. That's what made their relationship so awesome, and that was why he and Pam could never be.

"I got a woman," he said. "I wanna stay with her."

Pam shook her head. She jerked her tee shirt down angrily. "Then why you come over here, Charles?"

"I made a mistake," he said.

"Are you sure you're not making one *now*?"

He thought about that. There was a big possibility Nicole wouldn't take him back. If he stayed with Pam, he was guaranteed to have at least one of them.

"I made a lot of mistakes in my lifetime," he admitted. "But this ain't one of them. I love Nicole, and I wanna be with her."

With that he turned and exited the house, leaving Pam to deal with her moistness and his unbelievable rejection. She didn't think Charles did her wrong, but it would be a long time before she could give him and Nicole her blessings.

No. She didn't think she could ever do that.

PART SIX
BOILING POINT

CHAPTER 50

NICOLE GOT HOME from work with the usual hassles. The twins were happy and hyper, Shawn needed help with his homework, and Nicole simply wanted to relax. She wanted to take off her clothes and run a hot bath and marinate in the bubbles for at least an hour.

But that was crazy talk.

Instead she rolled up her sleeves and took half a pound of ground beef from the fridge. She pulled a box of Hamburger Helper from the cabinet and found her favorite pot under the stove. She got some water boiling and then went to help the twins change into something more comfortable. She did all of this before letting her hair down or even kicking off her pumps.

Charles called while Nicole was with the twins. She couldn't find her phone while it was ringing, but she found it in the living room a few minutes later. Her heart went into arrhythmia when she listened to the message he left her:

"Hey, Nicole. It's me, Chuck. Baby, I'm so sorry for what happened. I never meant to hurt you. I love you, Nicole. Call me back. I wanna come over there. I'm on my way. Call me."

Nicole's eyes were big and hopeful when the message ended. Charles was on his way over? What did that mean? Was his dilemma over? Did he decide who he wanted to be with?

Nicole knew she could get answers to all of these questions by simply calling him back, but she was almost too afraid to do so. She didn't know why she was so apprehensive, but she was.

She took a seat on the couch. Everything seemed to be moving very quickly. Her mouth was dry. Her fingers trembled. She took a deep breath and made the call. Her eyes darted fretfully while she waited for him to answer.

"Hello, Nicole?"

"Yeah. It's me."

"Baby, I'm so sorry." Charles voice was strong and powerful, yet he sounded as anxious and as worried as she was.

It sent chills through Nicole's entire body, to hear him like that. She couldn't speak.

"I wanna be with you," he said. "I wanna be with you, Nicole. I'm sorry I told you I was confused. I'm not confused. I love you. You're the only one I love. Do you forgive me, baby? Tell me you'll take me back."

Nicole panted as her body went from ice cold to El Paso warm in less than three seconds. Her eyes filled with tears. She put a hand over her mouth and sighed softly. She never experienced a myriad of emotions like this. Charles' declaration was exhilarating, but she couldn't respond.

He took her silence to mean she wouldn't take him back. "Please baby," he begged. "*Please Nicole. *I need you, baby. *I need you so bad.*"

Her tears flowed like water. Her heart thundered. She tried to tell him *Yes*, but her throat caught. She made a sound that wasn't a word at all.

"Can I come over?" he asked. "I'm on my way to see you. Can I come over?"

"Yes," she finally managed.

"Do you still love me, baby? Are you gonna take me back?"

"Yes," she said again. She felt like she was accepting his proposal for marriage. This was amazing. It was sublime. Surreal even.

"Alright, I'm on my way," Charles said. "I'll be there in ten minutes."

"Okay," Nicole said.

"I love you."

"I love you, too."

Nicole disconnected. She sat back in the sofa cushions, wondering if she might actually have a heart attack. After a few moments, her shock gave way to happiness, and a huge smile spread across her face.

He chose me!

She wiped the tears from her eyes and laughed out loud. Charles would probably never know how happy he just made her. Nicole couldn't remember the last time something made her feel this good.

Oh my God, I look a mess!

Nicole shot to her feet. She was cooking. She hadn't changed the kids into their play clothes yet, and Shawn was probably still procrastinating, unwilling to get started on his homework. Nicole had to deal with all of this, but first and foremost she had to fix her face. She started for her bedroom, but then she heard something that stopped her in her tracks.

It was a car door.

Nicole turned back and rushed to the front curtains. There was no way Charles was there already. She pulled the curtain back and peeked through her blinds, and what she saw pushed her to the verge of yet another heart attack – this one way more severe.

Byron stepped around his Buick and headed for the front door. He wore jeans with a wrinkled tee shirt. He looked a lot thinner than the last time Nicole saw him, maybe up to twenty pounds lighter. She saw that he was letting his hair grow out – but he wasn't combing it. She had never seen him so disheveled.

But his looks were not as important as what the hell he was doing there. *Shoulda called the police when he gave you those flowers!*

Stupid!

She kicked herself for being so kindhearted to her ex-boyfriend who had turned into quite the stalker. It was now clear: Byron did need to go to jail. But he wouldn't just go to jail if Charles caught him over there.

Oh hell...

Nicole's mind raced with the possibilities. In his current emotional state, Charles was likely to kill Byron – especially if Nicole was still arguing with him when Charles rounded the corner. Nicole's exhilaration over the reconciliation with her man was replaced with dread all over again. She was so stressed, her head was spinning as she opened the front door. She ran outside and cut Byron off in the middle of the front yard.

"What the hell is wrong with you?! What are you doing over here?"

"I just wanted to talk," he said. "Can't we talk?"

His eyes were nearly bloodshot. He spoke slowly, like he rehearsed his lines and didn't want to make a mistake. Or maybe there was some kind of misfire in his head that was causing a slight delay between his brain and his mouth.

Up close she saw that he was a lot skinnier than she first noticed. Not only were his cheeks sunken in, but nearly all of the fat lining his skull was missing. Byron usually kept his face clean-shaven, but now he had a struggling beard and goatee. His expression was deadpan. His eyes were ghoulish.

Fear was the last thing on Nicole's mind when she stepped outside, but now it was her only emotion. Her purse was in the living room, less than fifteen yards away. Her gun was inside her purse, tucked snugly inside a small holster.

Nicole looked in that direction and took a step back. Her front door was still wide open. If she ran, she could make it inside in two seconds. Byron could never catch her. But when she looked back at him, Byron had a gun of his own. It seemed to appear out of nowhere. One moment his hand was empty. The next second he had a huge gun. It was a .38, a long-nose revolver.

Nicole stared at it in disbelief. She met Byron's eyes again, and they were still chilling. His expression hadn't changed at all.

"Get in the car," he said, with the same slow, methodical speech. "We need to go somewhere, and talk."

Nicole was shaking her head. She took another step back. "Wha, what are you doing?"

"I just wanna talk," he said. "You won't never talk to me."

"I don't wanna talk to you." Her voice quavered. Everything was moving slowly now. She wondered how it had come to this. It was no doubt her fault, but *why* was it happening? And why *now*? She didn't deserve this. "Puh, put the gun away," she begged. "I didn't do nothing to you, Byron. Please, don't point that at me."

She was crying again. She took another step back. Byron didn't pursue her.

"Don't make me chase you," he said. Still very calm. He was evil and wickedly calm. "Do you want me to follow you in the house, or do you want to come with me?"

Nicole stopped in her tracks. Visions flashed before her eyes. Terrible visions. Bloody things. The twins. Shawn. Everything bloody. She fell apart. Agony took over her face and contracted it, pulling her lips down into a frown that was so exaggerated she looked like a sad clown's makeup.

"Please, Byron. Don't do this. Please stop."

"I won't hurt nobody, if you get in the car."

Nicole's body trembled. She knew he was lying. She remembered a self defense class she took when she was younger. The instructor told them to *Take a Stand!* in situations like this.

Whatever you do, don't get in their car, the instructor had said. *If he wants to rob you, he can do it right there. The only reason he wants you in the car is so he can take you somewhere isolated and do something much worst.*

If he tells you to come with him and he won't hurt you, he's lying through his teeth! If you go with him, he will try to rape you, and he might kill you. So you need to take a stand right there. He doesn't want to shoot you in a crowded parking lot. You need to scream as loud as you can. If he tries to drag you, go limp. If that doesn't work, fight with everything you have.

But whatever you do, do not get in his car.

Nicole remembered all of this as she nodded and headed for Byron's car. Everything she learned in that class was what it would take to save *her own* life. But the instructor never said what she should do if her children were in danger as well.

If Byron was going to kill her, which all signs indicated he would, Nicole didn't want to die in her front yard. The gunshot would no doubt send Shawn running to her defense. Nicole squeezed her eyes closed, not wanting to consider what Byron might do if Shawn came outside and saw his mother sprawled on the lawn.

Even if Byron ran away without hurting anyone else, Shawn would step off the porch and rush to Nicole's side. He'd be with her for countless agonizing minutes before someone arrived at the scene and took him away.

It was a morbid decision, but if she had to die, she didn't want her baby to see. This wasn't Shawn's fault, it was hers. She should've called the police when Byron violated the conditions of his restraining order the *first* time. But she didn't, and now it was too late.

"Please. Put the gun away. I'm getting in the car."

Byron lowered his weapon, and Nicole began to hyperventilate as she climbed into his Buick. Byron circled the vehicle, his eyes glued to her the whole time. He hopped behind the steering wheel and transferred the gun to his left hand. He kept it pointed at her, under his other arm, as he pulled away from the curb.

Nicole looked back at her house, and she thought she saw Shawn standing in the doorway. She wiped the tears from her eyes and looked again, but the Buick was moving fast, and her house was no longer in view.

CHARLES FELT GREAT when he pulled into Nicole's driveway five minutes later. He made the most bone-headed decision imaginable last Saturday. But somehow he was lucky enough to right his wrongs without losing the best woman he had ever known.

He wanted to wrap his arms around Nicole and never let her go. He jumped out of his car and hopped onto her porch like a man half his age. He had a big grin on his face, and it remained when Shawn answered a few moments later.

"Hey!" Charles said. "How you doing?"

The boy frowned. Charles knew he hurt Nicole last week, but he hoped Shawn didn't know about it. His smile slipped as he realized he may have to do a little more groveling.

"You alright?" he said.

Shawn nodded. "Mama not here."

Charles' unease intensified. "What you mean?"

"She left," Shawn said.

"When?"

"Five minutes ago."

"With who?"

Shawn didn't know if he should say.

Charles dug his cellphone from his pocket, but Shawn told him, "She don't got her phone."

"What?"

"She left it here," Shawn said.

Charles hoped this was some kind of joke. "She not in there, for real?"

The boy shook his head.

"She just up and left?"

"She left the stove on," Shawn said.

Charles felt a jolt in his chest. He knelt so he could look at the boy on his level.

"Look, Shawn, I don't know if your mama told you about the problems we had last week, but that's all over now. We not broke up. She still my girlfriend. I talked to her today, and she knows I was on my way over here.

"If she left without her cellphone, then it sounds like something might be wrong. I know she prolly don't want you to tell people her business, but this is different. This is an *emergency*. I need you to tell me what's going on."

Shawn was conflicted, but he understood the word *emergency* very well. Plus he'd been wondering the same thing. His mother would never leave without telling him where she was going. And she certainly wouldn't leave the stove on under any circumstance. He fidgeted, thinking maybe he should've called the police already.

"She went with Byron."

Charles' eyes widened. He felt sick to his stomach. "Byron? Ain't that her ex-boyfriend?"

Shawn nodded. "Uh huh."

Charles shook his head. What kind of game was this? Did Nicole run back to that chump already? Did she say Charles could come over and then leave with Byron just to hurt Charles' feelings?

No. That didn't make sense at all. Nicole wasn't vindictive like that. And Byron attacked her and her son. She would never go back to him. She was happy when Charles told her he was coming to see her. He could hear it in her voice.

"Ain't Byron the one that hurt her?"

Shawn nodded. Now he looked fretful, too.

"Did she tell you where she was going?"

Shawn shook his head. His eyes glistened with tears. "She didn't say nothing. She left the door open."

That was the last straw. Charles' heart began to knock in his chest. But he tried to remain calm, for Shawn's sake.

"You need to call 911," he told him. "Call the police and tell them everything that happened. Tell them your mama left with her old boyfriend that beat her up. Tell them she left the stove on and she didn't take her phone or tell you where she was going. Tell them she left the door wide open. Tell them just like that."

Shawn nodded. He was crying now. He felt like he failed his mother by not calling the police as soon as he saw her leaving. She told him to call 911 if he ever saw Byron again, but Shawn didn't.

Charles wanted to stay and comfort the boy, but he knew time was of the essence. If Byron took Nicole against her will, then she might be in grave danger. There was probably nothing Charles could do about it, but he had to try. He rose to his feet.

"What kind of car does Byron drive?"

"It's black and gray," Shawn said. "A Buick."

Charles stopped cold. He stared at Shawn so hard the boy went out of focus. Charles felt like he knew something important, but for the life of him he couldn't remember what it was. He racked his brain, and his subconscious gave it up: He saw that car. It was parked on Nicole's street Saturday night. There might have even been someone inside the car when Charles drove past it, but he couldn't say for sure.

Shawn saw the look of horror on Charles' face, and his little chest began to hitch.

"It's okay," Charles said. He knelt again hugged him tightly.

They never had this much contact before, but Shawn felt safe in Charles' huge arms.

"It's gon' be alright," he assured him. "And you doing just fine. You taking care of your brother and sister?"

Shawn nodded against the big man's shoulder.

"That's good," Charles said. "Now go in there and call the police, like I told you. I'm gonna go look for your mama right now."

He let him go, and Shawn looked a little braver than he did a second ago.

"I'll be back," Charles said. He jumped off the porch and raced to his car. Shawn said something, and Charles turned back to him. "What?"

"Sycamore Park," Shawn said again.

"What's that?"

"Byron used to take us over there," Shawn said. "He said it was our special place, 'cause don't nobody else be going over there..."

Charles didn't know what he was talking about. Sycamore Park was a dump. It used to be a beautiful place, back in the early eighties, but crack and gang violence changed all of that. In the mid nineties, the police were bagging two to three bodies in that hellhole every weekend. The city never shut the park down officially, but they did stop the Parks and Recreations crew from cleaning it up each week. It simply wasn't safe, for anybody.

Charles frowned, but then it struck him, why Shawn brought it up.

"You think that's where he took your mama?"

The boy nodded. "Byron said it was our special place."

Charles' jaw dropped. He put a hand over his face to hide it. He knew Nicole was in trouble, but this was much worse than he imagined. Again he tried not to let on how worried he was.

"Alright. You did good," he told Shawn. "It's good that you remembered that. Make sure you tell the police when they get here."

Shawn nodded and then disappeared inside the house.

Charles got in his car and struggled to get his key in the ignition; his hands were shaking so badly.

CHAPTER
51

IT TOOK CHARLES fifteen minutes to reach Sycamore Park. The drive was mind numbing. Charles sped. He honked his horn and banged the steering wheel whenever he got stuck behind a slow driver. As he got closer, he kept straining his ears, expecting to hear sirens soon. But he never did.

He knew Shawn called 911, but Charles didn't know how the investigative process would go. Would they send a few units to the park right away, or would they go to Nicole's house and question Shawn first? Either way, Charles figured he had a ten minute head start on them. But Byron had a head start as well. If he didn't take Nicole to the park, then Charles had no idea where they could be. Nicole didn't tell him too much about her crazy ex.

Sycamore Park was a large slice of land that stretched from Beach Street all the way down to Rosedale Avenue. The main attraction was a huge waterway that flowed through the landscape and met with the Trinity River on the north side of town.

Charles hadn't been to the park in at least ten years, but when he was a child his mother used to take him and Fred to the community center for daycare. Those were fond memories, but that was some time ago. Since then the park became a refuge for gangbangers, dopefiends and prostitutes. There were long, winding trails scattered throughout. In many places the sycamore trees were so tall, they created a canopy, blocking nearly all of the sunlight from reaching the ground.

Charles entered the park on the east side. It was five-thirty pm. The sun was barely starting to set, but a gloomy chill enveloped Charles as he turned off the main thoroughfare.

He could understand why people still brought their families here. During the daytime it was a regular park. It was a little overgrown, and there was a lot of debris clogging up the creek, but the picnic tables were still standing. The barbecue pits were bolted to the ground, so no one stole those either. There were a few areas that looked downright wholesome, so it made sense that Byron might think this was a nice place for a family outing.

But even in the daytime the danger signs were obvious. Gang graffiti marred every restroom and gazebo. The trashcans were missing or overflowing, and there were broken beer bottles everywhere. The creek itself had the foulest waters imaginable. The stench quickly filled Charles' car, even though he had the windows rolled up.

Not knowing which way Byron would've gone, Charles drove aimlessly, no more than ten miles per hour. There were already a few dopefiends on the prowl. They stalked the land like zombies, totally oblivious to the filth and the cockleburs collecting on their shoes and pants legs. Charles saw a handful of Johns too. They were parked conspicuously along the dirt roads, looking around anxiously while their date's head bobbed up and down in their lap.

Each minute that passed was like slow torture to Charles. He sat up in his seat with both hands on the steering wheel. His face was covered with sweat, his eyes wide and desperate. He rolled down his windows so he could listen as well as look, but there were no screams coming from any of the shady biking trails. All he heard was broken glass crunching under his tires, ghetto birds seeking a mate in the tall trees above.

After twenty minutes in the park, he was at his wits' end. Tears mingled with the sweat dripping off his chin. His heart was stressed. He felt like he had to vomit or die, he wasn't sure which. The thought of Nicole being with her abductor for so long was sickening. Charles didn't want to think about all of the horrible possibilities, but it was hard not to. Terrible images kept appearing in his mind.

If Shawn was wrong about the park, then where could they be? Or maybe the dirty deed had already been done. Maybe Charles drove by Nicole's body twice already, but he couldn't see her because of the overgrowth.

"*No...*" Charles shook his head, whimpering like a child. He wiped his face with a trembling hand and dug his cellphone from his pocket. There were no missed calls. Charles started to call Nicole's phone to see if she'd miraculously made it home somehow, but he saw something out of the corner of his eye that made him drop the phone and crane his neck all the way to the right.

He inhaled sharply and held the breath, still looking in that direction. His car kept rolling at the same slow pace. He soon passed the intersection. He looked straight again and got his breathing under control as he pulled over and parked. He stared into the rearview mirror, his eyes wet and wild, and then he wiped his face with the bottom of his tee shirt.

Charles didn't have a weapon on him. He hoped he wouldn't need one. He exited his vehicle quietly, looking right and then left. The street he was on was desolate. Ten feet behind him was a T-bone intersection. He headed that way, clinging to the shadows like a burglar. When he reached the intersection, he inched towards the corner and peered down the road he just passed.

The side street had a dense line of trees growing on either side. The trees were tall, and some of the branches stretched across the road, ushering an unnatural dusk that was perfect for prom night smooching or prostitution or something more sinister.

The side street was a dead end, and there was only one car parked on that shady stretch of road.

It was a black and gray Buick LeSabre.

NICOLE WONDERED WHO would raise her kids. Thoughts of rescue had long since been abandoned, ever since Byron brought her to the park. On the streets, she might have had a chance. She thought about leaping from the car several times. But Byron locked all of the doors. He swore he'd kill Nicole if her hands moved out of her lap.

She knew she was going to die anyway, so it shouldn't have mattered. But all of God's creatures value life more than anything else. Nicole kept telling herself that if she waited, there might be time to escape later. Except that time never came.

When Byron first entered the park, Nicole didn't know what to think. It was clear he was crazy. She hoped he was so delusional, he'd planned one last picnic. She thought she could surely make a run for it if he tried to set up for their last meal together. But Byron drove past all of his favorite picnic spots.

The deeper into the maze of degradation they went, the more assured Nicole was that her fate was sealed. If she made a run for it now, there was nowhere to go. There was no one there to help her. Byron would chase her down easily, and no one would hear her screams.

So she sat there, and she cried and she waited. She thought about her children while Byron ranted, mostly to himself. She thought Shawn might have called the police by now, but there were no sirens. It was just as well. Byron was parked at a dead-end, and he was constantly watching the only entrance.

He told Nicole he'd kill her and then himself if a car pulled up behind them. And she knew he'd do it. What did he have to lose? Kidnapping was nearly as bad as murder, as far as the courts were concerned.

Nicole had been crying so much, her whole face was red and raw. She sat quietly, with her hands still in her lap because that's where Byron told her to keep them. She trembled uncontrollably. Byron said something to her, but Nicole was thinking about the twins. She didn't respond at all. He said something else, and then he nudged her. She looked over at him drunkenly. Her eyes went first to the gun in his lap, still pointed squarely at her midsection, and then to his ugly face.

It was hard to believe she ever enjoyed kissing him. That didn't even seem like something that had happened in this lifetime.

"You hear that?" he asked.

Nicole shook her head. "No. I didn't hear nothing." She didn't hear anything the last twenty times he asked either. They'd been parked at this dead end for at least fifteen minutes while Byron decided what he wanted to do with her.

He looked around and checked his mirrors again. "I thought I heard something."

"You paranoid," she told him. "You paranoid 'cause you know you ain't doing right, Byron. You *know* this ain't right."

"Shht!" He held a finger up and stared straight ahead, listening intently. After a few seconds he sighed and nodded. "They coming for you. They not here yet. But I can feel it. They coming. You..." He looked her in the eyes. "You shoulda called me, Nicole. It didn't have to be like this. I never wanted it to be like this."

"Then let me go," she said. She'd been asking for the same thing for so long, the words barely had meaning. She didn't even ask like she thought he might do it. It was an empty prayer, like a condemned man's last words.

"It's, it's too late for that now," he said. "It's too late. You know it's too late. They gon' try to burn me, Nicole. They wanna burn me. I can see it." He scratched his head absently. "I can see it. They wanna burn me. They wanna. They do."

"I won't tell," she promised. "Just let me go. I won't tell nobody."

"No. You're a liar. You're always a liar." He frowned. "Why you didn't call me? All you had to do was call me. This wouldn't have happened. It wouldn't have – not if you called me."

"*Byron please...*"

"I gave you the card. The flowers. I told you to call me. I nee–"

"*Stop, Byron.*"

"I need you, Nicole. I needed you, but you weren't there for me. You were nev–"

"*Just stop.*"

"Shut up."

"No, Byron. I wanna go home. Ple–"

"Shut up! You shut up!" He sniffled. "You're gonna hear me out this time. You're gonna hear me out. You're gonna listen."

Her mouth snapped shut. She lowered her head and rubbed her face.

"I love you," he said. "I always have, Nicole. You can't say I don't love you. You can never say that." He waited for her to interrupt him again, but she remained mute. "But you played with my heart," he said.

"I didn't," she moaned.

"Yes you did," he said. "Yes you did. I put my heart in your hands, and you stepped on it. You stepped on it. You stepped on it so bad."

"Byron, I didn't."

"Why didn't you call me?" His voice and face cracked at the same time. He began to cry again. "Why didn't you call me? All I wanted was for you to call me."

She could barely make out what he was saying. His voice was muddled with sorrow.

"I was scared," she said. "I was scared to call you."

"Why? Why was you scared?"

"Because you was acting weird, Byron. Just like now! I didn't even do nothing to you. I don't deserve this."

"No! *It's me!*" he bellowed. He beat his chest like a gorilla. "It's me, Nicole. *I'm* the one who don't deserve this! I never hurt nobody. They always beat me down, but I never hurt nobody. You sent me to jail. You said I beat you!"

"Byron, just put the gun down. It ain't worth it. You know it ain't."

"You just wanna leave me again," he said. "I know you now." He stared at her like he unraveled a great mystery. "I know you now, Nicole. I know how you are."

"Pete?"

They both jumped. Their eyes darted to the driver's side window, and Nicole nearly screamed when she saw Charles standing there. Byron nearly screamed too. He looked from Charles to Nicole and then back again. He lowered his gun down by his left leg. He wiped his face briskly with his free hand. He stared at Charles like he might be a ghost.

"Wha, wha, wha, what? Wha, what?"

"Oh, my bad," Charles said. He surveyed the scene in a split second. And though he was elated to see Nicole alive, his expression didn't change at all. "I thought you was my partner, Pete," he said. "He told me to meet him somewhere over here. My bad."

Charles turned, back towards the T-bone intersection. Walking away was the hardest thing in the world to do, but he put one foot in front of the other and forced himself to get moving. He forced himself not to run. Forced himself not to look back.

Nicole didn't say a word, but the look in her eyes told the whole story. Byron kept his left hand out of view, and that told a story too. Charles knew he was armed. He knew Byron would be more agitated now as well. Charles couldn't think of any way he could get in that car without Byron getting a shot off, but he knew he had to do exactly that.

He made a right at the T-bone intersection, towards his own car. He pulled his cellphone from his pocket as soon as he was out of sight.

CHAPTER 52

BACK IN THE Buick, Nicole's heart was starting to beat with the rhythm of hope once again, and Byron was going completely bat shit. He turned in his seat and watched Charles until he was no longer in view. And then he returned his attention to Nicole. He brought the gun up and pointed it directly at her chest.

"Who was that?!"

"I don't know!" she screamed.

"Yeah you do! That was your boyfriend."

"No! I don't know him!"

"That was your boyfriend!"

"I don't know him! I swear! Please get that gun–"

"Shut up, bitch! You're fucking lying! You fucking liar!"

"I don't know him! I swear!"

"I saw him at your house," Byron said. He turned again and stared in the direction Charles had gone. The intersection was now deserted.

Nicole stared down the barrel of the gun. She brought a hand up to try to snatch it away from him, but Byron turned back to her and pulled it out of reach. And then he shoved it in her face.

"You want it? You want it?"

"*Stop!*" She backed away from him, but there was nowhere to go. She cowered, bringing her arms and hands over her face. But they wouldn't stop a bullet, and she knew it.

"*That's your boyfriend!*"

"*It's not!*" Nicole screamed. "*I don't know him! That's not him.*"

"*I'll kill you! You lying to me! I'll kill you!*"

She put her arms down and mustered all the defiance she had. "*That wasn't him!*"

Byron stared at her for a long time. Both of their breathing was ragged and hot. Both front windows were down, but the car was still hot. Way too hot. Finally Byron lowered the gun and took a deep breath. He turned again and checked the street. It was still empty. When he looked at her again, Nicole knew that he believed her.

"It, it's still too late," he said. "It's too late, Nicole. We gotta go. It's time to go."

"Alright," she said, panting hoarsely. "Alright. Let's go."

Byron nodded as he brought the gun up to her face again.

"*Stop!*" She pushed his hand away.

"We gotta go," he said. "We gotta go. You said you wanted to go."

"*I don't wanna die!*" she cried.

"But, but, but that's the only way," he said. "That's it, Nicole. That's the only way. There ain't no other way for us. We don't have no choice. It's the only, it's the only way. We can be together. It's the only way. You first, and then me. I'm sorry. It has to be like this. There's, it has to be."

She sucked air like a fish out of water. Twenty minutes ago she was prepared to die. But then she saw Charles, and she believed again. She believed there was a chance. Charles wouldn't let Byron kill her. He loved her. He was her knight in shining armor. But he was gone now. And whatever he was doing wasn't going to work because Byron was on edge. He wouldn't be fooled again. He...

They both went quiet at the same time. Like kittens following a flashlight beam, Nicole and Byron's eyes moved simultaneously. They both looked at the roof of the car, and they both heard the same sound cutting through the eerie silence.

BUHDDA-BUHDDA-BUHDDA-BUHDDA-BUHDDA-BUHDDA-BUHDDA

"What's that?" Byron asked.

"Nothing," Nicole said.

"That's a helicopter," he said.

She shook her head. "No."

He pulled the hammer back on his pistol. "They found us." He coughed roughly. "It's time."

"*No. Please.*"

"I'm sorry," he said. His face fell apart, and he began to sob again. "I'm so sorry."

Nicole stared down the barrel of the gun, but there was another sound that made her look away. This time it was a thrashing of bushes, something big coming towards them. She looked over Byron's shoulder just in time to see a huge, dark figure burst through the tree line, right across from the driver's door.

It was Charles.

He was scratched and bloodied, but Nicole didn't really see any of that. All she saw was his eyes and his teeth. They were both menacing. Ready for war.

Byron followed her gaze, but with a rumbling growl, Charles collided with the Buick before Byron knew what was coming. Charles didn't just hit the car, he seemed to go *through it*. Both of his huge arms were inside the vehicle before Byron could pull the trigger. The grizzly bear arms wrapped around Byron's throat like an anaconda, and Nicole shrieked as Charles yanked her stalker out of the window, as easily as he would pick up a rag doll.

Byron shrieked too. He screamed and kicked like a girl. He tried to cling to his car, but resistance was futile. Charles slammed him hard on the pavement and commenced to beat the living shit out of him. He swung with reckless abandon, his heavy fists impacting flesh and bone each time. Some of his strikes were hooks, some were elbows, some were hammer fists, like Charles was trying to pound a steak into the ground with his bare hands.

Byron lost consciousness long before the police rushed the scene and pulled Charles off of him, no doubt saving Byron's life.

CHAPTER 53

CHARLES MADE THE evening news.

A Channel Six helicopter was hovering overhead during his dramatic rescue. The cameraman zoomed in on Byron's Buick a few seconds before Charles burst through the bushes like Rambo. His pants were soiled and his shirt ripped. His short trip through the overgrowth left him with a myriad of scratches on his arms and torso. His chest and shoulder muscles were massive. A Hollywood makeup artist couldn't have concocted a more handsome, rugged and raw hero.

The ten o'clock news ran the suspenseful footage. Millions of people watched as Charles slammed into the car like a linebacker. The whole city was glued to the TV screen as Charles yanked Byron out of the window with hardly any effort. The news even showed the massive beat down Charles administered, but they cut the scene short when the police arrived and ordered Charles to lock his hands behind his head and lay down on his belly.

The first officer put a knee on Charles' spine and leaned all of his weight into it while they sorted out the particulars. The news didn't show any of that because no one wanted to take away from the true beauty of the story. The bottom line was Charles Hester was a hero. He single-handedly prevented a murder-suicide. He took his princess in his arms, and they walked off into the sunset. And the curtains closed, and everyone was happy.

The end.

ANOTHER THING THE news didn't show was the mind-numbing hours Charles and Nicole spent at the park, in the back of two separate ambulances and later at the police station. They had to answer so many questions, Charles began to feel like they were trying to prosecute him for something.

Finally he found the lead detective and told her, "Me and Nicole need to go *home*. We tired, and she ain't seen her kids in four hours. I know y'all trying to get your paperwork done, but some of this gon' have to wait 'til tomorrow."

To Charles' surprise, the detective apologized for the hassle and cut them loose. Nicole and Charles exited the police station five minutes later. She shivered under a large blanket one of the officers gave her when they first arrived. Charles had tape and gauze and shiny ointments covering the cuts and scratches he obtained during the rescue.

There were a few reporters waiting in the parking lot. They were eager for a full interview or at least a quick sound bite to close up the story they were putting together. Charles wasn't much of a public speaker, and the only thing on his mind was getting Nicole home. But he did pause long enough to give his final thoughts:

"I don't think I did nothing special. I knew he took her to the park, and I went looking for them. I was lucky to find her. I did what anybody would've done, for somebody they love."

He walked away after that, and the cameras got a nice shot of Charles escorting Nicole to his Bonneville. The reporters thought that was awesome. Tall, dark, handsome *and* humble... Charles was what this city needed; an everyday Joe who managed to defy the odds and do something extraordinary.

It didn't get any better.

WHEN THEY GOT home, Nicole was happy to see Wally's truck in her driveway. Shawn called him when the police arrived to get more information about Nicole's abduction. Wally was ecstatic that his sister made it through her ordeal safely, and he didn't lecture Nicole about not following through with her restraining order when her ex repeatedly made contact with her.

Even though Byron was safely tucked away in a Tarrant County Jail cell, Wally wanted to spend the night. He knew Nicole would probably have trouble sleeping. But she told him Charles was going to stay, and Wally was glad to hear it. This was Wally's first time meeting Charles, but he knew Nicole couldn't have found a better protector.

"He went through a briar patch to save you," Wally joked. "I don't know if I coulda done all that." He checked out Charles' battle scars. "Are you okay?"

Charles looked at his arms and shrugged. "It's just scratches. They put all this tape on here, make it look worse than it really is."

"You don't have to downplay it for me," Wally told him. "I know what you did, and it's a big deal. Nikki, she's like the only family I got. I don't know what I would do if something was to happen to her." Wally started to tear up. He looked Charles in the eyes. "If you ever need *anything* – I don't care what it is – you can always ask me. What you did for my sister, I can't put into words, how much I thank you."

"It's all good," Charles said.

He and Wally clasped hands and then came together for a brotherly hug. Wally still had tears in his eyes when Nicole walked him outside.

He asked her, "Is that the one you were telling me about? The stripper?"

"Yeah," Nicole said. She grinned.

"I'm glad I never talked noise about him," Wally said. "That's a big dude."

"Aww. He's just a big ol' teddy bear," Nicole said.

Wally laughed. "Well, I know *that* ain't true. But, um, you did good, sis. I'm glad he was there for you. How's everything between you two? Still going strong?"

"Yeah," Nicole said. "I love him. I think he's the one."

"That's good," Wally said. "I wish y'all the best. For real."

He gave her a long, comforting hug, and Nicole went back inside, happy to finally be alone with Charles and her children.

CHAPTER 54

THEY WATCHED THE ten o'clock news together. This was Nicole's first time seeing the action from overhead, and it confirmed what she already knew: Charles was spectacular. When he approached Byron's car the first time, Nicole didn't know what his plan was. She knew he called the police, but she never thought he'd take matters into his own hands rather than wait for them to respond. She certainly didn't think Charles was trekking through the dense overgrowth, hoping to catch Byron off guard.

Most of the people in their lives knew about the incident already, but there were still quite a few folks who didn't find out until they saw it on TV. They all called, virtually at the same time, and Nicole and Charles had to tell their story over and over again.

Fred thought his little brother lost his mind:

"Nigga, I just seen you on the news! You jumping out the bushes like Tarzan, beating some nigga's ass! What the hell you doing at Sycamore Park?"

Charles told him what happened, and Fred said, "Man, you taking this *straight and narrow* shit a little too far, ain't you? I know you said you was gon' stay legal kend shit, but you didn't say you was gon' start *helping* the police!" He laughed. "You got these gals out here thinking that's the way it's supposed to be. This bitch

asked me if I would do that to save her life. I told her *hell naw*!
You better get you a can of mace or something!"

Blanca, Angie, Twyla and Stella were the most boisterous.
They wanted to know when Charles and Nicole got back together,
how Charles knew she was at the park and why Nicole got into
Byron's car in the first place. Nicole answered all of their
questions, though she wanted nothing more than to crawl into bed
and recuperate from this crazy day.

Before she got off the phone with Blanca, her friend told
her, "I knew Charles was a good man! I told you, didn't I? I told
you from the very start!"

"Yeah, you did," Nicole said. She smiled and then yawned.
"Girl, I gotta go to sleep. I was tired when I got home from work,
and I feel a hundred times worse now."

"Is Charles staying the night with you?" Blanca asked.

"Yeah." Nicole felt warm, just thinking about it. "He said
he would."

"Can I be the maid of honor, at your wedding?" Blanca
asked.

Nicole chuckled. "Girl, you getting a little carried away,
ain't you?"

"Whatever," Blanca said. "Just remember I asked you
first!"

"Alright," Nicole said. "I'll remember."

She disconnected, and she and Charles decided to turn
their phones off for the rest of the night.

NICOLE FINALLY GOT in the shower at 12:15. Charles got
in the tub after her. Nicole got her kids tucked in their beds while
her man bathed. The twins didn't know anything bad had
happened today, but they were still excited because of the visits
from Uncle Wally and Charles and all of the late night phone calls.

Shawn was excited too, but he was also emotionally and
physically drained. He could barely keep his eyes open. Nicole
told him that although Charles was being hailed as a hero on the

news, Shawn was the true hero. If he didn't have such a good memory, Charles would've never known where to find her.

Shawn grinned and sighed pleasantly when she kissed him goodnight.

"I told you Mr. Charles would keep you safe," he said. "I knew he would."

"Yeah, you did," she said, a wistful tear glinting in her eye.

"Do I have to go to school tomorrow?" Shawn asked.

"No. Tomorrow everybody's staying home."

"Is Mr. Charles gonna be here?" Shawn wondered.

"Maybe," Nicole said. "I'll ask him. Would you like that?"

"Mmm hmm." Shawn pulled the sheets over his shoulders and closed his eyes.

Nicole kissed him again and rubbed his head tenderly. She heard him snoring lightly before she left the room.

BACK IN HER bathroom, Nicole found Charles at the sink, checking out the injuries he received during his ill-advised rescue. Because of a flood of adrenaline, Charles didn't feel any of the tree branches and shrubbery poking and cutting him as he blindsided the lowly kidnapper.

Looking at his body now, Charles knew that it was lucky he didn't put one of his eyes out. He threw caution to the wind as he ran through the rough vegetation. There were branches and thorns coming at him in all directions. He kept his hands up to protect his face, so his arms took most of the damage. All of his bruises were superficial, but some of the scratches were more than two inches long. There were large welts around the worst of them.

Nicole entered the bathroom and approached him from behind. He wore only a towel wrapped around his waist. She put her hands on his back, rubbing lightly. She put her arms under his and rubbed his chest and stomach, pausing each time she came across one of the cuts he took for her.

He turned to face her. Nicole continued to inspect his wounds. She touched them, very carefully, as if she was reading brail. She kissed them. And then she kissed his lips. They both remained silent.

He put his hands on her waist and kissed her passionately. Gradually Nicole felt an erection growing under his towel. She pulled the cloth loose and let it fall to the floor. She returned to the bedroom, losing articles of clothing along the way until she was completely nude. Charles followed her.

They made love that night, slow, sweet and ever so tenderly. Nicole knew she could never repay him for saving her life. She owed him everything she had, so she offered every bit of herself intimately. Their passion was like a ship lost at sea. They rode the waves together, and when the tide finally brought them back to the shore, she held onto Charles like it was just the two of them on deserted island.

She didn't have to tell him how much she loved him, but she did anyway, a few times, before they drifted off to sleep.

THE NEXT MORNING was Tuesday, but there would be no work or school for Nicole's household. The smell of toast and oatmeal coaxed Charles from his dreams at 9:30 am. Nicole brought him breakfast in bed, and this was just the beginning of the pampering she had in store for her hero, her knight in shining armor.

Charles ate heartily, and he was a little chagrined that he didn't have a change of clothes at Nicole's house. The stress from yesterday caught up with him overnight, and his whole body was sore. He wanted to lounge around with his woman and her kids, but he had to go home first to pick up at least one outfit.

Nicole told him he could stay with her for as long as he wanted, but Charles didn't want to get too far ahead of themselves. Shacking up was a big step. Charles was sure their relationship was headed in that direction, but he didn't think it should be brought on by a traumatic event.

"How long is it gonna take you?" Nicole asked when she walked him outside.

Charles had on the same pants he wore yesterday, but his shirt was too ripped and bloody to wear again. Nicole put it in a big freezer bag and tucked it away in her closet, as a keepsake. She gave Charles the biggest tee shirt in her dresser, but it wasn't big enough for Mr. Dripping Chocolate. The fabric stretched and clung to him like a Band-Aid. His nipples looked so enticing, Nicole had to stop herself from giving them a sensual squeeze.

"It won't take that long," Charles promised. "I'm just gonna change clothes and come right back."

"Don't take too long," she said.

She hugged him tightly. It was strange to Charles, to see her so dependent, almost needy. But he understood what she was going through, and he didn't mind the extra affection. Their ordeal had no doubt left her frightful, but things would mellow out soon.

Either way, he didn't think he could've been happier that day. He always dreamed he'd find a woman like Nicole. She loved him despite his flaws. She even put up with his distasteful job at Peeping Jane's. It was hard to believe they were on the verge of breaking up just two days ago.

He kissed the top of her head and told her, "I'll be right back. It won't take that long."

CHAPTER 55

CHARLES' HEAD WAS still in the clouds when he pulled into his apartment's parking lot twenty minutes later. He got out of his car, thinking about yesterday. Thinking about how surprised the police were when they realized he took Byron down all by himself, like a one man SWAT team.

The one thing Charles was *not* thinking about was DANGER. But, always a child of the ghetto, Charles turned and looked when he heard a car door open behind him. When he saw MikeyMike get out of the car, Charles thought it was very odd. When he saw a gun in MikeyMike's hand, Charles knew that his nigga moment, like most nigga moments, had finally bore fruit.

Mike told him, "What up with it now, homeboy?"

Charles started to shake his head.

Mike told him, "This HoovaLand, nigga!" and then he raised his arm.

And he started shooting.

POP! POP!

POP!POP!

POP!

EPILOGUE

CHAPTER 56

CHARLES MADE THE news again.

The Overbrook Meadows Telegram put his story on the front page. The headline read **LOCAL HERO GUNNED DOWN**. It was a city-wide tragedy. A lot of people in the media still wanted to interview Charles about his role in the takedown at Sycamore Park. They were shocked to learn that the muscle-bound man they saw in the video, who was so fit and full of life, was now struggling on a ventilator at Jackson Memorial.

The doctors said he wouldn't survive one minute without the life-giving tubes they crammed down his throat. Overall they gave him a 25% chance of survival.

NICOLE WAS NUMB, for the most part, for the first few days. Her friends worried that she had a breakdown. And it was understandable if she did. The incident with Byron would've pushed some of them over the edge. When you piled Charles' shooting on top of that, it was a recipe for disaster.

But Nicole didn't stay curled up in her bed like she wanted to. She got up every morning and dropped the kids off. She went to the hospital and stood by Charles' bed. She watched the machines beep. Watched Charles' chest rise and fall. She watched his eyes, his never-opening eyes. She held his hand and comforted him because one of the nurses told her that although Charles was not awake, he could still hear. It may be something Nicole said that brought him back to the world of the living. It was a long shot, but she had nothing to lose.

So she talked to him. She talked to him every day.

FRED CAME BY a few times. But he was no good in a tragedy, not helpful to anyone. Fred was raised in an environment where violence was the only answer to pain. His tears made him punch the walls and kick over furniture. They called security on him a few times, but the chaplain always came too, and she was able to talk him down before they had to kick him out of the hospital. Nicole didn't talk to Fred much. He made her anxious and angry.

When he wasn't at the hospital, Fred scoured the streets for information about who shot his brother. The streets eventually spilled the beans. Fred came to the trauma ward on day five in a different mood. He wasn't angry anymore. He was contemplative.

He pulled Nicole aside and told her the deed was done. Someone named MikeyMike was now deceased. Nicole stared at him for awhile, not sure how to respond to that. She finally walked away without responding at all. Fred followed her back to Charles' bedside, and he told his little brother the good news.

Charles didn't respond either. Fred left after a few minutes, looking a little dejected. Nicole did see him again for over a decade.

ON THE SIXTH day, Charles opened his eyes. Nicole wasn't there at the time. When she got to the hospital his nurse told her about it, and Nicole cursed herself for not spending the night with him. But she had three kids to look after. It was hard to keep them away from the hospital but still spend time with them every day.

Charles opened his eyes again around lunchtime, and Nicole was there for him this time. He looked at her, but that might have been wishful thinking. More likely he merely looked in her direction.

In any event, his eyes didn't remain open for very long. They swam in and out of focus and then fluttered, and then he went back to sleepy land. His nurse said he was drowsy from the morphine. Nicole knew that was partially true.

The other side of it was Charles was still struggling to live. Each breath he took might be his last. Nicole never knew if she was waiting for him to die or waiting for him to run towards the light. All she knew for sure was she was waiting, for something.

ON THE SEVENTH day Charles started to keep his eyes open for hours at a time. The doctors said this was a major improvement. They were able to speak to him about his condition, and Charles could respond somewhat. He could blink once for yes and twice for no.

That day Nicole enjoyed her visit with him for the first time. She asked him if he remembered what happened, and he blinked twice for *no*. She asked if the pain was very bad, and he blinked once for *yes*. She asked if he was going to keep fighting, and he blinked once for *yes*. She told him she loved him, and he blinked once. Nicole took that to mean *yes*, he loved her too.

ON THE EIGHTH day the trauma surgeon said Charles' left lung was no longer collapsed. She hoped it was repaired sufficiently for him to start breathing on his own. She said they were going to wean Charles off the ventilator; withdraw the tubes and "see what happens."

Nicole didn't like that plan at all. Plus her nurse already told her, "just between me and you," that they were eager to get Charles off the vent because he didn't have medical insurance. She said his care was costing the hospital $3,000 a day.

Nicole argued to the point of shouting, but her opinion only carried so much weight. She wasn't Charles' relative or his wife, and she certainly wasn't footing his medical bills. Plus she had never been to medical school, so the doctors weren't concerned with anything she had to say on the matter.

Either Charles was going to live or he wasn't. No hospital in the state had the time or charity to put this decision off indefinitely. So at 6:22 pm on a Wednesday evening, Nicole, the chaplain and a crowd of doctors and nurses all gathered in Charles' room for the big moment. Tears stained Nicole's cheeks as she watched them slide the tube out of Charles' throat. And then they all waited for the inevitable.

Charles' first breath without the vent was ragged and choppy. The next few were the same. But within thirty minutes he was breathing okay with just an oxygen tube in his nose. An hour after that, he cleared his throat and started talking.

CHAPTER 57

ON DAY NINE Charles' surgeons met with him and Nicole to give a prognosis and expectations for physical therapy. Nicole already knew about his injuries. She was there to support Charles.

He frowned when the doctor told him he got shot in the head. Surprisingly, this was his least traumatic injury. The bullet pierced the skin, above and to the left of his right eye, but the projectile did not penetrate his skull.

The doctor said this was a rare phenomenon, but not totally uncommon. She said the strangest case she knew of was with a victim who was shot in the forehead at point blank range. She said that for some reason the bullet skated to the left on that victim, travelled under his skin, alongside his skull, and then exited the very back of his head. She said Charles' injury was similar in nature, and he was lucky because his assailant was standing over him when he fired the headshot. That bullet was definitely meant to kill.

Charles' second wound was a gunshot to the left arm. This bullet got lodged in his humerus bone. The doctor said it was hell getting it out, but there would be no lasting damage here either. The worst part about this injury was that it immobilized Charles' arm at a time when he'd need it the most, for things like dragging his body around or using his new wheelchair.

Charles' third and final gunshot was to the midsection. This one was bad news from the start. When Charles first arrived at the hospital, his surgeon showed Nicole a diagram of all of the organs that were in the bullet's path when it entered Charles body. Later she told Nicole about the six feet of intestines they had to remove. Today she told Charles that the bullet would've gone all the way through his body, but it got lodged against one of his lumbar vertebrae.

They couldn't remove the bullet because it already caused some peripheral nerve damage, and they didn't want to make things worse. Yes, this nerve damage was the reason Charles could barely feel or move his lower extremities. No, the bullet wouldn't harm anything else if they left it there.

Nicole only saw Charles cry once in her whole life, and this was the day.

THE NEXT FOUR weeks were stressful, for everyone involved. The doctors were eager to send Charles on his merry way. Nicole was still fighting them at every step, demanding that they care for him as much as they would for someone who could actually pay for the services.

Charles was doing fairly well by then, and it was actually his preference that they let him go. He thought the hospital food was terrible, his room was depressing, and there was nothing more the surgeons could do for him. All that was left was for him to heal up, follow through with his rehabilitation and hopefully learn to use his legs again.

The odds of him ever making a track team or even going for a leisurely jog were slim to none. But if he gave it his all, his doctor said *maybe* he could get from the living room to the bathroom with just a cane one day. It wasn't a lot to look forward to, but it was something.

The only problem with leaving the hospital was Charles had nowhere to go. The manager at Windham Pointe was already threatening to evict him, and Fred had been arrested for murder.

Charles wanted to go back to his family in Joshua, but Nicole wouldn't hear of it.

"That's forty-five minutes away. I won't hardly ever see you."

"You don't have to see me that much," Charles told her. "I don't really want you to see me no way."

"So what you saying, you wanna break up?"

"We don't got no kind of relationship," he said. "I can't even get out of bed. This ain't what you want. You need to move on with your life."

Nicole wiped her tears and told him, "If you wanna break up with me over something I did wrong, that's fine. But I'm not leaving you over this. You can come stay with me when you get out."

"I can't do that."

"I been sitting next to your bed for over a month," she told him. "I ain't going nowhere, Charles. I'm always gon' be here for you."

"It's too hard," he complained. "It's gon' be too hard."

"No, going out with a stripper was hard," Nicole joked. "The rest of this, it's a piece of cake."

AND SO IT was that on Wednesday, May 8th, Nicole went to Jackson Memorial's trauma ward for the last time. She left with a wheelchair in her trunk and a very grateful Charles in the passenger seat. Later she would admit that she was a little naive and unrealistic in the beginning. She thought love would conquer all, and Charles would be back to his old self after a few days under her care.

That dream came crashing down before she even got Charles past her front door. Nicole's house wasn't handicap-accessible at all, and they had an accident two minutes after she pulled into her driveway. Nicole didn't realize how hard it was to get a fully grown man from a car into a wheelchair. Even worse, she tried to do it with half of his wheelchair on her driveway and the other half on her front lawn.

Charles didn't complain about the inevitable spill, and he didn't complain when Nicole couldn't get him up off the grass. After five minutes of struggling, a passing motorist stopped and helped put Charles back in his chair.

"You ain't gotta do this," Charles said when Nicole finally pushed him into the living room. "I could be at my grandmama's house."

Nicole was frustrated and sweaty. She told him, "Go ahead and leave. But I ain't gon' help you off the porch – *or drive you.*"

"So you kidnapping now?" he asked with a grin.

"Whatever it takes," she said, and then she turned and yelled down the hallway. "Shawn, Kevin, Keisha! Y'all come in here and say *Hi* to Mr. Charles!"

THE NEXT FEW months were filled with highs and lows. Sometimes it was hard to tell which was which. Nicole knew she put a lot of strain on their relationship by bringing Charles home. They were in love, but they were still in the baby stages of their commitment. There was a lot they had yet to learn about each other, and now they had to learn on the fly.

Even worse was Charles' high level of dependence. Shacking up prematurely was bad enough. But Nicole brought home a fragile life that needed more care and attention than the twins. Charles couldn't get in bed or go to the bathroom by himself. Nicole never had any training as a medical assistant, but she learned. Little by little.

Most of their bad days were caused by Charles' stubborn independence. He didn't want Nicole to help get him in or out of his chair, or bath him or wheel him around the tight corners in the house. He even resisted the patient care tech Nicole hired to help him while she was at work. If he dropped something, he would try to retrieve it for thirty minutes before he considered asking for help.

Nicole couldn't count the times she entered the bedroom or the bathroom and found Charles sprawled on the floor, struggling to get up, his face and chest slick with sweat.

"I got it," became his favorite catch phrase.

I don't need no help with that.

I can do this on my own.

No, you don't have to do it for me.

I got it.

I got it.

I said I got it.

But there were plenty of high points in Charles' recovery too. The thing he kept banking on was the fact that none of this was permanent. His arm was mostly healed before he left the hospital. And the bullet that skated around his skull didn't do much damage at all. There was a scar on the side of his forehead, but it wasn't that big. The exit wound in the back of his head was worse because his hair refused to grow over the scar tissue. Charles started shaving his head bald because of this. Fortunately Nicole thought he still looked very handsome.

The bullet still lodged next to Charles spine caused the most damage, but it wasn't the end of the world. The doctor told him that unlike the *central* nervous system, the *peripheral* nervous system could heal. Charles could wiggle his toes before he got discharged from Jackson Memorial. And after a week at Nicole's house, he could move his whole foot.

Physical therapy became his best friend. He worked out a lot in prison, and it was easy for him to start exercising again. Five days a week his therapist picked him up at two o'clock, and Charles returned weary but excited at dinner time. He was always eager to show Nicole that he could do more than he could the day before.

She cried the day he stumbled through the front door on arm crutches, saying, "I ain't gon' be using that wheel chair no more."

She cried again the first time she saw him get out of bed and make it to the bathroom on his own. He leaned heavily on every wall and doorframe along the way, but he still did it.

All by himself.

CHAPTER 58

ON AUGUST 16TH, Charles went back to the hospital for another gastro surgery. When the doctor sewed him up again, Charles no longer had to use a colostomy bag.

Two weeks later Charles completed his last day of physical therapy, and he enrolled himself in the new "*Mr. Charles Workout Plan.*" Nicole, Shawn, CJ and Shay joined the class too. The regimen included jogging, at least five days a week, pushups every morning, sit ups every night and weight lifting every other day.

Charles was the only one who followed through 100%, but everyone participated to some degree. Nicole lost ten pounds and flattened her abs that summer. Shawn's biceps got noticeably bigger, and Charles gained 52 pounds, putting him back at a hefty 218. He weighed 234 before he got shot, but he thought he looked leaner and more fit now, even with the jagged scars on his belly.

Those scars would forever be a reminder of what could happen *when keeping it real goes wrong.*

ON MONDAY, SEPTEMBER 9th Charles started his first day as an AC/Heating repairman for Climate Kings. This was the same company he interviewed with nearly a year ago. The manager remembered Charles, and he was upset to hear that Charles still hadn't found a job after all this time. Of course

Charles didn't tell them he was incapacitated for most of the months in question.

On Tuesday the following week, Fred was convicted of murdering Michael, aka MikeyMike, Cooper. The prosecutor didn't have a strong case, so Fred was able to plea bargain for a fifteen year sentence. He'd be eligible for parole after serving ten.

The next Saturday Charles emptied his public storage unit. Nicole, Wally and a couple of his friends stuffed all of Charles belongings in there back when Charles first moved in with Nicole. Charles was surprised to see everything was still in pristine condition.

He kept his favorite recliner and his big screen TV and sold everything else. He added that money to his first check from Climate Kings and went to the jewelry store for a gift for Nicole.

When she got home from work, Charles surprised her with two dozen roses as well. He dropped to one knee in the living room with the flowers in one hand and a small, velvet box in the other. He looked just as handsome as the day Nicole met him, even more so now because Nicole watched him crawl back from the brink of death. She nursed him and nurtured him, and Charles was now a part of her, as much as Shawn and the twins.

She dropped a bag of groceries and put a hand over her mouth, tears already twinkling in her eyes. Shawn was excited too. He picked up the groceries, but he didn't take them to the kitchen just yet. Even the twins piped down for this solemn and monumental occasion.

"Here, baby."

Charles gave Nicole the roses. She cradled them against her chest. Charles took her left hand in his. Nicole squealed and squirmed like a school girl. Charles chuckled.

"Baby, you something else. You know I wanna marry you. Why you acting like it's a big shock."

"It is," she said. "I dreamed about it. This is a dream come true." Her face was warm. Her whole body was hot and tingly.

"Alright," Charles said. He opened the box, and Nicole squealed again when she saw the ring he got for her. Charles held her hand and looked her in the eyes. His smile was dazzling. Everything about him was sexy, even his freshly shaved head.

"I want to tell you," Charles said, "that when I first came over here, I didn't think we was ready. I thought you was only taking care of me because of how I saved you, from that crazy dude."

Nicole was shaking her head, but Charles kept talking.

"I know you prolly don't see it like that, but the fact of the matter is I saved your life, Nikki. And then you turned right around and saved mine."

"I didn't save your life," Nicole said. She was gushing with excitement.

"Yes you did," he said. "I can't think of nobody that would've done what you did for me."

"It wasn't because–"

"Ah..." He held a finger up. "What I'm trying to say is I saved your life and you saved mine, so we even now, right?"

Nicole nodded, still glowing, though she was confused by this proposal.

"So if we even," he said, "then you know that I don't wanna marry you out of *gratitude*; because I feel like I owe it to you because of what you done for me. I wanna marry you because you're the most beautiful woman in the world, and I love you more than I ever loved anybody else. You my soul mate. You complete me. You're everything I ever wanted – and more. That's why I wanna be with you for the rest of my life. So, will you mar–?"

"Yes!" Nicole screamed.

She jumped into his arms as soon as he slid the ring on her finger and rose to his feet. She kicked her legs up in the air, and Charles lifted her with no problem at all. The twins rushed him too. Charles was strong enough to pick both of them up with one arm while still holding Nicole aloft in the other. Everyone had big, Christmas morning smiles.

"So, do I still have to call you *Mister* Charles?" Shawn asked before he took the groceries to the kitchen.

"What you wanna call me?" Charles asked him. He put the twins down and wrapped both arms around his fiancé. Nicole smothered him with kisses.

"I dunno. *Dad*?" Shawn said.

Charles smiled. His heart sighed. "Yeah man. I'd like that. I'd like that a lot."

KEITH THOMAS WALKER

ABOUT THE AUTHOR

Keith Thomas Walker, known as the Master of Romantic Suspense and Urban Fiction, is the author of more than four dozen novels, including *Fixin' Tyrone*, *Life After*, *The Realest Ever*, the *Backslide* series, the *Brick House* series, the *Finley High* series, the *Asha and Boom* series, and the *Blurred Lines* series. Keith's books transcend all genres. He has published romance, urban fiction, mystery/thriller, teen/young adult, Christian, poetry and erotica. Originally from Fort Worth, he is a graduate of Texas Wesleyan University. Keith has won numerous awards in the categories of "Best Male Author," "Best Romance," "Best Urban Fiction," "Best Young Adult Romance," "Best Duo," "Book of the Year," and "Author of the Year," from several book clubs and organizations. Visit him at www.keiththomaswalker.com.